Last Dance

Aaron L Bratcher

Download today for **FREE**

http://AaronLBratcher.com

Last Dance

Book Cover Design by Aaron L Bratcher

Check out the author's website
https://AaronLBratcher.com

CHAPTER 1

The store was crowded. Shoppers filled the aisles to take advantage of the big sale. "We've never had a Black Friday sale this big! We're rolling back the clock two full years. Get 1982 prices today!" Televisions from the small portable to the large 32 inch screen lined the wall, broadcasting their message in unison as shoppers crowded the aisles in an attempt to get that special item.

"Keep up Stephanie, this place is a madhouse." Ray spoke over the closest television and looked back to his daughter before turning down the next aisle.

Stephanie tucked her ash blonde hair behind her ear as she followed. "I'm here daddy. What are we getting?"

The televisions droned on. "We now return you to our special presentation of The Nutcracker with limited interruptions."

Stephanie stopped and stared at the closest screen, entranced and oblivious to the world around her. The graceful dancers stepped and turned to the music; Stephanie's eyes took in every detail. She felt a hand on her shoulder and she jumped with a short cry and turned to see her father.

"Didn't mean to scare you." He looked up at the screen and then back to her. "You ready to go?" He smiled.

Stephanie nodded and fell in beside her father. "Is that what you're getting Mom for Christmas?"

Ray handed the portable CD player to her. "Think she'll like it?"

"Yep. Definitely." She looked back to the televisions and stared at them as they fell out of sight before turning her attention back to her father. "Know what I want for Christmas?"

"A doll?"

"Nope."

"How about a nice necklace?"

"Nope. Wait, did you get me a necklace?"

Ray smiled. "I can't..."

"Well, that's not what I want. I want dance lessons so I can become a ballerina. Papa says I want to do it soon so I can get muscle, um..."

"Memory?"

"Yeah. Muscle memory."

"I think your grandfather says too much. When were you talking to him?"

1

"Today. He got home this morning and called me. Said we could watch The Nutcracker together."

"Of course he did." His voice was flat. He paused a second before continuing in a regular voice. "He really got you into this ballet thing, didn't he? Always watching The Nutcracker with you?"

"Someday, I'm going to do that on Broadway!" She turned and held her hand out, hitting her father with the box and nearly dropping it.

"Careful!" Ray grabbed the box from Stephanie and held onto it. "Don't want to break it before we even buy it."

"Sorry."

Both remained silent as they made their purchase and walked out to the car. "Kick the snow off your shoes before getting in."

Stephanie looked around at the shoveled parking lot and then down at her near bare boots before doing as asked. As they drove she ran her finger over the bag. "Daddy?"

"Yes sweetie?" Ray looked ahead as they drove along the snow and ice covered street seeing only a few other cars.

"Why can't I have dance lessons?"

Ray sighed. "Sweetie we've covered this. It's not the dance lessons I'm opposed to, but what it might lead to that I'm afraid of. Show business is not a good life." Ray waited for a response and not hearing one he looked over at his eight-year-old daughter, his face softening as her brilliant blue eyes filled with tears. "Does it really mean that much to you?"

Stephanie nodded her head.

Ray glanced at the road as they started to cross a bridge and then back to Stephanie. The corners of his lips curled up. "I think…"

A strong gust of wind blasted across the bridge, pushing the back end of the car across the slippery surface. Ray spun the wheel counter-clockwise and slammed vainly on the brakes. Stephanie's eyes went wide and she grabbed at the door handle. She didn't even have time to scream as a large truck driving in the opposite direction slammed into the car.

"Dad!" Rose whispered the name and stood from the chair next to Stephanie.

"I got here as fast as I could. Traffic has really picked up. How is she?"

Stephanie opened her eyes halfway and saw her mom and grandfather looking at her from across the room.

"Papa?" Her lips made the motion as the word came out as a slight exhale. Stephanie closed her eyes.

Lucas hugged his daughter-in-law and continued in hushed tones. "What happened?"

Wiping tears from her eyes Rose pulled back. "They got blown across the bridge into oncoming traffic."

"How is Ray?"

Rose closed her eyes and shook her head as tears started anew. "He... he's in surgery."

Lucas held her again, trying his best to comfort her. "But Stephanie's okay?"

"She's a little banged up, but she's going to be okay. Where's Mom?"

"She was visiting a friend for the weekend. You remember Carly? No? Well she should be here in a while." Lucas' stomach made a loud gurgling sound.

"Is that your stomach?"

Lucas grinned. "I was just about to make breakfast when you called."

"The cafeteria is on the ground floor. Why don't you get something?"

Lucas kissed her on the cheek and walked out into the hallway, closing the door behind himself. He looked left and right. "Okay, now which way to the elevators." As he turned to go back into the room an orderly walked by. "Excuse me, but which way to the elevators?"

The young man paused and pointed behind himself. "That way, turn right and you'll see them." He then continued on.

"Thanks." Lucas followed the man's directions and found himself at the elevator. As he stood there, two police officers in conversation joined him.

The doors opened and a nurse stepped off. Lucas held his hand out in offering to the officers who then stepped on. Lucas followed them onto the elevator.

One of them pressed the ground floor. "Think she'll live?"

"I heard something about brain hemorrhaging that couldn't be stopped. She probably only has a few hours."

"That's so sad at such a young age."

The doors opened and the officers got off as they continued talking. Lucas stood there gripping the railing as the doors closed in front of him. After a second the doors opened again with the officers looking at him.

"You okay sir?"

Lucas cleared his throat. "Yes. I think I just have the wrong floor."

"If you need something, you let us know. Okay?"

"Okay. Thanks." Lucas reached forward and hit the button to the first floor.

"You're back already? Did you change your mind?" Rose looked up from the chair she sat on next to Stephanie's bed.

"I wasn't as hungry as I thought. Um, are you sure she's okay?"

Stephanie opened her eyes and tried to take in a deep breath, wincing as she did.

"Positive. Some bruises and a cracked rib and a broken wrist, but otherwise okay. Why?"

"Mommy?"

Rose stood and looked down on Stephanie. "Mommy's right here." She drew her finger along Stephanie's forehead and pushed the ash blonde hair behind her ear.

As Lucas walked toward the bed, a doctor came in behind him. "Mrs. Starr?"

Rose looked up. "Doctor. Any news on Ray?"

"He's just gotten out of surgery and he's now resting."

The worry lines on Rose's face smoothed away. "Oh, thank God. When can I see him?"

"He's unconscious, but you can see him any time." The doctor approached Stephanie. "How are you feeling young lady?"

"Okay, I guess. What's wrong with Daddy?"

The doctor smiled. "Nothing now so you needn't worry that pretty little head any more. How's the cast?" The doctor reached over her body to pick up her left arm. "You'll have quite a story to tell your friends. You going to have them sign it?"

"Sign it?"

"Sure. It's an old tradition from back when even I was a kid. If you get a cast you have all of your friends and teachers sign it."

Rose smiled. "I'm sure she'll have it full of signatures before it's taken off."

"Everything is looking good here. Make sure she doesn't take a bath with the cast. When she takes a shower, cover it with a plastic bag. Let me sign some paperwork and you and your daughter can go home."

"We'll want to see Ray first."

"Of course. Any time you like. He's in room 324." The doctor left the room after writing Ray's room number on the white board.

"I want to see Daddy." Lucas helped Stephanie as she awkwardly climbed out of the bed and headed to the bathroom to change into her clothes. From inside the bathroom her small voice came out. "Mom?"

Rose walked over to the door. "Yes?" She didn't hear anything. "You okay sweetie?"

"I need help. I can't get this shirt on. It hurts."

Rose smiled and went inside and after a few minutes they both came out.

Lucas paused at the door of Ray's room. Inside Ray lay on the bed and next to him sat his mother with her head bowed. Hearing the footsteps of Lucas and the others, Mary looked up, tears in her eyes. She stood as Lucas went over to her.

"I just got here." She put her arms around Lucas and her head onto his chest.

As Lucas and Mary held each other, Stephanie and Rose went over to the bed. Rose took Ray's hand into her own. Stephanie looked at all the head wrapping and the equipment hooked up to him. "Daddy?"

Rose put her hand on Stephanie's back. "He can't hear you."

Stephanie looked at her mom in confusion. "If he wakes up he can hear me." She looked at her dad again. She started to reach out to his arm, but seeing the IV drip in his arm she stopped. "Daddy?"

Mary walked over to Stephanie and put her hand onto her back. "Oh I believe he can hear you dear. He just can't respond."

4

Stephanie looked up at her grandmother and then looked back to Ray. "Get better daddy so you can come home."

"Rose, would you like us to take her home with us so you can stay here?"

"Would you?"

Mary pulled her lips into a straight line, as much of a smile as she could muster. "We'd be happy to." She put her hand on Ray's arm, leaned over and kissed him on the cheek. "You'll be home soon. I'm sure of it."

Lucas held his hand out to Stephanie. "You hungry?" Stephanie nodded and took his hand. "You want to go to IHOP? I know it's your favorite."

"Thanks Mom. Thanks Dad. I don't know what I would do without you." Rose hugged Mary and Lucas.

Mary held on to her. "He'll be okay dear. You'll see. Stephanie can stay the night at our place. Do you want us to bring you anything?"

Rose shook her head and then let go. "No. I'll be okay."

Lucas looked at Stephanie as she ate her pancake. "How does your head feel sweetie?"

Stephanie kept chewing her food as she answered. "It's okay, but my chest hurts sometimes."

"When you breath in a lot and when you turn certain ways or walk hard?"

"Yeah. How did you know?"

Lucas smiled. "You're not the only one to have had a cracked rib. On stage during rehearsal once, the man working the canvas drops lost control of a sand bag and it hit me in the chest."

"I remember that. The way you whined when you got home, you would think you were going to die."

"You crack a couple of ribs and see how you feel. Besides I didn't whine that much." He winked at Stephanie who giggled. "Finish eating and we can go home. In the morning we'll go back and see your dad."

"Can we get Frankie?"

"Frankie?"

"Of course we can." Mary turned to Lucas. "Frankie is her stuffed animal. You need to be around more often so you know these things." She turned back to Stephanie. "We might as well get your jammies and tooth brush too."

Stephanie climbed into bed keeping her cast off the mattress as she carried her stuffed bunny, but stayed sitting up. "I want to pray for daddy."

"Of course dear." Mary and Lucas bowed their heads.

Stephanie put her bunny next to her pillow and then closed her eyes and folded her hands. "Dear God, please bring my daddy home. Amen." She opened her eyes. "Do you think he'll be home tomorrow?"

"He just might." Mary kissed her on the cheek.

"Good night." Lucas kissed her on the cheek and left the room, closing the door behind himself.

Stephanie laid down, still getting used to her cast. Falling asleep took time because every time she moved, her body would ache a little. After what felt like hours, though in reality it was 30 minutes, she fell asleep.

"Stephanie." She felt a hand on her shoulder. "Stephanie."

"Hmmm?"

"You need to get up. We have to go to the hospital."

Stephanie opened her eyes to see her grandfather standing over her with her coat. The light poured in from the hallway as she got up. In the hallway, she could hear her grandmother blowing her nose. With her eyes half closed she absently grabbed her bunny and trudged behind them toward the garage. Someone, probably her grandfather, helped her get into the car and made sure the buckle was secure. She fell asleep again before the car left the driveway.

"Here we go."

"Daddy?" Stephanie opened her eyes to see Lucas unbuckling her belt. Behind him stood her grandmother, wiping tears from her eyes.

"No, it's your papa. We're here. We need to go inside."

Stephanie nodded and took the offered hand. As she walked along the hall, she became more alert and look around. They were already on the third floor. Up ahead she recognized her dad's room. When they entered, her brow furled. Her mom sat in the chair next to an empty bed. Rose looked up, revealing a tear streaked face. She stood and went to Stephanie, embracing her in a big hug.

"Ouch! Mommy, you're hurting me! Where's daddy?"

Rose loosened her grip and held Stephanie back at arm's length. "Your daddy... he." She took in a shuddering breath as her bottom lip quivered. "Your daddy went home."

CHAPTER 2

Stephanie gripped her bunny and cried. Rose immediately pulled her close again. Soon after, Mary and Lucas were there holding on to both of them.

"It's going to be okay. We'll be okay." Rose held on to Stephanie for a while longer before pulling away.

Lucas wiped a tear away from below his eye. "When did he die? What happened? On the phone you just said there was a complication."

Rose shook her head. "I don't know what happened. Everything was fine and then he slipped into a coma. That's when I called you. Shortly after that he died. I... I don't know. They think he may have had a brain embolism."

Mary held onto Lucas. "My boy. My sweet boy." When she turned her head, she noticed the doctor at the doorway.

The doctor walked into the room. "I'm sorry to interrupt. I just wanted to give you this and see if there's anything I can do for you." He handed Rose a manilla envelope.

"What is it?"

"A copy of the death certificate and some other information you may find useful." His voice remained soft and subdued.

"Thanks." She took the offered envelope and looked down at Stephanie. "I guess it's time for us to go home."

"I'm not sure how I feel." Mary wiped her eyes as Lucas drove following Rose and Stephanie to their house. "I have so many conflicting emotions."

"It's not right for parents to bury their own child." Lucas shook his head and wiped tears from his cheek with the back of his hand.

Mary nodded. "And poor Rose and Stephanie. To lose a husband and father. They'll be needing you more than ever."

"I hadn't thought of that. After the holidays the company is going on tour."

"For how long?"

"A couple of months." Lucas pulled into the driveway behind Rose and and got out of the car. He continued talking after Mary got out. "I can get them some tickets. I could at least see them on the weekends."

"It's a start." Mary walked around the front of the car and held onto Lucas as she watched Stephanie get out of her own car, gripping her bunny as if it were her only connection to life. "She looks so lost."

Lucas and Mary walked into the garage where Rose had parked. He put his other arm around Rose and gave her a small hug before they went inside the house. Inside, the rabbit moved from one arm to the next as Lucas helped Stephanie take her coat off. She continued to stand there, almost oblivious to her surroundings. Lucas took her hand and led her to a chair where she sat down.

Rose watched as Lucas took care of Stephanie. "I think I must have looked the same way when my dad died. Just sort of lost in my own mind. I remember how my mom cried for weeks on end." She paused for a couple of seconds. "I guess in the end the grief was just too much for her."

Lucas came up beside her and put his arm around her. "Shhhhh. Don't you talk like that. We're here for you both. You won't be like your mom."

Rose leaned her head up against his body and sighed. "Thanks Dad."

Mary came out of the kitchen with a couple cups of coffee, handing one first to Lucas and then one to Rose. "Will you be needing some help with the funeral arrangements?"

"I haven't even had time to think about it. We never discussed where we want to be buried. I guess we thought we had time."

"Lucas and I are going to be buried at Mason Gardens. It's a nice place."

Rose stepped back and looked at them with her mouth open. "How are you two doing this? I am so sorry. I've not even thought about how you must feel."

Mary swallowed and shrugged before looking down. "It's hard to lose your only son."

Lucas put his arm around Mary and looked at Rose. "There's just something unnatural about burying your own children. It's not easy."

Stephanie sat expressionless as they lowered her father into the ground. On one side of her sat her mother, the other her grandfather with her grandmother next to him. After the service, various people walked by and picked up a flower from the table standing by the grave site. After dropping the flower onto the casket they stopped by to give their condolences. At first they were family members, people she saw only so often at weddings and other such affairs or not at all. Then there were strange faces and voices each saying how sorry they were for her.

After nearly everyone had gone, Rose stood and held out her hand to Stephanie. "Come on baby, we need to go say goodbye."

Stephanie stood and took the offered hand. As her mom took a step forward toward the coffin, Stephanie stood still and held her other hand out to Lucas. "Papa." It was the first word she said in the past two days.

"Just about there… and done." The nurse finished taking off the cast. "Why don't you move your hand around and tell me how it feels."

Stephanie complied and hesitantly moved her hand.

"Feels a little stiff? What you need to do is try to move it around every few minutes. If it's still stiff after a week, then we can do some physical therapy."

Lucas patted Stephanie's shoulder. "Don't worry sweetie, I'll make sure you get everything you need."

"Thanks papa."

The nurse handed Lucas a sheet of paper. "This is everything you need to know. If you feel physical therapy is needed, just give us a call and we'll get you set up."

"Just in time for Christmas, eh sweetie?"

Stephanie gave a half smile.

"You getting excited about Christmas?" Lucas glanced briefly toward Stephanie and then back toward the road. Snow fell against the windshield to be pushed to the side by the wiper blades. The parking lots of various businesses were full as shoppers made the most of the weekend before Christmas.

"I guess."

"I would think you would be very excited. It's only two days away."

"Papa stop!" Stephanie squeezed her eyes closed and held her hands out to the dashboard as she yelled.

Already slowing down as they neared the red light, Lucas pressed the brake harder and brought the car to a near immediate stop 10 feet away from the stop line.

"What!? What's wrong?"

"You almost went into the cars!"

Concern replaced alarm as Lucas looked at Stephanie. "We're okay. Let me pull up a little." Lucas looked into the mirror at the car just inches from his back bumper with a man inside shaking his hands in frustration as he mouthed something. "Yes, we're okay. See?"

A tear went down Stephanie's cheek as they drove on toward her home. "I'm sorry papa. I was scared."

"It's okay sweetie." Lucas remained quiet for the few remaining blocks to Stephanie's home. He spoke up again as they had pulled up into the driveway and were entering her house. "They're showing The Nutcracker in a little bit. You want to watch it while we wait for your mom to come home?"

Stephanie shook her head.

"Are you sure? You love watching The Nutcracker."

"I just don't want to. I'm going to take a nap."

Lucas gave her a hug and watched as she walked to her bedroom. He sat down and turned on the television and changed the channel until he found the program. He glanced toward Stephanie's bedroom and turned up the volume. Maybe she would join him.

Stephanie closed her bedroom door. As she walked over to her window, she looked down at her hand and tried to move it around a little more.. She looked out at all the fresh snow on the ground. The snowfall had diminished to only a few stray flakes on the wind. A snow plow drove by spraying the contents of the street onto the side of the road. Further down the street she could see a couple of boys making a snowman.

Her dad would probably be asking if she wanted to make a snowman. Maybe Papa would like to make one. She turned to her door and then heard The Nutcracker presentation from the television. Tears welled up and spilled over onto her cheeks. She ran to her bed and sobbed into her pillow.

Lucas turned off the television when he heard Rose coming inside the front door. The television was turned low as he watched a different program.

"Hey Dad." She looked around the living room. "Where's Stephanie?"

"Taking a nap."

"Really?" She walked down the hall to Stephanie's room and quietly opened the door. Stephanie lay on her stomach with her face toward the door, clearly asleep. After closing the door, Rose joined Lucas back in the living room. "How did it go?"

"Well her cast is off and she needs to work her wrist to get back full mobility. I'm sure she'll be fine in no time, but if not she can have physical therapy. She's obviously still upset. Nearly scared me to death on the way home."

"Oh?"

"Was coming to a red light and she screamed for me to stop. Guy behind us almost ended up in the back seat."

"Poor dear. I'm hoping her special Christmas present will lift her spirits." Lucas raised an eyebrow so Rose continued in a lowered voice. "She's getting dance lessons."

"When? Was this after Ray…?"

"No, no. I finally convinced him that it's every little girl's dream to be a dancer and that it's just a fad and that she will outgrow it."

"I know how much he was against it."

"She pestered him every chance she got. When he finally relented, he thought it would be fun to keep up pretenses."

"I'm sure she'll love it. If anything can put some spark into her that should be it. What time do you want us over on Christmas?"

"I think I can hold her off until about eight. Is that too early?"

Lucas smiled and gave Rose a kiss on the cheek. "We'll see you then."

"Stephanie?" Rose had opened the bedroom door and peeked her head inside. "Baby?" She spoke up a little louder. Stephanie opened her eyes. "There you are. Merry Christmas!"

"It's Christmas?"

"Yes it is. I'm surprised you're not up. Papa and grandma will be here soon. Why don't you get up and get dressed, okay?" She closed the door leaving Stephanie alone.

Stephanie sat up and brought her left hand up to her mouth as she yawned. She looked at her wrist and moved it around wincing a little as she hit the end of her range of motion. The sun peeked up over the horizon into her bedroom window. She stood and stared out the window for a couple of minutes. A light snow drifted down covering everything in sight had a fresh blanket of snow. It made everything so quiet and peaceful. As she looked out, her grandparents drove up and into the driveway. "Oh! They're here."

Her pajamas flew onto her unmade bed and she quickly put on some jeans and a sweater before heading out to the living room. When her feet landed on the cold wood flooring in the hallway she turned around and ran back to her bedroom to put on some socks. She grabbed some pink socks, but then threw them back into the drawer to grab some red and green socks with little bells on them. The little bells tinkled as she ran back into the living room and slid to a stop near the door where her grandparents were coming inside. "Merry Christmas!"

Lucas laughed. "Merry Christmas. Here, why don't you put this bag of gifts under the tree." He handed two large bags to Stephanie.

"Isn't that the sweater we gave you last year?" Mary pulled at the sweater's sleeves feeling the fabric before letting go.

"Uh huh."

Rose came toward them from out of the kitchen. "Merry Christmas! I have some coffee in the kitchen. Here, let me get your coats."

Lucas brushed some snow off Mary's coat before helping her get it off. "It's definitely a white Christmas this year. Remember how last year we just had a bunch of dead grass in the yard?"

Rose took the coat from Lucas and waited as he took off his own. "I do. Such a nice treat."

"Are all of these presents for me?"

"No, there's some in there for your mom and grandmother too."

"Here's one for you Papa!"

Lucas headed toward the seating area. "We better all get over there before she decides to open all the presents herself."

Stephanie sat cross-legged with a smile on her face in front of the tree as everyone came over and sat down. As they sat, her expression turned more somber. "Who's going to read the story?"

"I'll read it." Lucas pointed up on the shelf. "Hand it to me, will you?"

Stephanie stood and walked over to the book shelf that held an assortment of books and games and a couple of pictures. She grabbed a worn leather bound book and handed it to her grandfather who proceeded to read the story of Jesus' birth.

"I think it's my turn to play Santa." Rose stood and took the red hat with white trim from the side of the tree and put it on in a ceremonial way. She picked through the packages and handed one to everyone.

Stephanie pointed to the tree. "What's that envelope on the tree?"

Lucas laughed. "She's learning fast."

Rose glanced at the envelope. "I thought maybe we would do that one last."

Stephanie gasped. "It's a good one! Let me open it first, please?"

"Okay." With her eyes sparkling and the corner of her lips upturned as she tried to hide her smile, Rose handed the envelope to Stephanie.

Stephanie opened the envelope and pulled out a folded paper. As she read, her smile vanished and she dropped the paper and envelope and ran from the room crying.

Everyone watched as she ran off. Lucas turned to Rose. "Now what's that all about?"

"I don't know." Rose stood and headed toward Stephanie's room with Lucas and Mary close behind. She stepped past the open door and went over to Stephanie as she cried into her pillow. "Stephanie? What's wrong?"

"It's my fault. It's all my fault."

Rose rubbed Stephanie's back. "What is?"

Stephanie pulled her head up and looked at them. "Daddy's dead and it's all my fault!"

CHAPTER 3

"It's not your fault."

"No it isn't!"

"That's not true!" The responses all came in a rush. Rose sat down next to Stephanie. "Baby, why do you think that?"

"Because I was asking for dance lessons. It's all my fault!"

"Oh baby." Rose hugged Stephanie as she continued. "It isn't your fault. Nobody could've known how icy that bridge would be."

"I know he doesn't want me to dance."

Rose held her back a little so she could look into her eyes. "Your father is the one that said it was okay. He even went down and talked with the dance instructor before buying the lessons."

Stephanie stared at her mother for five seconds before responding. "He did?"

"Yes."

"But he said he didn't want me to dance."

"Baby, he never had a problem with you dancing really." She looked at Lucas. "He was just afraid of other things. But after I talked to him and once he talked to the teacher, he was okay with it."

Stephanie looked down and slightly shook her head. "He was looking at me when the truck hit us."

"That's not your fault. Look at me. The truck driver said that the wind blew you and your dad across the road right in front of him." Rose held her close and rubbed her back. "It will be okay." She continued to hold her as she got her own emotions under control. After she let go, she stood. "You know your daddy got you some other Christmas gifts too. Want to see what they are?"

Stephanie sniffed and nodded before standing up. Lucas and Mary each gave her a hug before she headed to the living room. Just as she turned the corner she announced, "I want to see the necklace Daddy bought me."

"How did you know about that?"

Lucas hummed as he packed his suitcase. As he closed the lid, the phone sitting on the nightstand rang. He picked it up. "Good morning. Oh Stephanie, good morning sweetie." He switched the phone to his shoulder and cupped it with his cheek as he struggled to zip the overpacked bag. "That's today?" The phone fell to the floor. Lucas bent down, making one of his knees pop as he picked it up. "Hello? Sorry, I dropped the phone. When is it?" He looked at his watch and sighed. "Yes, of course I'll be there. Wait, what?" He hefted his suitcase up and carried it as far as the cord to the phone would allow him. "You definitely need ballet slippers. Yes, and leotards too." The suitcase made a thud against the wood flooring as he set it down. "Okay, I'll meet you and your mom at the dance studio. I love you too sweetie."

Mary came to the bedroom doorway. "You have time for breakfast before you go?"

Lucas hung up the phone and followed Mary to the kitchen. "Turns out I'll be leaving later than I thought. Stephanie wants me to come to her first lesson so I'm going to get a later flight." He grabbed a cup from the cupboard and poured himself some coffee. "I'm supposed to meet her and Rose at the dance studio in an hour."

Mary put down a plate of eggs and toast on the table at his seat and returned to the cooking range to prepare some more eggs.

"Thank you." Lucas sat down. "No bacon?"

"You eat way too much bacon. It isn't good for you."

"I like bacon." He continued to sit as Mary cooked her food. "I'm not sure why I need to be there."

"I explained this to you."

Lucas sighed. "I guess I didn't realize all that it involved. Are you coming?" He looked at his watch on his wrist again and watched as Mary sat down next to him.

Mary smiled. "I can't. I have a class of my own to teach." She looked at his plate. "You waited."

"I do have some manners." They prayed and ate together before Lucas left.

"Papa!" Stephanie ran up to Lucas and hugged him as he entered. The dance studio consisted of a large open space with one wall lined from the wooden floor to ceiling with mirrors, a long horizontal bar attached to the wall, a piano and some sound equipment sat in one corner and hard plastic chairs lined the wall for guests to sit in.

An involuntary grin took over his face as she hugged him. "Don't you look nice. Turn around, let me see."

Stephanie modeled her new outfit to him. "Isn't it pretty?"

"It certainly is. It looks like they're about to start, you better get over there."

Stephanie ran up to the bar, where the girls were asked to stand.

"Thanks for coming Dad." Rose hugged Lucas before they both sat down. "I don't think she would have done this without you here."

"Really? She's wanted to do this all year."

"I know. I think it has something to do with Ray's death."

Lucas nodded absently as they watched the class get in order.

"Good morning students and welcome! We at the Riverside Ballet Theater know that coming here today is an exciting thing and we want to help you become the best dancers you can be. My name is Miss Stanley." She paused as a couple of the girls giggled. "Yes, my name is Miss Stanley and today we will be talking about how we stand, and a little bit on how we move. Now, our first thing today is standing. I want you all to put your feet together and turn your toes out. Make sure, you turn your entire leg. Okay, now look at me. Imagine someone is pulling on your hair at the top of your head. Got it? Good, now stand tall so it doesn't hurt. Don't stand on your toes, keep those heels on the floor. Good. Put your shoulders back, and look up."

As the instructor gave the last visual, she walked up to the first of the girls in the line. "You want to turn your entire leg. See how when I move my feet, my knee and my upper leg move also. If you just move your foot at your ankle, you'll hurt yourself. Okay good, now straighten up." She moved from one girl to the other correcting each girl girls stance. Eventually she got to Stephanie and stopped to look at her. "Move your head up a little. Perfect."

Rose leaned in to Lucas. "I wish you could be here all the time."

"I gotta go where the work is."

"Oh, you're home."

Lucas looked up from the newspaper he held in his hands. "I got home last night. You don't remember me kissing you as I got into bed?"

"No." Mary pulled a cup out of the cupboard and poured herself some coffee.

"You even talked to me for a minute before passing out again."

Mary kissed Lucas and sat down. "I must have been sleep talking. What did I say?"

"You were lecturing me about missing Stephanie's birthday party last week." He held the paper with one hand while and picked up his coffee to drink.

"Well it isn't every day your only grandchild turns 13. Did you at least call her?" Lucas nodded as he set his cup down. "Good. You know that's what alienated you from Ray. Always missing his birthdays and activities. She needs you."

"I know. I know. I'll make it up to her." He smiled to himself as he picked up his paper again.

"Uh huh. Well at least you're here for her performance today."

Lucas dropped his hands onto the table. "That's today? I thought it was next week."

Mary shook her head. "It's a wonder you ever get to anything on time."

Lucas folded the paper and stood. "That's why I have you." He kissed her. "I better get dressed."

Lucas and Mary took a few steps into the large auditorium and stopped to look around for Rose. Mary pointed up toward the front. "There she is, down there."

They could see Rose beaming as they approached her. "You need to get a copy of the program. Stephanie has a leading role."

Mary took the offered program and looked at it as Lucas looked over her shoulder. "Oh! There she is. 'Stephanie Starr' as Cinderella."

Lucas smiled. "Our little Starr is growing up. Let me go get a couple copies of the program." As he walked back up the aisle toward the entrance he paused. "Mark?"

The thin man with dark rimmed glasses looked up from his seat. He stared at Lucas a second before smiling and standing up. "Mr. Starr?"

Lucas shook Mark's hand. "I thought it was you. What brings you here? Someone in the show?"

"My nephew, Phillip, is in this thing. His parents had to go out of town for the weekend so I said he could stay with me. How about you?"

"My granddaughter is playing the part of Cinderella. What have you been up to?"

"Oh, same old, same old, Doing good."

"That's great. How's your dad?"

"He's doing okay. Still working at the pharmacy, but he's hoping to retire in a few more years."

"Good to hear." Lucas gestured toward the empty seat next to Mark. "Wife visiting the bathroom?"

Mark looked at the empty seat and then back to Lucas. "No, just an empty seat. I never could find the time."

"Oh. Well you have some years yet. I better go and get the programs. Good to see you." Lucas continued up the path and picked up a couple of programs from the stand and then returned to his seat.

"Who was that?" Mary took the programs from Lucas and put them into her purse as he sat down.

"Mark Phelps. You know, Joe Phelps' son."

Rose perked up. "Does he have a sister named Janie?"

"Yes, do you know him?"

"No, I think he was a senior when I started high school. I had some classes with Janie."

The room fell silent as the lights were dimmed. A light applause greeted Miss Stanley as she walked on stage toward the center with the spotlight following her. With her head held high and shoulders back, each foot moved forward with the toe pointed down at a slight angle to land with cat-like precision. "Good morning and thank you all for coming. We're all so very delighted to have you at our show. We at the Riverside Ballet Theater strive for excellence in ..."

Lucas leaned in toward Mary and whispered into her ear. "Do we really need to hear a commercial? We're already customers."

"Shhhh. You be good. We're here for Stephanie."

"... and enjoy the show." The woman walked off the stage and the room went black with only the emergency exit signs offering light.

After a moment, the curtains drew back and stage lights grew in intensity to reveal the scene. In the corner Stephanie wore a drab dress and held a broom while two others sat at a table in white and pink clothing holding some playing cards. Once the curtain reached the edge of the stage, the dancers went into motion. Stephanie had her gaze cast down to the floor and swept with a broom, gracefully moving across the floor while the other two at the table started to move their legs in dance poses as they played cards. Stephanie kept glancing out to the audience and nearly went off-stage before catching herself and placing the broom against the oval mirror that stood in a crafted wooden frame. She took out a cloth and dusted the mirror. When she raised her hand with the cloth, she winced a little and straightened her wrist, keeping it straight as she continued to dust.

Lucas leaned in to Mary and whispered into her ear. "Did you see that?"

She scowled and whispered back. "See what?"

"Her expression. It looked like she was in pain."

Mary watched for a few seconds and leaned toward Lucas. "She seems okay."

Presented with only music and the choreography of the dance, the audience could still easily follow the story. They laughed at the antics of the stepsisters as they 'learned' how to dance and gasped in appreciation of Cinderella's ball gown. When the glass slipper had to be tried on the feet of the step sisters, everyone laughed as members of the royal court and then members of the household tried to remove the slipper from one of the sisters. In the end, after her identity had been discovered, everyone encircled Cinderella and transformed her into a lovely bride. The audience clapped and cheered as the entire cast came onto the stage to take a bow.

A boy passed by Stephanie as she came from behind the stage dressed again in her street clothes. "When are you going to learn to dance, Stephanie?"

She scowled at him. "When you learn to shut your mouth!" She looked around and finding her family, ran over to them. "Papa! You made it." She nearly knocked him down as she hugged him. "What did you think? Did you like it?"

Lucas laughed. "I loved it. You definitely looked beautiful in that wedding dress. I bet when you do get married, though, you'll be even more beautiful."

Stephanie backed up. "Oh, I won't be getting married."

"No? Why not?"

"Boys don't like me."

"Well you're still young. Someday boys will find you irresistible."

"Nope. And I don't care."

"Well what if we were to have the last dance at your wedding together? Would that make it worthwhile?"

Stephanie looked up with her eyes and rolled them from one side to the other as she gave it some thought. "Well... that would be nice." She looked back at him. "You promise?"

"I promise." He smiled at her and then looked down at her wrist. "How's your wrist been feeling?"

"Fine. Why?"

"Mr. Starr." The dance instructor walked up and shook Lucas' hand. "I think that if you missed this performance Stephanie would have dropped dead. When you missed her birthday last week, the entire class got to hear her whining about it. It was near impossible to get her to focus on preparing for this performance."

"Yes." Lucas looked from the corner of his eye toward his wife. "I'm getting it from every direction. I'll make every effort to make her birthdays in the future."

"Well good. Stephanie could be our best dancer and I would hate to see her waste away because of her grandfather's absence." Without a further word she glided off, with her head held high, to talk to other parents.

"I swear, it's like that woman is always dancing." Lucas took Stephanie by each hand. "I am sorry I missed your birthday."

"It's okay Papa. I'm glad you got to see me dance."

"It was beautiful." He did a broad sweep of the stage with his hand as he talked. "You dominated the show. However, as reminded by your grandmother, it isn't every day you turn 13. So I want to make it up to you. In fact, I want to make it up to all of you." He stepped back and looked at his wife and daughter-in-law as he reached into the breast pocket of his sport jacket and pulled out some tickets.

"What is it?" Rose looked at the tickets she took from his hand and gasped.

CHAPTER 4

"What?" Stephanie tried to peek at the tickets.

Mary took the tickets from Rose and looked at them. "Oh, Lucas!" She looked up at him.

"I know." His entire face smiled at her. "Where we first met."

"What is it?" Stephanie took the tickets from her grandmother who continued to look at Lucas. "Oh! Theater tickets!"

"Those aren't just theater tickets, my dear." Lucas looked away from Mary and took the tickets from Stephanie. "These are tickets to the Chicago Theater. Best seats in the house, I guarantee it."

"What am I supposed to do with my class?"

"I'll try to get some time off of work."

"No need to worry either of you." Lucas looked to Mary "I already checked and you have three days off because the university has a holiday." He then turned his attention to Rose. "And you will have the week off with pay. I talked to your boss and you're over due."

"Oh Dad, I don't know what to say."

"It's been so long since I've been there. Oh, this is going to be wonderful." Mary kissed Lucas on the cheek.

Stephanie watched the interaction then took the tickets from his hand to look at them some more.

"What should I pack?" Stephanie tucked her blond hair behind her ear and stared into the closet.

"Something nice." The answer came from across the hallway as Rose packed her own bag.

Stephanie moved a couple of items across the bar and frowned. "I don't know. I may not have something nice enough."

"Sure you do. Why don't you wear that black dress with the sequins going down the side."

Stephanie pulled a few more items across to reveal the dress. "I can't wear that. It's too small."

A moment later Rose came up beside her with a sigh. "It is not too small, here." She pulled the dress out of the closet and held it up to Stephanie. "Oh. It is too small."

"See? I told you!"

"It looks like you've outgrown these." She held another dress up to Stephanie then put it back before stepping back to look at the handful of dresses hanging in the closet. Rose's face slowly grew into a smile. "Well, I guess we'll need to find something to wear while we're in Chicago."

"Oh yes! I can get some new shoes, and a small purse…"

"Now hold on. I said we can get something to wear, not an entire ensemble."

Stephanie frowned. "I guess that's okay too." As her mom walked away, she picked up a pair of black shoes from the floor. "How about some new shoes?"

"The ones you have are fine."

With her lips twisted, Stephanie put the shoes out by her bed. "At least flying will be nice."

After they had landed at Chicago O'Hare Airport, Mary headed to the line of pay phones in the airport with Rose and Stephanie behind her. "Let me call Lucas and tell him we're here." She opened her purse and pulled out a small address book and opened the first page. She set it down on the small metal shelf hanging below the phone. There were several numbers crossed out down the page.

With a scowl on her face, she looked at the numbers crossed out that were written on the side too. She turned the page and frowned. Then her eyes brightened. "Oh yes." She turned to the back of the book and saw the number written there. She picked up the phone and put in a quarter before dialing.

Stephanie looked around the airport as her grandmother dialed and asked for Lucas. There were so many people moving in the cavernous building. She stepped in closer to her mom and grandmother.

"… ahead of schedule. Sure, she's right here."

Stephanie reached for the phone, but Mary passed it to Rose. Stephanie tried to grab the phone from her mom who just batted her hand away. "Hi Dad… Yeah?"

"I want to talk to him!"

"Oh, I'm sure that would fine." Rose gave Stephanie a stern look as she tried again to take the phone from her mom. "Okay, sure… I'm not sure, let me ask." She turned to Stephanie. "Do you want to talk to Papa?"

"Duh, yeah!"

"Stop grabbing the phone like that. It's very rude and don't talk to me like that." She handed the phone to Stephanie.

"Hi Papa!… Yes, the flight was fun. When will we see you?… Okay, I love you too!" She put the phone back. "He said he is waiting for us at the hotel."

"Brrrr. I didn't think I would need to bring a jacket in June." Rose folded her arms around her to shield herself from the wind as they waited for the cab driver to put their luggage into the trunk. "Look at my arms. Goosebumps!"

"Now you know why they call it the Windy City. Did you bring sweaters?"

Rose nodded to the trunk of the car where the cab driver had just closed the lid. He came over and opened the door for them to climb inside.

Stephanie rubbed her arms after she sat between her mother and grandmother. "Why couldn't we have been in here while he put the luggage into the trunk?"

The driver closed his own door as he sat down behind the wheel and looked at Rose through the rearview mirror. With a thick Russian accent he asked where they were going.

"The Drake Hotel."

Mary leaned back with her eyes closed as they traveled toward the city while Stephanie and Rose looked at everything. As they reached the edge of the city, Mary opened her eyes and pointed to the city skyline. "See that big black building with the two white antennas? That's the Sears Tower. Maybe tomorrow we can go up to the sky deck."

The cab driver hit a button on the meter and looked back at Rose. She handed him some money. After giving her the change he got out of the cab and put their suitcases onto the sidewalk before opening the door.

A man came up to the car door in a black outfit with the name of the hotel embroidered onto the shirt. "Welcome to The Drake, may I take your luggage?"

"Yes, thank you." Rose stepped back to allow the man to grab the suitcases and place them onto the nearby cart.

Lucas came out of the hotel toward them. "Ah, there you are."

"Papa!" Stephanie walked over to him and gave him a hug.

"Come inside, this place is really something. Presidents have visited here you know." He gave Rose and Mary hugs and led them inside. "It is even said that Al Capone may have spent some time here."

"Who?" Stephanie scowled over at Lucas.

"I think you've lost her, Dad."

"Okay, well did you know the 10th floor is haunted?"

Stephanie's eyes got big. "Haunted?"

"Yep. By the 'Lady in Red.' They say she jumped out of a window shortly after the place opened up because she found her husband with another woman."

"Which floor are we on?"

"Let's find out." They had reached the main desk. Lucas addressed the woman behind the counter. "Starr, party of three." After the woman verified Rose's I.D., she handed them a couple of keys. Lucas looked at the number stamped on it. "Oh, I guess you won't get to see the ghost."

Rose turned her head to cough, hiding a smile. "Let's go see our room."

"Allow me." The man with their luggage took one of their keys and led them to an elevator, pushing the luggage cart. After showing them to their room, the man carried their luggage in. Lucas gave him a tip and he left.

Mary closed the door behind the man. "I never know how much to tip."

"A dollar a bag is right these days. I have to get back to the theater. I just wanted to see you guys once you got here. You have everything under control?"

Mary gave him a kiss on the cheek and smiled. "Us girls have it under control."

"Yes, Papa. Us girls have it under control."

Lucas chuckled as he opened the door to leave. "Okay, after the performance tonight, just wait a few minutes for the theater to clear before you come to the back stage. I'll show you around and let you meet the crew. There is a fascinating history to this theater. Tomorrow you can go up the Sears Tower or anything else you like."

"Yes, yes." Mary waved him off. "You go and I'll show them around. I grew up here you know." Mary closed the door behind him as he departed and looked at Rose and Stephanie. "Who wants to go shopping?"

Mary's mouth stood agape. "What happened to Marshall Fields?" She looked around and then back again. "There's the clock. This is State Street. Macy's bought them out?" She looked at Rose.

"I guess so. Do you want to go someplace else?"

"No, we're here. Let's go inside."

Once inside, finding something for Stephanie became a priority. They went to the proper department and browsed around. Her mom held a dress up to her. "What do you think of this?"

"I don't want red. If I wear that then I'm the 'Lady in Red.' Then I'll have to kill myself."

"Don't be so melodramatic. It's just a story, it didn't happen."

Mary handed Rose a black dress. "You can never go wrong with black."

Rose held the dress up to Stephanie. "I don't know, it's a little short on her."

Stephanie looked down at the dress as she held her leg up a little. "It's not too short. See? It's almost down to the top of my knees."

Rose handed the dress back to Mary and accepted another one. She held it up against Stephanie and frowned. "Hmmm. This may take some time."

Stephanie gasped and pushed the dress aside and ran over to another rack. She pulled off a dress from the end and held it up against herself. "This is it! It's perfect!" She turned around so her mom and grandmother could see. The long black dress had a straight neck line across the top with three hollow stars made of sequins across the top.

"That is nice." Rose took it from her and turned it around to look at the back. The v-shaped back came to a point at the middle of the back. "This is very nice." She looked at the price tag and cringed. "Oh, I don't know Baby."

"How much is it?" Mary looked at the tag and then looked up at Stephanie. "Well, she is a Starr. Let me help you out with that."

"Are you sure?"

Before Mary even had a chance to respond, Stephanie hugged her. "Oh, thank you Grandma!"

Mary patted her on the back. "You're welcome! Now let's go get you some new shoes and a purse to go with it."

"Mom! It's too much."

Mary looked at Rose with a smile. "It's a grandmother's job to spoil her grand-children."

Rose adjusted Stephanie's hair as they got out of the cab. The sliver chain of Stephanie's necklace glinted. "Nobody can see the necklace, you should have just left it back at the room."

"I always wear the necklace. Oh look! There's Papa's name!" The marquee prominently displayed his name for the lead role. After showing their tickets at the entrance, they walked inside and Stephanie immediately stopped. "Wow." Her gaze went up to the chandelier hanging from the high ceiling. Her eyes slowly took in the entire lobby.

Rose gently guided her forward toward the stairs as other patrons came in behind them. "Watch your step."

When they got to their seats, Stephanie stood by the railing to inspect every detail her eyes could take in. When the lights dimmed they were able to finally convince her to sit and watch her grandfather play the lead role in Death of a Salesman.

From the opening act to Willy's death, Stephanie watched with rapt attention. After the applause died, her mom asked what she thought of it. "It was sad. Let's go and see Papa."

The trio worked their way to the back-stage entrance where they got some resistance from the guard stationed there. "Look, ladies. I just got here for this evening's performance. If Mr. Starr said anything to anyone, it would have been to Lou who isn't here."

While the guard talked, Mary had been digging into her purse and pulled out her driver's license. "See? Mary Starr. I'm his wife. And this is his daughter and granddaughter."

The guard looked at it. "My apologies, ma'am. You can never be too careful."

Stephanie walked ahead of the other two and came into a large area where a couple of the actors were standing around while Lucas sat on a bench rubbing his leg. The actress who had portrayed Linda sat next to him with her hand on his shoulder. When she saw Stephanie, she took her hand down. Lucas looked over and saw Stephanie. "Hey, Sweetie!"

Stephanie slowed down as she approached and watched him rub his leg. "Hey Papa." She gave him a hug after which he resumed to rub his upper leg. "Did you hurt your leg?"

Rose and Mary came into view and approached as he answered. "No, I'm just getting old. They hurt a little when I'm on them for some time." He stood and kissed Mary and then Rose. He turned to Stephanie "Is that a new dress?"

Stephanie turned around for him. "Like it?"

"Yes, it's perfect."

"I know, right?"

"Let me introduce you to the team. This is Veronica. She played the part of Linda." Veronica stood and smiled. "And over there stuffing sandwiches into their mouths are Jeremy and Frank. Hey guys, come over here and say hi to my family."

Jeremy grinned as he approached. "You must be Stephanie." He held out his hand to her. "Lucas here talks about you all the time. You're a dancer?"

"Mhmm." Stephanie shook his hand.

Frank shook each of their hands and then headed back to finish eating with Jeremy 10 seconds behind him.

Lucas pointed to some other people walking around. "Of course there are people responsible for the props, lighting, and other stage hands that we pick up locally."

"This place…" Lucas sat down and motioned with his hand. "has a very interesting history. They had a form of air-conditioning before conventional air-conditioning became available."

"Oh? How's that?" Mary sat down next to Lucas where Veronica had been sitting and put her hand on his leg.

"There's a tunnel far underground used a long time ago to transport coal, I think, on a track with small cars. They had air ducts that led down to this tunnel and they would draw air up from it to cool off the audience."

Stephanie yawned.

"Okay, maybe it isn't that interesting. You guys about ready to go?" As he stood, Mary stood also and held on to his arm.

Rose tucked Stephanie's hair behind her ear. "I think our little Starr is definitely ready."

Lucas led them to a side door. "You guys figure out what you're going to do tomorrow?" He opened the door and led them out into the alley.

"You know I lived here for several years before I moved away and I don't think I ever went up the Sears Tower. If it's not too cloudy, we could do that."

"You can always take them to the aquarium and the museum. They're close by. I think they have a special pass for the both of them."

Rose perked up. "Oh, that sounds nice. What do you think, Baby?"

As they got closer to the end of the alley, three young men who looked to be in their early 20s stood and walked toward them. They all wore the same style blue jean jacket and had belts with large buckles prominently displayed. As they walked, they spread out and pulled off their belts and swung them around their heads with the heavy buckles making a whooshing sound as they circled the men's heads.

CHAPTER 5

Stephanie's eyes went wide and she took a step backward as she watched the men.

Light poured into the alley from the street behind the men as they advanced, casting their faces in shadow.

"We're not looking for any trouble." Lucas positioned himself in front of the ladies and held his hands up a little above his waist.

"Shut up old man." The young man in the center took a couple of steps forward as he addressed Lucas. "Throw down your wallet and jewelry and maybe you'll get out of here without getting hurt."

One of the two in back spoke up to their leader. "Hey Bobby, she's pretty. I bet she would like to show us a good time."

"The little girl? Or her mommy?" the other man laughed at his own retort.

Rose grabbed Stephanie's hand and pulled her toward herself and then whispered to her while looking on at the men. "Run back! Go get help."

But Stephanie couldn't let go of her mother's hand. Like a deer caught in the headlight of an oncoming car, her legs remained frozen with fear and she couldn't tear her gaze away.

Lucas stepped forward a step. "You leave them alone." He looked closely at the three faces. "You leave now, Bobby, and we won't even mention this to the police."

Bobby's face turned into a sneer as he ran forward the few steps between himself and Lucas. Lucas stepped forward inside the arc of the flying buckle and landed a punch solidly into Bobby's face. Bobby took a step back, shock on his face, and shook his head as the other two came forward. Lucas blocked one of the buckles with his arm, however the other landed squarely onto the left side of his head.

"Papa!" Stephanie ran forward, letting go of her mother's hand, to Lucas and crouched down by him as he sat on the ground holding his hand over his head. Blood flowed freely through his fingers.

"Hey! Stop right there!"

Everyone looked up to see a police officer running toward them. Bobby lowered the fist he had raised to hit Stephanie and ran with the other two away from the officer past Rose and Mary. Bobby shoved Rose aside as he and the others ran past to the other end of the alley. They turned the corner and disappeared out of sight. Rose and Mary rushed over to the side of Lucas.

The officer grabbed the mouth piece clipped to his shirt and pressed the button. "This is Officer Duncan, I'm in the alley by The Chicago Theater. I'm going to need an ambulance." He let go and squatted down next to the still dazed Lucas. He put his arm onto his shoulder. "Mister, can you hear me? The ambulance is on its way."

Mary reached out her hand and then pulled it back. "Oh Honey, why did you do that?"

Lucas' lips moved, but nobody could hear what he said before he slumped against Stephanie.

Stephanie tried her best to keep his head from hitting the pitted asphalt. "Papa! Papa!"

A paramedic held a cold pack to Lucas' head as he came to. "Welcome back."

Lucas raised his hand and touched the cold pack and looked around. "I guess I'm not as fast as I used to be. Am I going to need some stitches? I would rather not."

"I got the bleeding to stop. You might get by with some butterfly bandages and liquid skin. Other than that, how do you feel?"

"Like I got hit in the head by a brick."

"What were you thinking, Dad?" Rose stood next the police officer with her arm around Mary.

"You gotta stand up against guys like that. Here, help me up." The paramedic helped Lucas sit up.

"I'm going to need a statement from all of you. Did you get a good look at them?" Officer Duncan pulled out a pen and a pad of paper.

Stephanie looked up from beside Lucas. "One of them was named Bobby."

"I got a good look at them. There were three. Yes, the leader is named Bobby. I would say he's five foot ten with light brown hair. The others were about his height. They were all wearing blue jean jackets and black jeans. I didn't see the color of the shirts under the jackets. They were all caucasian and one of them had dishwater blonde hair and bushy eyebrows with a scar on his left cheek. The last one had very dark hair. I couldn't see the color of their eyes from lack of light."

Stephanie stared wide-eyed at her grandfather. "Wow. How did you remember all of that?"

"Back when we started dating, your Papa helped the F.B.I. with a case." Mary gave a half smile to Lucas.

Stephanie looked between Mary and Lucas. "You did?"

Lucas nodded. "Yes I did. They gave me some tips on specific things to remember for identifying someone."

The police officer pocketed his pen. "I've dealt with Bobby and his boys before. I assume you want to press charges?"

"Of course. I'll need to come in tomorrow?"

While the officer and Lucas exchanged information, Stephanie took off her shoes and massaged her feet. The paramedic noticed. "Feet giving you problems?"

"Oh, it's nothing."

"I'm here. Let me take a look."

Stephanie held on to her foot for a second before shifting it forward toward the man. He took the foot and moved it in a circular motion and then moved the toes and the lower foot. "You're pretty hard on your feet. You should get some better shoes."

"I'm a ballerina."

"Ooooh. Okay." He remained silent for a minute as he massaged the other foot a little. "You're pretty young. You should probably look at doing something else. Then you won't have to worry about your feet always hurting."

Stephanie jerked her foot back. "What!? How can you say that? I love dancing." As she said this, she put her shoes on and stood.

"I didn't mean to upset you."

Stephanie walked away.

"Stephanie? Where you going?" Rose sighed and walked after her. "I better go get her before she finds more trouble."

Lucas knocked on the room door and waited. Not getting a response, he knocked again. "Hmmm did they leave for the Sears Tower already?" He looked at his watch. "Only nine."

The door opened. Stephanie stood in her pajamas with her hair a tangled mess and her eyes half closed. "Hi Papa." She turned around and went back inside and climbed into the bed with her mother.

Lucas followed her inside and closed the door. "Wow. Last night must have been exhausting. See any ghosts?"

"No. No ghosts, just blood. My dress is ruined."

"Baby, we'll take it to the dry cleaner first thing today and see what they say." Rose got up from the bed, walked over to Lucas and gave him a hug and kissed his cheek. "Morning Dad. How are you feeling?"

"Doing pretty good. Just a little sore."

Rose opened a drawer, pulled out some clothes and then went into the bathroom and closed the door.

Lucas walked over to Mary's bed and sat next to her. "Morning Honey." He leaned down and gave her a kiss. "You guys order breakfast?"

Mary kept her eyes closed. "We're on vacation. It's a mandatory thing to sleep in when you're on vacation."

"So you haven't ordered breakfast?"

Mary opened her eyes and stared at him. "You could have been killed last night."

"You know I don't like to be bullied. Besides, they didn't look like the killing type."

"That doesn't matter. Our bodies can't take as much any more. You got hit on the head."

Lucas touched the area gently and winced. "I'll be more careful. I promise."

Mary patted his hand. "You better be. I expect to have you around for a few more years."

"Once you guys are ready, there's a bakery nearby that has some danishes with hickory smoked bacon pieces baked right in."

Mary gasped. "It's a wonder you aren't fat the way you eat."

Rose came out of the bathroom fully clothed, walked over to the windows and drew back the curtains. The sun light reflected off the lake and flooded the room.

"Mom!" Stephanie threw the covers over her head.

"Wow. Did you know that Sears was already in their financial decline before they finished building this place?" Lucas looked up from the pamphlet he had picked up as they got into the long line for the elevator that would take them to the observation deck.

Stephanie glanced at him from the corner of her eye. "Papa. No more history lessons. It's Summer Vacation."

"So that means the learning has to stop?"

"Yes!"

Lucas shook his head and continued to read as Mary looked over his shoulder and read.

Rose smiled. "I heard they're building something taller in Malaysia."

"You too Mom?"

Rose looked at her daughter with wide eyes and drew the back of her thumb across her closed mouth.

"I can't believe what he said." Stephanie said it out lout to nobody in particular.

Rose looked around at the others in line. "I didn't hear anything unusual. Who said what?"

"Last night. He said I should stop dancing."

"Oh Baby, he was just trying to be helpful. You don't need to worry about what he said."

Lucas put the pamphlet into his back pocket and took Stephanie's hand. He stepped back so their arms were stretched out. "And you..." He gave a little pull and Stephanie twirled around, wrapping his arm around herself as she got close to him. "... love to dance. And remember..."

Stephanie grinned up at him. "You get the last dance at my wedding. I know, but I still don't think that's going to happen." The large elevator doors opened. Stephanie let go of her grandfather and stepped up next to the people in front of them. "Oh! Let's go!"

Stephanie stared at the back of the large man in front of her and crinkled up her nose before muttering something under her breath.

"What's that?" Rose leaned in to hear her better, but Stephanie muttered so low she still couldn't hear. "What?"

"I said I'm going to suffocate in here."

"Oh, stop it. You'll be fine."

When the elevator doors opened, they had to wait as everyone else got off. After stepping off, Stephanie made a show to her mom of taking in a few deep breaths. Her mom smiled and shook her head and went over to the large window with Stephanie in tow. Even without clouds in the sky, a slight haze hung visibly over the city.

Mary put her hand across Stephanie's shoulder and pointed. "Over there, dear, right next to the lake? That's Shedd's Aquarium and across the street is the Field Museum. We'll visit the aquarium after this. The museum is pretty big so we'll want to go there tomorrow."

Stephanie nodded and looked around at the city and the lake. Her eyes followed the waterline right up to the glass. That's when she noticed the boy looking at her. He looked away and toward the window four feet in front of him. She watched as he looked down at his feet and slowly took a step toward it before looking up again. He took in a deep breath and then looked at Stephanie again. She smirked and put her toes and her forehead up against the glass and looked straight down to the streets before looking over at him again. The large boy swallowed and took another small step toward the glass and stopped. When he looked at Stephanie, his face had lost its coloring. He turned and quickly walked away from the window and her.

"Some people just can't make the cut." Stephanie smiled to herself and looked to the aquarium.

Stephanie stared at the long tentacles of the giant 40 foot squid suspended from the ceiling and shivered. "That can't be real."

Lucas leaned close and whispered into her ear. "It is." He pointed at a sign on the wall.

"Ewww." She shivered again. "Why did we come here?"

Rose smiled at her. "I love the aquarium It's so peaceful and so many different kinds of fish. I want to see if they have any seahorses."

Mary laughed. "I bet I can guess why you like them."

Stephanie looked from one to the other. "Why?"

Lucas smiled. "Sweetie, they're so excited about sea horses because it's the boys that get pregnant."

"Really?"

"Yep. Let's go see if they have any." Lucas followed Mary and Rose.

As they walked through the aquarium, Stephanie noticed a large group of people gathered by the large tank and slowed down. Stephanie stopped to watch the five performers as the woman gave a narrative of a merman trying to win the affection of a mermaid in love with someone else. Her mom and grandparents were engaged in conversation and were looking at the small tanks to the side where it wasn't so crowded. They moved on, not realizing Stephanie had stopped.

Stephanie gasped and jumped as Lucas put his hand on her shoulder. "Oh! You scared me." Her voice came out in a hoarse whisper.

Lucas leaned in close to her and whispered. "You scared us. We didn't know where you went to." Lucas looked up at the tank and continued to whisper. "You finish watching this, Sweetie, and I'll tell your mom where you are."

Stephanie followed him. "No, I'm done."

"You sure? Looks like they just got started."

She shrugged and followed him to where her mom and grandmother were looking at a spitter fish. Her mom gave her a hug. "There you are. Got lost in the crowd?"

"She was watching an underwater ballet."

Mary smiled. "That's our little Starr. Always into the ballet."

Stephanie remained silent as they continued through the aquarium. Lucas put his hand on her shoulder. "You okay?". She nodded, but remained silent.

When they were about to leave Stephanie sighed. "Maybe he was right."

"Who, Baby?"

"The paramedic. Maybe he was right. Maybe I should give up ballet."

CHAPTER 6

Rose scowled. "Now why would you say that?"

Stephanie's face turned red as everyone looked at her. She looked down and swept the tip of her toes along the flooring. "Just what he said and some other things. Maybe he's right. Today, while they were doing their under water ballet, I was wondering if someday I would end up doing a show I didn't even like. And Miss Stanley is always rubbing her feet when we come in for class. She's all alone. I sometimes wonder, is that my future? To be a lonely old maid teaching a class?" She looked up at everyone and then looked at her grandfather. "How can I save the last dance for you if I never get married?"

Lucas' face softened. "Come here Sweetie." He hugged Stephanie as she got close and held on to her for several seconds as she sniffed and wiped her eyes before he said anything. "If I've learned anything in life it's this. Be true to yourself, to your family, and to God. You do that and everything else will fall into place. Life is never ever what you expect it to be. You'll think that you have it all planned out and then something happens that you didn't expect that will send your life in a completely different direction." He looked at Mary and smiled. "When I met your grandmother, I was dating someone else. I had no idea that I would be marrying her."

"He's right Dear. You know how much your Papa loves to act, but there are several plays I've seen him turn down over the years because he doesn't like them. And there's all kinds of dancing. You've been doing ballet, but you can go to a school that teaches lots of modern dancing styles. Who knows? Maybe you'll be in a movie because of your dancing talent, or you could be an instructor who is married, or maybe something else. I don't know and neither do you."

Stephanie listened as her grandparents tried to console her. "I don't know. Maybe I just need to take a break."

Rose caressed Stephanie's face while her grandfather continued to hug her. "Baby, you've been dancing long before you started dance lessons. It's who you are. If you want to take a break, that's okay. Just listen to your Papa. Be true to yourself."

Rose and Stephanie entered the dry cleaners and walked up to the counter where an asian woman stood. As Rose opened her mouth to say something the employee cut her off. "Starr. Yes, beautiful dress. Very pretty. We were able to get the blood stains off. You wait here and I go get." She walked to the back of the store and then came back with the dress on a hanger. "See? No blood." She placed it flat onto the counter top for Rose and Stephanie to see. After giving them time to look, she turned it over. "Pretty dress. So glad we could save it. Sad story. Your grandfather okay?"

Stephanie couldn't help but smile as the woman talked. "Yes, he's okay. Thank you."

"Oh, I'm so happy. You want, I put dress into bag for you." She didn't wait for an answer and pulled out a clear bag to place over the dress and handed it to Rose.

Rose looked at the three stars that adorned the top of the dress and then looked to Stephanie. "No matter what you do, I just know that you'll be a star. When we get home tomorrow we'll let Miss Stanley know whatever you decide together. It'll be fine."

Stephanie smiled. "Thanks Mom."

Stephanie dropped her bag into the back seat of the car before climbing into the passenger seat. Rose waited until she buckled up before backing down the driveway. "I'm surprised you're bringing your clothes."

"Someone might be able to use them."

"Oh." Rose drove in silence for a while. "How do you think she'll take the news?"

"She'll probably be sad to see me go, but there are others that will be happy to take my place. She'll get over it." They arrived early so Stephanie could give her news in private. Stephanie got out of the car, grabbed her gear, and walked toward the entrance when she noticed her mom still in the car. "I thought you were coming too?"

Rose smiled and got out of the car. "Sorry Baby. Just thinking of when you started your lessons. You were so cute in that outfit."

"Yeah, I remember. Papa was there too. It was so long ago." She nodded to the car at the end of the parking lot next to Miss Stanley's car as her mom got next to her. "I wonder who that is."

"Maybe a new student. You ready?"

Stephanie nodded and walked up the ramp ahead of her mother and into the building. When she stepped inside she stopped. Her mother nearly ran into her.

"Why did you stop? Oh." Rose followed Stephanie's gawking stare and saw Miss Stanley pulling away from a kiss.

Miss Stanley pulled on her dress a little. "You surprised me."

"I'll see you later?" The man took a step back.

Miss Stanley's eyes sparkled. "After eight?"

"Sounds great." The man walked toward Stephanie and Rose to leave the building. "Ladies."

Stephanie watched him leave and then turned toward her teacher. "Miss Stanley?"

"Yes?"

"When did you get a boyfriend?" Stephanie walked toward her, leaving her mom to pick up the bag she had dropped at the sight of the kiss.

Miss Stanley smiled. "Last week. He saw me at the grocery store and asked for my number. At first I had no intention of giving it to him, but it felt like... I don't know. He seemed so genuine and kind."

"He's gorgeous!"

Her teacher laughed and grinned. "And there's that too. You're here early. Everything okay?"

Stephanie looked at her teacher for a second and then down at the bag her mother had placed next to her. "Um, Yes. I think so." She picked up her bag. "I just wanted to get here early to do some warm-ups. Let me go change. I'll be right back."

———————————

Lucas walked off the stage as the audience continued their applause.

"Always leave them wanting more, eh Lucas?" The stage hand patted Lucas on the back.

"Wouldn't have it any other way." His smile faded from his face as he walked away. He found a chair and sat down with a groan and rubbed his left leg.

"Leg bothering you again?" Veronica walked over to him and put her arm over his shoulders. "It seems to be every day now. When are you going to visit the doctor?"

Lucas sighed. "I guess I can't put it off any longer. I'll see one next week after Stephanie's birthday."

"I remember her. She was adorable. How old is she now?"

"Sixteen. I kept missing her birthdays, but no more. If I miss this one, I don't think she'd ever forgive me."

Veronica laughed. "Oh, she adores you. I'm sure she would get over it." She kissed him on the cheek. "Be safe." She walked toward her dressing room and looked back. "Any news yet on where our next location is to be?"

Lucas shook his head. "I haven't heard anything yet. They're cutting this one close."

Veronica shrugged. "It isn't the first time." She disappeared into her room and closed the door.

Lucas stood and gingerly walked to his own room where his cell phone rang. By the time he got there, it had stopped. He looked at it and saw that Mary had called. "Probably reminding me of Stephanie's birthday party next week." He called her back and got to hear about Stephanie's birthday party the following week. After he finished his call, he put the phone on the table where it rang again. He smiled and opened it up to answer it. "Hello, Sweetie… Yes, I'm flying home first thing tomorrow morning so I'll be able to make it. What would you like for your birthday?" He looked around for some paper and something to write with. After finding it he paused. "A what? How do you spell that?" He wrote down some items and scowled as he looked at the list. "Okay, I'll see what I can do… I love you too."

Lucas walked out of the building with his suitcase and squinted as the head-lights of a turning truck temporarily blinded him. The brakes screeched and the truck came to a halt in front of him. The driver hopped out and ran to the back jerked the rolling door up. He grabbed a bundle of newspapers with one hand and pulled the door down with the other in a fluid motion. He ran up to and un-locked the empty kiosk to drop in the stack of freshly printed papers. The man nodded to him and ran around the front of the idling truck to hop through the open space into the driver seat. With a grind, the driver put the truck into gear and a cloud of sooty smoke shot out of the exhaust pipe as he drove toward the next corner to repeat the procedure.

Lucas put his suitcase down and hailed a cab as he caught his breath. "I guess I'm older than I thought."

The cab stopped and Lucas got into the car as the driver put his suitcase into the back. When the driver got in, he looked back at Lucas and stared hard at him. "Do I know you?"

Lucas looked back at the driver and shrugged. "I don't think so. I don't live around here. I'm just on tour with my company for a stage play."

"That's it! Yeah, I just saw you the other day with my girl. Took her out for our anniversary. You were good!"

"I'm glad you liked the show. Thank you."

"You know, the way you sort of limped across the stage looked so real. Can't wait to tell Laquel how I met the man from the show. To the airport?"

"Yeah." Lucas rubbed his leg and frowned.

When they arrived, the driver held a piece of paper and pen in front of Lucas. "If you don't mind? Laquel would love it." Lucas smiled and signed the paper. "Is that Lucas Starr? Hey, alright! You have a good flight now."

Lucas stared out the window of the plane as it raced down the runway and watched as the pink and reddish hues of the sky shifted to a peach color. In the blink of an eye, the sun peeked over the horizon like a bright pinpoint in the sky against the dark surface of the earth. The plane turned and the rising sun disap-peared behind them. Once they reached the cruising altitude of 36,000 feet, the captain turned off the seatbelt sign and the flight attendants slowly moved the drink cart down the aisle.

Lucas gratefully accepted a drink and set it on the little seat tray. He pulled down the window cover and closed his eyes and just as he was starting to slip into unconsciousness his leg spasmed in pain and he knocked the drink off his tray onto the man next to him. He closed his eyes and gritted his teeth as he tried to endure the deep throbbing pain.

"Whoa!" The man in the center seat picked up the cup and held it out for Lucas when he saw the eyes of Lucas squeezed tightly shut. "Sir, are you okay?"

Breathing heavily, Lucas opened his eyes and turned to the man. "I am so sorry." His face grimaced as he tried to pick up the ice cubes and put them into the empty cup. The other passenger by the aisle offered her napkins in assistance.

The man hit the button over his seat and soon a flight attendant arrived. She opened the overhead bin and pulled out a terry cloth towel and handed it to the man so he could clean up the spill. When she looked up at Lucas, she saw him gritting his teeth. "Sir, are you okay?"

"My leg is just killing me. Can I get some aspirin or something?"

"Of course." She went to the station at the back of the plane and came back with a couple of aspirin and a cup of water. Lucas took it and after much shifting around and rubbing of his leg, finally got to sleep.

"Sir?"

Lucas opened his eyes and saw the two passengers next to him and the flight attendant all looking at him.

"We're about to land. Would you please bring your seat upright?" The attendant waited for Lucas to move his seat upright before continuing on her trek up the aisle to prepare for the landing.

"Glad one of us could sleep. I can never sleep when I'm flying." The man bent the corner of the page in his book before closing it.

Lucas blinked and filled his lungs with air and held it for a second before letting it out. "Normally I can't either. Guess I really needed it." Lucas pushed up the window cover and looked out the window to see the familiar landscape. Lucas rubbed his leg as he continued to watch the land get closer and closer until, with a bump, the plane landed.

"This your final stop?"

Lucas looked at the man. "Huh?"

"I said, is this your final stop?"

"Yes. I'm here for my granddaughter's birthday."

"Oh, that's nice. How old is she?"

"Sixteen. She'll be sixteen."

"Scary age. Driving, dating. My daughter is 18. She's off to college this fall. I just hope she doesn't wind up pregnant."

"Well, I'm sure you raised her up right."

Lucas thanked the cab driver and carried his suitcase up to his house. He worked his way to the bedroom and opened the door to find his wife reading in bed. "Oh, you're up. Good morning."

"Good morning." She got up and gave him a kiss. "You made it home."

He smiled. "And with time to spare."

"How early did you leave? I bet you're exhausted."

"Actually, I was able to sleep on the plane so I'm awake."

"That's new."

"Yeah. I'm going to get Stephanie her gift. You want to come?"

"I'm still in my pajamas. You go. I have some stuff around here I need to do. She said she already told you what she wants?"

"She called yesterday right after you did. Gave me a list of possible items, but I don't know what half of them are." He pulled the list out of his pocket.

Mary laughed. "You better get going then."

Lucas was pleased to find the thin Saturday morning traffic moving. He glanced down at the list. "Let's see, where can I find an MP3 player? What *is* an MP3 player?" He looked up and did a small correction to the direction of the car. "I guess I could go…" He gritted his teeth and squinted as pain shot through his leg. As his leg spasmed, he pulled his hand down on the steering wheel causing the car to swerve.

CHAPTER 7

"Papa?" Stephanie sat up in her bed and listened. Not hearing anything she got up and went down the hallway and into the empty living room. She scowled and headed into the kitchen to find it also empty. "Hmmm." She walked over to the phone that hung on the wall and dialed her grandfather's mobile number. "Come on. Pick up." Hearing it go into voice mail, she sighed and held the button to hang it up and started to put the handset back onto the wall holder when she changed her mind and dialed her grandmother. "Hi Grandma, I'm sorry that I'm calling you so early... oh good. Yeah, I was wondering if you've heard from Papa... he did? Oh. I just tried calling him and he didn't answer. I'm worried... Oh, that would be great. Thanks... I love you too."

Stephanie put the phone back on the wall and sat down on a kitchen chair. Before she fully sat on the seat she stood and went to her room and got dressed. She paced her room for 15 seconds and then sat down on her bed. "Oh God, please let him be okay." She stood and went into her mom's room. "Mom! You gotta get up."

"No, you're practice isn't for a few more hours."

"You gotta get up. There's something wrong with Papa."

Rose rolled over and sat up. "What? What happened?"

"I don't know, but I just know something happened to him. Get up!"

Rose dropped back onto the bed. "Stephanie, I had a long night. Talk to me in an hour."

"Mom... please."

Rose opened her eyes and saw Stephanie crying. "Okay. Give me a minute. Did you try calling him?"

"Yes and there's no answer. I also called Grandma and she said she would call back and she hasn't. I just know something happened."

"Close the door and give me a minute. Go make some coffee for me, will ya?"

Stephanie closed the door behind herself and went to make the coffee. After it had finished brewing she poured some into a cup and put in the sugar and cream as her mother liked and was about to take it to her when her mom appeared at the kitchen doorway. "Okay, bring it with. We gotta go."

"Where?"

"Oh. I don't…" The phone rang. Stephanie ran over and answered it. "Hello?" She listened for a few seconds before she choked up. "Mhmm." She held the phone out to her mom.

"Hello? Hi Mom." As she listened she brought her hand up to her mouth. "Okay. We'll be right there."

Stephanie didn't wait for her mom to finish hanging up the phone before she headed through the door into the garage. She waited for her mom to come to the car.

Rose got into the driver seat. "How did you know something was wrong?"

"I don't know. I just… I don't know. I woke up and had this awful feeling. Mom… a car accident." Tears welled up and poured down her cheeks.

"I know Baby, I know."

"It's Daddy all over again." Stephanie caressed the chain hanging around her neck.

Rose put her hand on Stephanie's leg and drove toward the hospital in silence.

Stephanie stopped at the open door while her mom walked past her into the hospital. Her mom turned. "Stephanie?"

"I don't know if I can do this."

Rose walked back to her, took her hand, and held her eyes with her own. "We'll do it together. Okay?"

Stephanie took a deep breath and nodded. Holding her mom's hand she walked into the hospital. It looked different than she remembered with things in different places and rooms laid out differently. As they wandered the hospital, she let go of her mom's hand.

Even her mom got confused. At one time and they had to turn around to go back to a different waiting room where a nurse worked at her station. "Excuse me."

The nurse looked up from her computer. "Yes?"

"We're looking for a patient named Lucas Starr."

The nurse tapped some keys on the keyboard. "He's in the I.C.U." She pointed to her right. "Go through those double doors, turn right. In about 20 yards, you'll see some elevators. Go up to the third floor and when you get off, turn left back toward this direction and when you get to the first hallway, you'll need to turn right. Okay?"

Rose stood looking at the double doors. "I think so."

The nurse smiled. "There will be signs. Just get to the elevators and go to the third floor. Elevators are through the doors and to the right. You'll be fine."

Rose nodded and led Stephanie through the doors that were indicated at the far end of the waiting room. Turning right they walked until they found the elevators. When they got off on the third floor, the wall across from the elevator had a sign pointing them toward the I.C.U.

As they got closer, Stephanie grabbed her mom's hand again. When they got into the large room, her eyes scanned the beds to find her grandfather. When she saw him, she let out her breath that she had been holding since they walked in. "Papa." She let go of Rose's hand and ran to the bed. Despite the attached I.V., she grabbed his hand while tears streamed down her face.

"Mom." Rose gave Mary a hug. "How is he? What happened?"

Mary sighed and sat down. "On his way to get Stephanie her birthday gift and somehow he lost control of the car causing it to roll. He's in a coma. They also…" She glanced at Stephanie and then looked back at Rose. "We'll talk more later."

Rose nodded and went to find chairs for Stephanie and herself.

"Stephanie, are you hungry?"

Stephanie looked up at her mom, looked down at the chair she sat in, and then looked back up at her. "When did you bring a chair?"

Rose smiled. "About half an hour ago. You never had any breakfast, are you hungry? Let's go get something to eat."

Mary stood and joined Rose. "We can all go together."

Stephanie looked at Lucas and then back to them. "Bring me an apple?"

"Okay." Rose leaned down and hugged Stephanie before she and Mary left. When they came back, they saw that Stephanie had turned her chair to face the bed and had leaned over and rested her head next to his legs and fallen asleep.

"Poor thing. This morning must have been exhausting for her." Mary went and found a small blanket and put it over Stephanie.

"Stephanie? Stephanie?"

Stephanie sat up and opened her eyes half-way, closed them and then opened them again only half-way. She took in a deep breath and looked around. "Hmmm?"

Rose stood by her holding out Mary's cell phone. "Why don't you call Miss Stanley and let her know you won't make it today?"

Stephanie gawked at the phone for a few seconds before taking it. "She got married. Her name is Mrs. Parker now." She yawned and opened her eyes fully and looked at Lucas. "Any change?"

"No Baby. No change."

Stephanie opened the phone and dialed the dance studio. "Hi Mrs. Parker, it's Stephanie. I can't make it in today… Yeah, my Papa is in the hospital… Tomorrow?" She looked up at her mom who shrugged. "Maybe, I don't know yet… okay I will. Thanks." She closed the phone and handed it back to her mom. "She says to take my time and that she has an announcement for us when we do come in."

"Mrs. Starr?"

Mary and Rose both looked over and then Mary stood. "Mark? When did you become a doctor?"

Mark hugged her. "I've been a doctor for several years now." He looked at Lucas in the bed. "I heard he was in here, I'm so sorry."

"Thanks. This is my daughter-in-law, Rose, and my granddaughter Stephanie. Rose already knows you."

Mark shook Rose's hand. "You do?"

Rose smiled. "Well, not exactly. I had some classes with Janie in school."

"Ah." He shook Stephanie's hand. "The one who played Cinderella a few years ago?"

"Yes."

"That was actually quite enjoyable. I don't normally care for ballet, that's something my nephew is in, but I liked that." He pulled a card out of his pocket and handed it to Mary. "I have to continue my rounds, but if you need anything at all, have some questions that need answered, you just call my beeper. Okay?" He hugged Mary again. "Again, I am so sorry. Mr. Starr was always so nice to me growing up. Rose, Stephanie, good to meet you."

Rose looked at the card in Mary's hand. "That's nice."

"He's single, too."

"Oh mom." Rose looked down at the card again.

Mrs. Parker taped her toes as Stephanie walked into the studio. She looked up and smiled. "Hi Stephanie, how's your grandfather?"

Stephanie shook her head. "Still no change. It's been more than three weeks and still no change."

"I'm sorry. With your appearance, I thought perhaps he was well. Did you have a nice birthday party?" She finished her task and slipped on her slippers, grabbed a small wrapped package on the floor, and glided over to Stephanie.

"No, my mom is trying to get me away from the hospital. I canceled my birthday party."

Mrs. Parker held out the package to Stephanie. "Happy birthday."

"Oh." She took the package and opened it to reveal a pair of very old ballet slippers. The color had faded and the toes were scuffed. She looked quizzically at her teacher. "Are these...?"

"They belonged to Anna Pavlova..."

Stephanie gasped. "The ones from your office!? I couldn't possibly take them."

"You can and you will. I have ..." She paused and cleared her throat. "It has been my most wonderful privilege to be your teacher over the years. As you know, they were my inspiration to start dancing. I hope these will inspire you to continue in the art in the many years you have ahead of you."

Stephanie tilted her head. "Are you going somewhere?"

"You missed the announcement in your long absence. Mr. Parker has been offered a job out of state. We will be moving in less than a month." She looked around the nearly empty studio. "I have almost everything packed up for when I find a new place to teach." She sighed. "I'm going to miss this place."

Stephanie's body went limp as she stood looking at her teacher. She looked around and realized she hadn't noticed the missing piano and other items. She looked back at Mrs. Parker. "I..."

"Perhaps we can have one last lesson to see if you can get that posture just right, yes?"

"Nobody else is coming in?"

Mrs. Parker turned away. "Classes ended last week." She took in a deep breath and held it a second before letting it go. "No, this... this will be a private lesson." She wiped her eye, straightened her shoulders and turned to Stephanie. "Now... go to the bar and show me first position."

A man pounded a 'For Sale' sign into the ground as Rose drove Stephanie away from the ballet studio. "When it rains, it pours. So much happening these days." Stephanie stayed fixated on the sign as they drove past. "What did she give you?"

"The ballet slippers of Anna Pavlova. Her grandmother had given them to her."

"She's famous?"

Stephanie turned to look at the road ahead, her voice still flat. "Yes."

"That was very kind of her. I bet you'll miss her." She waited for a response but didn't get one. "You feel like seeing Papa?"

"Okay."

When they got to the hospital, Stephanie and Rose parked by a different door than the one they had parked near that fateful morning. This entrance allowed them to get to the I.C.U. with more efficiency. After Rose got out of the car she closed the door and turned to find Mark right beside her.

"Hey there, perfect timing, I was just taking a break when I saw you pulling in." He kissed her. Rose gestured toward the car with her head. "Oh, She's not at ballet?"

Stephanie stood by the car, gawking at her mother and the doctor. "What... when did this happen?"

Rose cleared her throat and looked at Stephanie. "Mark and I have been seeing each other for a while now. I wanted to tell you, but I wasn't sure how you would take it."

Stephanie put her hand to her face, shook her head, and then lowered her hand. "I gotta go see how Papa is doing." She went in ahead of them into the hospital. When she got to the room where here grandfather lay, Stephanie went over to her grandfather's bed and looked at him. He had gotten so thin. She kissed him on the cheek and told him the news of the ballet studio closing down and the gift she received. "I wish you could have been there Papa. Mrs. Parker said I never had better form. And she cried Papa. I didn't think I would ever see her get so emotional. You know how she is, always so formal so she wouldn't let me see, but I knew she was crying."

Mark and Rose came in and walked over to Mary where he handed her some papers. He looked over at Stephanie. "I think it's good that she's here too. This is definitely a family decision."

Rose looked up at him. "I don't think I could have gotten by these past few weeks without you." She looked toward Stephanie and found her watching them. "Baby, there's something else we need to talk about."

Stephanie's shoulders sagged. "There's more?"

Mary set the papers down onto a nearby table. "Honey..." She swallowed. "Honey, your Papa's in pretty bad shape. It's been over three weeks and we don't know if he'll ever recover."

Stephanie stepped closer to the bed and put her hand onto the side rail. "Papa will be just fine. You'll see."

"Perhaps. But even if he does come out of the coma, we don't know how he would be. You wouldn't want him to be a vegetable for the rest of his life. This is hard on me too, but sometimes you have to just accept things."

"No... you can't." Tears streamed down her face and her voice quivered. "You can't do this. I won't let you! Papa will be fine. He has to be."

Rose walked up to Stephanie and put her hand onto her shoulder. "Baby, there's something else you don't know."

CHAPTER 8

Stephanie collapsed into the chair next to her. "There's more?"

"Baby, Papa has bone cancer. Remember how he would rub his legs after performing? The cancer was causing him pain."

Mary walked over to Stephanie and put her hand onto her shoulder. "This is hard, I know. But, maybe it's for the best. You know, even if he came out of this he may not remember who you are, your mom, or even me. He might not be able to talk. There's so much about the brain we don't know. Then he has to battle the cancer? I don't want him to suffer. Maybe we should let him go."

Stephanie looked at her mom with Dr. Phelps standing a little behind her then up to her grandma and then over to Lucas as he lay on the bed with I.V. and monitoring equipment hooked up to him. She shook her head and stood. "No. We have to give him a chance."

"Honey, it's been three weeks. You think this is easy for me? Do you think I want to lose my husband? But look at him." She paused as Stephanie glanced at Lucas. "This is no way to exist. It's not living."

Tears streamed down Stephanie's cheeks as she voiced her frustration. "Not yet!"

Mary recoiled and looked to Rose and Mark as if searching for support. She sighed and patted Stephanie on the back. "Okay, not yet."

Stephanie held onto Lucas' hand with both of her hands and closed her eyes. "Oh God, please let him wake up." She looked at Lucas. "Remember, you said you would have the last dance at my wedding. You promised. So you gotta wake up." She watched him for a minute and sighed. She sat down again and put her forehead down onto his hand. "Papa, please wake up."

Mary walked away from Stephanie over to Rose who gave her a hug. Mary pulled back, wiping tears from her eyes. "Let's wait a couple more days."

Rose nodded. "Okay."

"Papa, please wake up."

Lucas felt a hand holding his own and slowly opened his eyes and looked around at the unfamiliar surroundings. He turned his head slightly and looked at Stephanie. He made a brief quiet sound in his throat.

Stephanie's head jerked up, her eyes and cheeks still wet from the crying. "Papa?" Lucas cleared his throat as everyone approached the bed. Stephanie involuntarily squeezed his hand as she asked him in an even voice, "Papa? Can you say my name? Who am I?"

Lucas scowled and opened his mouth to speak but nothing came out. He cleared his throat and tried again. "Stephanie." The word was almost a croak, his voice rough from not being used for so long.

She took in a shuddering breath and looked at the others who had gathered around the bed. "He remembers me!"

Mary teared up and leaned down and hugged Lucas. "Oh, Honey. I thought I had lost you."

"Ow." Lucas pulled on his hand and Stephanie let go. As everyone talked at once, Lucas raised his hand up toward his face and closed his eyes.

Mark put his hand onto Rose and Mary's shoulders. "I think it would probably be best to let him get some rest. He'll need some time to get oriented. Why don't you come back in the morning? I'll schedule an MRI for tomorrow afternoon."

Mary gave Lucas' hand a squeeze and bent down and kissed his cheek. "I'll be back tomorrow."

Rose kissed his cheek and followed Mary away from the bed. She looked back to see Stephanie still standing by the bed. She went over and hugged her. "Come on Stephanie. You can come back with Grandma first thing in the morning."

"Bye Papa. I love you." She kissed his cheek and followed her mom out of the room as Lucas watched them leave. Within a few minutes, a natural sleep overtook him.

Mary set her coffee down on the table next to the bed. She looked over and saw Lucas watching her. "Oh, you're awake." She leaned over and kissed him. "How you feeling?"

Lucas grunted a little. "Sore. No Rose or Stephanie?"

"Rose is working and Stephanie is in the cafeteria getting herself something to eat." She held his hand. "I'm glad you're okay. I…" she choked up. "Never mind. I'm glad you're back with us."

"I saw Mark yesterday. Didn't know he was a doctor."

Mary smiled. "He's just like his dad, never tells anything unless you ask."

Lucas rolled his eyes. "I did ask and he still didn't exactly say. I asked him, 'How long have I been here?' Know what he said?" Mary shook her head. "He said 'Long enough to give us a scare.'" He looked at Mary. "How long have I been here?"

Stephanie walked over eating an apple, a smile on her face. "Hi Papa." She leaned over and kissed his cheek. "I just saw Dr. Phelps and he said that they're going to move you to a different room today."

"Sweetie, how long have I been here?"

Stephanie looked up at her grandmother then looked back at her grandfather. "Three weeks."

Lucas took a deep breath and looked up at the ceiling. "Three weeks." After a second he looked back at Stephanie. "That means I missed your birthday. Again. I'm sorry."

Stephanie put her head onto his chest. "I'm glad you're alive."

"Did Mark say anything else Dear?"

Lucas looked over at Mary. "Not really. Just said he wanted to run some tests on me today to check my head. Said there's something else he needed to talk to me about once I feel up to it."

"Mr. Starr, it's good to see you awake." The nurse came in and picked up the chart at the foot of his bed, looked up at the equipment and wrote down some numbers. After she put the clipboard back, she walked over next to Mary. "This woman has been here every waking moment. And your granddaughter had to be dragged away to do her dance class. Your family loves you very much." She paused as Mary and Stephanie echoed her sentiment. "You ready to go to your new room?" Lucas nodded and the nurse removed the attached equipment from him. "We'll leave the I.V. If you ladies will just follow us, we'll take this young man to his new room."

An orderly that had been standing nearby came over and helped the nurse get the bed into motion as Mary and Stephanie followed behind. Stephanie leaned over to whisper into her grandmother's ear. "When Papa was talking about getting his head checked, I kept waiting for him to say something about them finding something in it."

"I'm sure he'll get his humor back soon." She looked at Stephanie up and down. "When did you get taller than me?"

Dr. Phelps walked in with another doctor to find Lucas talking to Mary and Stephanie. The food tray hung over the bed, mostly untouched. "Good morning Mr. Starr. How are you feeling today?"

"Mark, I'm doing okay." He rubbed his left leg as he spoke.

"That's good to hear. I see you've been rubbing your leg a lot. When did the pain start?"

Lucas looked down at his leg and then at the other doctor. The smile on his face faded. "A couple years ago, I would get a little pain after being on my feet for a couple of hours. I figured it was because of old age, but in the past few months it suddenly started to get a lot worse." He paused. "You already found something, didn't you?"

Mark nodded. "When you were admitted after the car crash, we did a lot blood work. There were some indications you might have cancer. After talking to Mrs. Starr and hearing about your leg pain, we did a small test and found that you have Osteosarcoma. A type of bone cancer. This is Dr. Baral, the oncologist on staff here. He'll be working with me and a dietitian for your treatment."

As Mark talked, Mary grabbed Lucas' hand. "A dietitian?"

Dr. Baral nodded. "Yes, ma'am. The body needs materials from many varieties of fruits and vegetables to make it work right. Especially in times of sickness. What you eat, and how much of it, makes a big impact on your wellbeing." He indicated the breakfast tray. "Are you not hungry?"

Lucas shook his head. "No, haven't had much of an appetite lately." He looked at Mark. "So, how much longer do I have to live? A month? A year?"

"That largely depends on you. The cancer has not metastasized, so your long-term survival looks good. Chances are you could live to be 90. Just listen to Dr. Baral and the dietitian and your treatment should go well." He glanced at Stephanie and smiled. "And make sure she doesn't eat all of your apples. They're good for you." Stephanie smiled and looked at her grandfather. "I'll leave you with Dr. Baral for now and check up on you later."

Dr. Baral thanked Mark and then looked at the chart at the foot of Lucas' bed briefly before addressing Lucas again. "Dr. Phelps is a kind man and I am glad he is a friend of yours to help you through this. You have an unusual case as this is not something normally associated with adults. Also, judging from what you said, it wasn't initially aggressive which is also unusual." He took a deep breath and looked Lucas in the eyes. "Let's see what we can do to keep you from losing your leg."

Mary gasped and tightened her grip on Lucas' hand. "His leg?

Stephanie remained silent as tears stung her eyes.

Rose came into the room to find Stephanie looking at a magazine with Lucas while Mary napped. She walked up and kept her voice low. "What are you guys looking at?"

"A travel magazine. Papa says he wants to go to the beach when he's strong enough."

Rose soundlessly said "Oh" and nodded her head. "Bought it in the gift shop?"

Stephanie looked up from the magazine. "Actually Dr. Phelps brought it to us after he heard Papa talking about the beach."

"That's nice. Find any place you want to go?"

Lucas gave a small smile. "All of these places are for the rich. But it's still nice to look."

"Oh! Look at this one Papa!" Stephanie showed her grandfather a villa on a beach scattered with palm trees. "It's so beautiful. Maybe I can go there for my honeymoon." She looked up at her mom. "Think you'll marry Dr. Phelps?"

Rose stood still for a second. "I don't know. We just started dating."

Stephanie looked back at the magazine. "He's nice." She turned the page a couple more times. "We could always stay in an old light house." She showed the picture to her grandfather.

Lucas glanced up at Rose as she stared at her daughter, winked, and looked back at the magazine. "Can't say I've ever done that. Not sure if I can climb all of those stairs though."

"True. Hmmm." She twisted her lips and continued to flip through the magazine.

An orderly came in with a wheelchair. "Good evening, Mr. Starr. You have an MRI scheduled?" Lucas nodded. "I'm sorry it's taken so long. The normal operator had a small incident with his car and was late getting in by a couple of hours. I understand you were in a car crash yourself?" He came over as he talked. Stephanie and her mom got out of the way so he could help Lucas out of the bed and into the chair.

"Yes. Apparently I flipped the car over and hit my head. Put me into a coma."

"That's quite the ordeal. I'm glad to see you've come through okay." He turned to Rose and Stephanie. "We'll be back in about 30 minutes. It's a simple scan of the head."

Lucas turned toward them as he got wheeled out the door. "We'll see if there's anything left up there."

"See? I told you he would get his humor back." Mary smiled at Stephanie from across the room.

Mary stopped short at the entrance to keep from bumping into a woman coming out as she and the others returned from the cafeteria. "Excuse me. I'm sorry."

"No, I'm sorry. I'm looking for Mr. Starr."

"He should be back any time. He had to get an MRI." As she spoke, Lucas appeared from around the corner down the hall with a different orderly pushing his wheelchair. "Oh, there he is now."

The woman stepped back into the room to wait as Lucas got pushed into the room. The orderly moved to assist him into the bed, but got waved away by Lucas. She waited until the orderly had left before introducing herself. "Good evening. Mr. Starr?"

"That's me."

The woman smiled. "Hi, I'm Mrs. Cunningham. The dietitian on staff here."

"So you're not a doctor?"

"No sir, but I do have a Master's Degree in Nutrition." She smiled and raised her eyebrows. "Think that'll do?" Lucas smiled in return so she continued. "Tonight we're going to start you on a special diet. It's designed to help you gain some of your weight back and keep you in shape as you begin your chemo next week. I understand you've had a recent loss of appetite so the doctor should give you something to stimulate it. Even with that, you may find you aren't hungry at your prescribed snack time. I need you to eat anyway." She paused. "Any questions so far?"

"This is the first I've heard of the chemo."

"Oh?" She looked down at her notes. "Dr. Baral should have said something by now. I'll double-check his schedule. I know he's taking a day off this week, but I thought that was tomorrow." She held up a legal pad with an attached pen. "Who should get this? It's to keep track of your overall feeling and, um, bodily functions."

Mary stepped toward the woman. "I'll take that. If we leave it to him, you'll never get anything written down."

"Good. Also, here is the prepared diet plan."

Lucas held his hand out for the stapled papers and once Mary handed them to him he looked them over. "No bacon? No coffee?"

Mary smiled. "I always said all that bacon wasn't good for you."

Lucas sighed and continued to look at the papers. "So what's for dinner tonight?"

"Tonight you'll have fish with some greens, a whole grain bread, and some fruit." Mrs. Cunningham looked at Stephanie. "You're Stephanie?" Stephanie nodded. "Dr. Phelps says I should make sure you don't eat Mr. Starr's apples." Stephanie gasped as the others laughed.

Mary and Stephanie came in the next morning to find Dr. Baral talking to Lucas. He nodded at them in greeting as he continued. "... a high dose chemotherapy to quickly knock out the cancer. Normally I don't like to take this approach as it will also kill more good cells, but it looks like you may have had this for a while and it has quickly accelerated. After that, we'll be doing a stem cell transplant. So I have some good news and bad news. Which do you want first?"

"I could use some good news, so go ahead and give that to me first."

"The stem cells will be yours so there won't be any rejection."

"If that's the good news, then what's the bad?"

CHAPTER 9

"The bad news is that we need to perform a small surgery to collect some marrow from your good leg and then in a few months, after treatment is done, we'll need to do another surgery to put it into your leg with cancer. I have the initial surgery scheduled for you in two days time. Is there anything you need from me?"

"A way out of this?"

"It won't be easy, but I believe this is the best way." Without another word, he turned and left the room.

Lucas looked over at Mary and Stephanie with a grim expression. "Guess I'm stuck in here for a little longer."

"I'm sorry Honey. I wish I could do something."

"It is what it is. We'll get through this." He looked at Stephanie. "Want my apple?"

"I can't. Dr. Phelps said you're supposed to eat them."

"I'm too full. I could eat it and get sick, but then it would just go to waste. If you eat it then it won't be wasted."

Mary handed the apple to Stephanie. "Did you ever find out why Dr. Baral wasn't here yesterday?"

"I guess Mrs. Cunningham had the wrong day written down. Guess she couldn't read his handwriting either."

"Your mom is concerned with all the time you're spending at the hospital." Mary picked up a tray in the cafeteria and handed it to Stephanie.

"I'm okay."

Mary pointed to a sandwich and Stephanie nodded. She put it onto the tray along with another one. "Maybe you should spend some time with your friends. Summer is almost over. You'll be going back to school soon."

"Papa needs me. I can see my friends at school."

"Oh Honey, I know how much you love your Papa. I just gotta wonder if… what if this doesn't end well? Would he want your last memories of him to be in the hospital? Would you want that?"

Stephanie sighed. "Grandma, remember when we went to Chicago and those guys were swinging their belts at us and how he stood up to them and punched that guy in the face?"

"Yes, I do."

"I was so scared, but he wasn't. That's the memory of him I'll always have. My brave Papa who's always there to protect me."

Mary sniffed and pulled out a tissue from her purse to wipe her eyes and blow her nose. "Yes, he's a brave man. You're so much like him you know."

"I am?"

Mary smiled at her. "So full of life and so strong. It's no wonder he loves you so much." She walked up to the cashier as Stephanie held the tray of food and drink. "Your poor father, he never got the attention he wanted from his father and tended to shrink away into his own self instead of fighting for what he wanted. Looking back, I think that just made the situation worse. And then you came along, so energetic and outgoing, I think he felt he was in constant competition for your affection."

"Good evening Mrs. Starr. Stephanie."

Mary and Stephanie turned to see Dr. Phelps coming up to the cashier with a sandwich and drink in-hand.

"Is Papa okay?"

"He's still in surgery, but everything is still looking good."

"Would you like to eat with us? My mom isn't here, but we don't mind. Do we grandma?"

"Not at all."

Mark paid the cashier and looked at his watch. "I have a few minutes. Thanks."

Stephanie kept watching him as they ate. After he and Mary exchanged pleasantries about the weather and the plans for the chemotherapy he turned to Stephanie. "You're awfully quiet. You doing okay in all of this?"

"Pretty much. Just hoping he's okay."

Mark forced a half-smile. "I'm sure he'll be fine. If you ladies will excuse me, I need to go."

Stephanie watched him go and then turned to her grandmother. "I like him. You think he and mom will get married?"

Mary shrugged. "Who knows? Let's go see if your Papa is out of surgery." They stood and put their trash into the trash can and tray on the top. "Why this interest in Mark and your mother's relationship?"

"She's so sad sometimes. She looks at some pictures and cries. I want her to be happy and he's nice."

When they got back to the room, Rose sat next to an unconscious Lucas. "He just got back. There's a message on the answering machine for you Steph. A girl named Brittney asking if you want to go to the mall tomorrow. Isn't that the girl from dance class?"

"Yes, she is."

"I have the number here. Maybe you can use your grandma's phone and call her back."

Stephanie looked from one to the other and frowned. "I can see her at school."

"True, but you don't want to be rude. It's just a phone call. And who knows? Maybe you'll decide that you can spend some time with her tomorrow at the mall after all."

Stephanie glared at her mom for several seconds. "Fine. Grandma, can I use your phone?"

Mary picked her phone up from the side table as she watched the television and opened it. "Hello? Hi, Honey... Yes, he's up but... I don't... " She sighed. "Yes, I can come get you. Are you home yet?... At the school. Okay, give me a few minutes." She turned off the television and walked into the kitchen where Lucas sat staring at his small plate of food and glass of water. "Not hungry?"

"I think I am, but the smell alone is almost making me sick."

"You liked it enough yesterday."

Lucas looked up at her and shook his head. "I can't eat this."

"Well at least drink the water. You don't want to get dehydrated. Stephanie just called and wants to come over to visit."

Lucas nodded as he picked up the water. He held it near his mouth, took a couple of breaths and then gulped down three swallows before setting it down with a grimace. He closed his eyes and took in a few breaths before opening them. "I used to use water to wash bad tastes out. Now it is the bad taste."

"Maybe a little ice cream to help?" Lucas raised his shoulders an inch so Mary put a little ice cream into a bowl and set it in front of him. "Maybe that will help. You think you're okay for Stephanie to visit?"

"If you don't bring her, you know she'll find her own way over so you might as well get her."

"True. Okay, I'll be back in a few. You going to be okay?"

Lucas waved her away with his hand as he picked up his spoon to try the ice cream.

Mary pulled up next to the sidewalk where Stephanie stood talking to another girl. Stephanie waved goodbye and got into the car. "Who was that?"

"That's Brittney."

"Oh, okay. Now your Papa's having a hard day so you can't stay long."

"I just need his help with this assignment."

"What assignment is that?"

"Well you know how much Papa likes those stories of old places? In American History we're covering immigration and I thought he could help me with my report on Ellis Island so it can be more interesting. I'm sure he has some old stories he can tell me."

"He's definitely the man for that. We'll see how it goes."

When they entered the kitchen, an empty plate and a tipped over glass sat on the table. Water lay puddled up next to the glass and dripping onto the floor.

Stephanie looked around. "What happened?"

"I think I know. Will you clean this up? I gotta go check on Lucas." Mary left Stephanie to clean up the mess and went to the bedroom to find Lucas changing his shirt. "You okay?"

Lucas pulled his lips into a straight line. "Sorry about the mess in the kitchen. Give me a minute and I'll clean it up."

"Don't worry about it. Stephanie is cleaning it up. Have you been taking your anti-nausea medication?"

He sighed. "I think it came up with the water and food." He raised his voice. "I try to take it, but every day it seems I should take it at a different time! I expect the treatment to be one day, but they reschedule it for the next week! I can't wait for this to be over!" Mary remained silent and looked at him from across the room. "Sorry. This is so hard. So frustrating."

"I know. We're almost done. Only two more treatments to go." She paused. "Stephanie says she wants some help with her homework."

Lucas tossed his dirty shirt into the laundry basket. "Let me see if I can get some of the stench from my mouth."

Mary closed her eyes as she heard him gagging in the bathroom while he tried to brush his teeth. "Oh Lord. Please help him get through this." She returned to the kitchen to find everything cleaned up and Stephanie eating a banana.

"Is Papa okay?"

"He will be, Honey. He will be."

Lucas came into the kitchen and smiled at Stephanie. "Hey Sweetie."

"Papa? Your mouth is bleeding."

He put his finger up to his mouth and touched his tongue before looking at it to see blood. "Great. Be right back."

Mary put her hand on Stephanie's shoulder as they both watched him head back toward the bedroom. "That happens sometimes, you don't need to worry."

"I hope I never get cancer."

"I hope you never do either. Do you want something else to eat?"

"You don't have any apples?"

"They were hurting his mouth. We have some peaches."

Stephanie curled her nose. "I don't like the fuzz."

"Oh, that's right. Wait, isn't your mom working late tonight?"

Stephanie nodded as she stood and walked to the refrigerator to look inside.

"Why don't you eat with us then?"

"Okay."

"What's okay?" Lucas walked into the kitchen wearing another shirt.

"Stephanie's going to have dinner with us."

"Ah. That is okay." He smiled. "So, what's the rush to get over here?"

Stephanie closed the refrigerator and walked up to him and hugged him. "I just wanted to see you."

"Oh really?" He hugged her back. "A little birdie told me you wanted some help with your homework."

Stephanie stepped back. "Maybe a little. I'm doing a report on immigration through Ellis Island for my American History. I thought maybe you would have some stories I could add." She walked over to her book bag and pulled out a textbook and a notebook. "You know, 'cause you're into that sort of thing."

Lucas sat down at the table. "Stories of Ellis Island? You came to the right place. Let me tell you…"

Stephanie stared at the painting in the waiting room. "I'm really starting to hate that painting."

"What painting is that?" Rose looked to see what Stephanie was referring to.

"That one. Any of them. All of them. Spending too much time in this place. Waiting."

Rose put her arm around Stephanie and pulled her close. "It will be okay. After this, you won't have to come back to the hospital for a long, long time."

Stephanie nodded as she kept close to her mother. She saw Dr. Phelps walk in and sat upright.

"Mrs. Starr, Rose, Stephanie. Mr. Starr is out of his surgery and recovering in room 212. You're free to go see him, but it might be awhile before he regains consciousness. In a few days he can leave, but he'll have to be back daily for a check-up." He handed Mary some papers. "He'll need to take it easy for a while. The less walking the better. After that, his real recovery should begin."

"Thank you Mark." Rose stood. "For all you did. We appreciate it." She kissed him on the cheek and walked out with Stephanie and Mary behind her.

After they walked away, Stephanie ran up to walk next to her mom. "I don't understand why you're not dating anymore. He's nice."

"He is and I like him, but he is… uncertain? I don't know. I thought it best we stop seeing each other until he can figure out what he wants in the relationship."

When they found the room, Lucas lay unconscious. Rose and Mary sat in chairs while Stephanie stood by his bed staring at him. "He's so thin."

"He had a hard time finding something he could eat. One day he would like something and then the next he couldn't stand the taste of it. We had to keep a variety of things around the house so that he could eat." Mary sighed. "That chemotherapy was hard on him."

"When he gets out, we should take him to the pancake house for dinner. Think he can eat there?"

Lucas spoke up from the bed. "They have some good smoked bacon there." Stephanie turned back toward Lucas and Mary and Rose stood and came over to him. "Looks like I made it through."

Mary squeezed his hand. "I knew you would. How do you feel?"

Lucas took in a deep breath. "A little out of touch. Disconnected from myself."

"Once the anesthesia wares off, you'll be fine. Any feeling of sickness?"

"No. When do I leave? I am in desperate need of some good bacon."

Lucas picked a strip of bacon up from his plate and took a bite. He closed his eyes and savored the flavor. "Mmmmm. I have missed this." He opened his eyes. "What are you all staring at?"

Stephanie laughed. "You're too funny."

"Miss?" Lucas held his hand up to get the waitress' attention. "Will you get me another order of this bacon? It's delicious."

Mary's mouth dropped open. "Is that all you're going to eat is bacon?"

"I just might. I have been through a terrible ordeal and I deserve a treat."

Rose joined Stephanie in laughing and soon Mary laughed too.

Lucas took another bite and gave a big grin as he chewed and swallowed. "How would you guys feel about doing something different this year for Thanksgiving?"

Stephanie picked up some of her bacon. "Like having bacon?" She took a bite.

"No, no. Nothing that radical. I had something else in mind."

CHAPTER 10

"What'd you have in mind, Dad?"

"I know someone with a beach house in Miami Beach." Stephanie's eyes grew wide as she listened. "It's a vacation home and is usually empty most of the year. I think by then, I should be strong enough to go on a trip."

Stephanie clapped her hands. "That would be awesome. Yes, please let's do that! Oh! Can I bring Brittany?"

Rose answered her. "I don't know Steph. I'm sure her family would like her to be with them on the holiday."

"No, it's okay. Her sister got to go with her friend to Orlando last year for Thanksgiving."

"Mom? Dad? What do you think?"

Lucas looked at Mary. "I'm okay with it if Brittany's parents are."

Mary shrugged. "The more the merrier."

"Yay! Thank you! Thank you! I'll ask her tomorrow at school."

Stephanie ran up to the edge of the water and watched the small frothy waves wash over her feet. As the water pulled back out to the ocean, sand shifted under her feet and flowed over the tops. Brittany came up alongside her, both with large smiles on their faces.

Rose called out to them. "Stephanie, Brittany. You guys need some suntan lotion."

The girls ran back to the spot where a blanket lay spread out next to a rented umbrella and chairs upon which Mary and Lucas sat. Rose handed them the lotion after she put some on herself.

Stephanie took the bottle. "This is the perfect spot. I could spend all day here." She looked around as other people came onto the beach and set down their supplies. A boat in the distance zipping across the water mesmerized her. "Oh, I would love to be on that boat." She felt the bottle of lotion being taken from her. "What…?"

Brittany poured some lotion onto her hand. "Let me do your back and you can do mine." She motioned for Stephanie to turn around and put it on her back. "My sister came back looking like a lobster last year. So we need to make sure we do this every two hours."

"Oh yeah, I remember. She looked terrible." Stephanie looked for the boat, but couldn't find it again. "Papa, can we go on a boat?"

"Baby, why don't we just enjoy the beach today?" Rose took back the bottle of lotion and put it into her bag.

"Beat you to the water!" Brittany ran off toward the water with Stephanie a few steps behind.

Rose adjusted the umbrella forward to protect Mary and Lucas from the intense sunlight. "How's that?"

Mary smiled. "Perfect Dear. Thank you." She turned to Lucas. "How are you holding up? Your legs okay?"

Lucas watched the girls laughing and splashing each other in the surf. "I couldn't be better. Legs don't hurt at all. I think this is exactly what the doctor ordered."

"Actually I'm glad Stephanie could bring a friend." Rose sat back down on the blanket and watched the girls. "Do you think we can rent a boat?"

"My friend said that we want to look at the intracoastal for things like that. We can rent jet skis or go tubing or parasailing there and the water is a lot calmer."

Stephanie came running up to them. "We found a jellyfish! You gotta come see!"

Mary and Rose got up and waited for Lucas as he got up. Everyone followed Stephanie as she ran forward to where Brittany stood on the beach. When they arrived, she pointed toward a translucent blob with bits of dark colors inside of it on the sand.

Lucas walked up to it and bent down. "That's a jellyfish alright." He reached down to pick it up.

Mary gasped. "What are you doing? You're going to get stung!"

"Eh. It's small and there aren't any tentacles. I think I'm okay." He stood with it in his hand. "Want to hold it?"

Stephanie stepped back. "No way!"

"I will." Brittany came up close and looked at it. "What's it feel like?"

"Hmmm. Like cooked egg white? Best way to know is to hold it yourself. Here hold out your hand." He held his hand near Brittany who put one hand out. Lucas dropped the jellyfish into her hand.

Brittany looked at it and then touched it with a finger from her other hand before she dropped it.

Stephanie shook her hands as she watched. "Ewwwww. How can you touch it?"

Lucas laughed. "You girls are funny." He headed back to the protection of the umbrella.

After Brittany vigorously swished her hand in the water, she and Stephanie went up to the blanket and laid in the sun to 'work on their tan.'

"Hey Steph. You up?"

Stephanie turned in her bed. "No."

"Yes you are. What do you want to do today?"

"I want to sleep. You're supposed to sleep in when you're on vacation."

Brittany grabbed her pillow and threw it at Stephanie. "Time to get up."

Stephanie grabbed the pillow and put it under her own. "Ah, much better."

"Come on! Seriously, what do you want to do today?"

Stephanie turned toward Brittany. "Papa said we can do whatever we want. I want to go on a boat. Maybe go tubing."

Brittany's eyes got wide. "I've never been tubing. Think we can go?"

"Watch the master. Come on." Stephanie climbed out of bed and silently opened the bedroom door. She kept her voice low as she spoke. "You get out a frying pan and I'll get the bacon and eggs. Keep quiet." Stephanie went to the refrigerator and got out some bacon and eggs and took them to the cook top where Brittany had set out a couple of pans. "My Papa used to get up early, but since he got cancer he's been sleeping more."

The girls cooked the entire package of bacon before starting the eggs. As the eggs were frying, Brittany put four slices of bread into the toaster and helped Stephanie blot the bacon on sheets of paper towel when the smoke alarm pierced the quiet with sonic blasts.

"Oh no!" Brittany ran over to the smoking toaster and pushed up on the lever to reveal blackened toast.

Stephanie ran over to the smoke alarm and waved her hand at it to no avail. In desperation, she blew at it as she continued to wave her hand. Brittany rushed over and waved her hand at it too. A moment later, a towel appeared next to them waving at the smoke alarm. Stephanie looked over to see her Papa waving the towel.

"Oh darn. I wanted to surprise you."

Lucas laughed. "Oh, I'm surprised." After the alarm stopped beeping he put the towel down.

"So breakfast is ready?"

Brittany and Stephanie both turned to see Rose and Mary standing inside the doorway.

Rose walked over to the cupboard for some plates. "It was nice of you to make breakfast."

Brittany walked toward the toaster. "Yeah, but I think the toaster is broken. The dial is almost all the way down, but it still got burnt."

Mary walked over and unplugged the toaster. After carrying it to the trashcan, she turned it upside down and dumped the large accumulation of crumbs that had collected on the bottom. "That should help." She handed the toaster to Brittany. "Try it now."

Lucas grabbed a piece of bacon from the plate. "You girls figure out what you want to do today?"

"Hey! You're supposed to wait." Stephanie took the plate from the counter and set it on the dining table away from her grandfather. "We thought it would be fun to go tubing."

After everything and everyone got settled at the table and they had prayed, Lucas grabbed a few pieces of bacon and put them onto his plate. "So, tubing eh?"

"Hi, I'm Matt and I'll be your driver. Welcome to Fun in the Sun Water Sports. What are we doing today?" Matt sported a white t-shirt with the company's logo and red shorts. His sun bleached hair stood in sharp contrast to his dark sunglasses and tanned skin.

Stephanie and Brittany looked at Matt and then whispered to each other and giggled.

"The girls will be tubing."

Matt looked at everyone else and then back to Lucas. "Just the two of them?"

"Yes."

"Alright. I'll need these forms filled out and signed and then we can get started."

Lucas filled out the forms while Matt got life vests for everyone from the closet. "You guys have special plans for tomorrow?"

Rose accepted the vest from Matt. "I don't know. Dad, what are we doing tomorrow? It's Thanksgiving."

Lucas handed the clipboard back to Matt and put on his own vest. "There are several restaurants in the area. We'll make reservations tonight."

Matt helped everyone onto the boat and attached the large inflatable to the back of the boat before getting in himself. "There's an area up ahead that is generally free of water traffic. Just another company and ourselves use it." He looked at Brittany and smiled. "You going by yourself or you riding with her?"

Brittany and Stephanie looked at each other and then back to Matt and answered in unison. "Together."

Stephanie pulled her hair out of her face and let it fly in the wind as the boat picked up speed. She leaned her body up against the side of the boat and put her hand out into the spray of water. She looked over at Brittany to see her eyes closed and a smile on her face as her dark hair flew behind her. Her mom and grandparents were looking at and talking about various items along the shore as they sped by.

After speeding along for 10 minutes the boat slowed down and stopped. Matt walked to the back of the boat and put the tube into the water. He turned to Brittany "Okay. I'll need you to come here and get onto the middle of the tube."

Brittany reached Matt and held onto his hand as he helped her onto the tube. As she grabbed his hand, she looked at Stephanie and gave a big smile. After she situated herself on the tube, Matt reached out for Stephanie's hand and had Brittany move a little to the side as Stephanie got onto the tube also.

"Hold onto the handles. If you want me go faster, just put your finger into the air and make a wide circle. If you need me to slow down or stop, just put a fist into the air. Okay?" The girls nodded. "Okay, let's have some fun." He worked his way to the front of the boat and got behind the wheel. After starting the engine he shifted it out of neutral and moved the boat away from the tube.

Brittany smiled at Stephanie. "I think I'm in love."

Stephanie opened her mouth to reply when the rope pulled them. "Oh."

At first they moved slowly, but then they picked up speed and the tube bumped about. Stephanie raised her finger and spun it around and then grabbed the handle. Matt turned the boat so that the tube went over the wake. With grins on their faces, the girls both spun their fingers in the air and grabbed onto the handles again. Matt sped up some and meandered the boat so that the girls were jumping over the waves created by the boat. Soon they were clinging onto the handles as their bodies were flung about in the air. It wasn't long before first Stephanie and then Brittany were flung from the tube.

Matt brought the boat around with the tube in tow. "You okay?"

"That was great!" Stephanie pulled herself up onto the tube and then helped Brittany. "Let's do it again!"

Rose scowled "You sure you're okay?"

"This is awesome!" Brittany replied.

Matt pulled the boat away and soon had the girls clinging on again moving them from one side of the wake to the other. With practice they learned to lean their bodies into the pull of the tube and were able to survive jumping the wake. In their allocated half hour, they only fell off two more times before being towed back to the boat for the trip back.

Stephanie looked at her arm after she climbed back onto the boat. "I think I banged it on your head. Look at that bruise." She looked at her grandfather. "That was so much fun!"

"Fun? That was terrifying! I thought for sure you were going crash on top of each other in the water or maybe you were going to flip over in the air and crash down and knock yourself out."

Stephanie sat next to him and gave him a hug. "Thanks Papa!"

"Thanks Mr. Starr."

Lucas shook his head and hugged Stephanie back. "You're welcome. I'm glad you had fun. Let's go back to the beach where the only thing you have to worry about are the sharks."

Rose looked at Lucas. "Sharks?"

"I am thankful to be on this trip with you guys." Brittany looked to Stephanie. "Your turn."

"Okay." Stephanie looked at her grandfather. "I am grateful that my Papa is alive." Everyone around the table nodded. "I am also grateful to be here and I am grateful to Mrs. Parker for all she taught me before she had to leave." She looked at her mom. "Your turn."

Rose sighed. "I know we're all grateful to have Dad alive with us. Even tho it didn't work out with Mark, I'm glad he was there for me and we had that short time together. I do hope he decides to make it something more in the future." She looked at Mary.

Mary grabbed Lucas' hand. "I'm so thankful to have you." She let go of his hand and got a tissue from her purse and blew her nose.

"Seems to be a common theme." Lucas smiled around at the table as everyone looked at him. "I'm thankful to God for sparing my life and letting me have this time with you all. Let's eat." As everyone ate, Lucas spoke up again. "Pretty soon you girls will be graduating. What will you do after that?"

Stephanie swallowed the food she had in her mouth. "I haven't fully made up my mind. I do miss dancing…"

"Not me. When Mrs. Parker announced that the school was closing, I was actually relieved. I had been thinking of quitting anyway, but didn't want to be a quitter. You know? Anyway, this summer I had that job at the veterinarian office and I am sold. That is completely what I want to do the rest of my life."

"I thought you loved to dance."

"Not really, that's your thing. It's just that your passion for it was contagious. None of us wanted to let you down. You or Mrs. Parker. "

Stephanie blushed. "I had no idea."

CHAPTER 11

Rose leaned toward Stephanie. "See? Your love of dancing has an effect on others. You shouldn't give it up."

"So Brittany. How do you become a veterinarian?" Lucas took another bite as he listened.

"Dr. Orson said that I need to take a pre-med track in both high school and college. After that I go to vet school."

Stephanie watched Brittany, not taking her eyes off of her as she nibbled on her dinner roll. "What's in a pre-med track?"

"Chemistry, biology and math mostly."

Stephanie rolled her eyes. "Ugh. You know how much I hate biology."

Brittany laughed. "Remember when we had to dissect that cow's eye?"

"Oh my goodness I thought I would to faint."

Mary chuckled. "When Stephanie was about five, she insisted that she would never kiss boys because they had germs."

Everyone except Stephanie laughed.

Stephanie frowned. "I think I'm well past that now."

Brittany leaned over and bumped her with her shoulder. "So you saying you would kiss Matt?"

Stephanie gasped. "I'm sure you would! He was totally into you. Do I have a sign on my head that says back off? He never even looked at me."

"I'm sure you were imaging it, you're beautiful." Lucas rolled his eyes. "I would imagine that if you went to a dancing school, Stephanie, it would be a lot like what I did. Various method and style classes on the profession. Though I had to learn singing and dancing on my own after the fact. After some acting, I learned quickly that I could get the better roles if I knew how to sing and dance. What dances are they teaching these days?"

"Jazz, hiphop, and some other modern dances from around the world mostly I guess."

"Hmmm. That's what I feared. All the modern stuff and nothing of the classics." Lucas shook his head as he took another bite of food.

"Like what, Papa?"

"Well…" He swallowed. "There's a whole history of dance just from the past 50 years that you'll be missing that could be very useful. A career in dancing means you could be in commercials, movies, on-stage musicals. So you might be asked to do Jazz, but you might also be asked to do Swing or Ballroom Waltz dancing or who knows what else? Besides, when I have the last dance at your wedding, I think we should do something that gets everyone's attention." Lucas winked at Stephanie.

Stephanie nodded. "If it ever happens, our last dance does need to be special. Maybe you could teach me something?"

Brittany sat up straighter. "Oh, I would love to see that!"

Mary looked at Brittany. "You would?"

"Of course. Watching Stephanie dance with her grandfather? This has got to be something worth watching."

Lucas looked around at the living room space of the beach house. "I think…"

Stephanie went to the coffee table in the middle of the room. "Want me to move this?"

"No. Actually I think we may not be able to do this in here. It's too small."

"We could do it on the beach."

"Not a bad idea. Let's try that."

Stephanie and Lucas went out the wide glass door of the kitchen that led them down a small flight of stairs onto the beach with everyone else in tow. Rose grabbed her camera off the counter as they left the house. The low tide caused the water to recede leaving a flat and smooth area of damp sand.

Lucas walked out onto the sand. "Yes, this should do nicely. Okay, I think we should learn the Waltz. It would be just perfect for your reception." He held his left hand out and let Stephanie take it with her right and stand before him with her free hand on his shoulder and his other hand on her waist. He smiled as he looked her up and down. "Well, you definitely have a good posture, but your feet should be facing forward."

Stephanie adjusted her feet. "Sorry. Habit."

"Okay, the moves are simple. I'll move my feet and you just mirror what I do. At first, you can just look down to see what I'm doing. Once you have the steps, you just hold your head high and look at me as we dance. Ready?"

Stephanie nodded and as her grandfather moved and counted in groups of three, she mirrored his movements with her own feet. After they had done the basic step a couple of times, she looked up and smiled as they continued to dance, ignoring the strangers on the beach that had stopped to watch them.

Rose took a few pictures. "You two look absolutely beautiful."

Brittany sat cross-legged on Stephanie's bed with a school book across her lap. "What was that talk at the beach about college?"

"Huh?" Stephanie looked up from her own book. "What talk?"

"When we were at the beach, you said you didn't know what you were doing after high school. I assumed you would be going to a dance school."

"I don't know. It's been so long since I danced. With my mom working, and no dance school nearby after Mrs. Parker closed her school, I haven't been active. No other school is close enough. Then there's my dad."

"Your dad?" Brittany scowled.

Stephanie looked down. "I know, he's been dead for eight years." She looked back up. "But every time I had a performance, I felt guilty."

"Why?"

"Because my dad didn't want me to become a professional dancer. He said that it isn't a good life and that being on the road just ruins families. He and Papa didn't get along so well because Papa was always on the road." Stephanie sighed. "Mom's right tho, I do love to dance."

Brittany looked at Stephanie for a moment. "You are a beautiful dancer. I can't imagine your dad wanting you to give up on your dreams." She looked down at her book and then back up. "You ready for the Shakespeare test tomorrow?"

Stephanie shrugged. "As ready as I'll ever be." She closed her book. "Let's go watch some T.V."

Stephanie watched as Brittany drove away before heading to her bedroom. She sat on her bed and stared at the end table where a photo of her father stood in a black frame. Her silver-chained necklace hung down from it. She reached over and gently picked it up off the frame. She had once accidentally broke the chain. After her mom found a place to repair it, Stephanie decided it best to not wear it except on special occasions. She ran her finger along the hollow silver heart pendant. She made a mental note that she would have to ask her mom to get some cleaner and put the necklace back onto the frame.

She stood and went to her closet, opened the door and pulled a box down from the shelf. She tucked the box under her arm, glanced back at the photo of her dad, and then left her bedroom and headed to the living room where she sat down and opened the box. Inside were the ballet slippers given to her by Mrs. Parker. She stared at them for a full minute before reaching in and taking them out. She slipped her own shoes off and put the slippers onto the floor next to her own feet. Of course she could never wear them. However, seeing them next to her own feet made her shiver. She put them back into the box and put the lid on.

After sitting for another minute, Stephanie walked over to the bookshelf and pulled down the most recent video tape her mom had made of a performance. She put it into the player and stood back to watch herself on the television. It wasn't long before she the music and movement captured her.

She closed her eyes to listen and soon found herself mirroring the movements on the television. She couldn't help herself. When the presentation had finished, she opened her eyes and stared at the black screen. She rewound the tape and put the video back onto the shelf and sighed. "I'm sorry daddy, but I need to dance."

Lucas sat across from Stephanie at his kitchen table as she looked through a dozen school brochures. He picked one up that Stephanie had just set aside. "What's wrong with this one?" He opened it up and looked at it.

"Papa, that's the pile for schools I'm going to apply to." She scanned the brochure laid on the table before her and moved it to the pile destined for the trash.

"Ah! Okay, now it's making more sense." He studied the brochure in his hand. "I bet your mom would like this one. It's in-state so the tuition will be lower."

Stephanie looked to see which one he held. "Yeah, mom got all excited when that one came in. It looks nice, but I don't know yet."

"You don't want this to be a burden for your mom." He set the brochure back from where he had gotten it. "An in-state college would save a lot of money and I'm sure she would like you to be close."

Stephanie looked up. "Mom says I can go to any school I want because daddy had insurance and she's set part of it aside for college." She scowled as she looked at the latest school. "This one... " She turned the page.

"This one?"

"Huh?" She looked up, her face returning to normal.

"You said, 'This one.'"

"Oh." She looked down at the brochure again. "I think... I think this is the one that Mrs. Parker went to." She turned the page. "Sometimes she would talk about when she went to college and the dancing she did there." She turned another page. "I'm almost certain this is the place."

"If you have her contact information, maybe you could ask her for a letter of recommendation to send with your applications."

Stephanie's eyes went wide and she looked up at her grandfather. "I think mom has it! That's a great idea!" She stood and ran around the table to hug him.

Lucas chuckled and patted her back. "It's good to know I still have them now and again. Have you given any thought to your audition routine?"

Stephanie pulled back, her mouth open and her eyebrows furled in anxiety. "Audition?"

"Well yes. Dance schools traditionally accept on a percentage of those that want to attend. You need to audition and be accepted."

"I don't know. I mean I dance around the house, but nothing like when I went to school and did performances. Will I be good enough?"

Lucas smiled. "You'll be fine. It's like riding a bicycle. You'll need to put together a routine that goes with a musical piece and practice it until it's flawless."

"How long does it have to be?"

"If it's anything like acting, probably five to seven minutes. You should probably call the school to find out."

Stephanie nodded. "I can do that." She refocused on Lucas. "You really think I'm good enough?"

"Of course you are! I've seen you dance and you're a beautiful dancer."

"Okay, there's a fork coming up." Lucas looked down at the map he held in his hand. "You want to go right."

"More of a turn than a fork." Rose made the indicated turn. "You feel like you're ready for this?" She looked into the rearview mirror at Stephanie.

"I've been practicing the routine for three weeks. It isn't Swan Lake, but I think it's good. Mrs. Parker said I should mix in a little modern to make an impression."

Lucas glanced back. "You don't sound too happy about that."

Stephanie grimaced. "I'm not. Ballet should be ballet. You don't mix it with other dance styles. But Mrs. Parker said it's a common thing to do for auditions."

"We're passing highway 12. When is my next turn?" Rose looked at Lucas and then back to the road.

"We're looking for Flushing Highway. Another 30 miles or so." Lucas turned back to Stephanie. "Did she give you any other tips?"

"Nothing more than when we did a normal performance. Eye contact and let the emotions of the music pour through me."

After arriving at the school, Rose pulled the car into the parking lot and turned off the engine and looked at her watch. "Right on schedule. Want to look around a little?" She turned to Stephanie.

"No. I want to check in and get this over with."

Rose nodded and walked with Lucas as Stephanie led the way into the auditorium. They walked toward the front where the young women and men waited in line to get their position for the audition.

"Stephanie Starr." Stephanie gave her name and waited as the woman ran her finger down the list on the clipboard and stopped at her name.

She wrote something down and looked up and smiled. "Like you were born to the profession. You're number 12."

Stephanie nodded and turned to Rose and Lucas and took the duffle bag from her mom. "I'm going to go get ready."

"You want help with the make-up?"

"No, I got it." She walked off, leaving the other two to find a place to sit as they waited. When she came back her body was covered in black with her hair up in a bun and her face a pale white from the pressed powder while her lips were a burgundy color. "Do I look okay?"

Lucas' eyes went a little wide and he looked at Rose who had a smile on her face and told her how she looked great. He looked back at Stephanie. "It's more goth than I expected."

"Papa. It isn't goth, it's death. The music starts out lively, but then is mostly sad."

He mouthed 'Oh' and nodded. "Then you definitely fit the part."

"I'm so nervous. I haven't performed in front of judges before."

Rose put her arm around Stephanie and pulled her close. "Oh, Baby. You'll be fine. Just do your best and show them the great dancer I know you are."

Stephanie took in a deep breath. "I gotta go wait with the others." She hugged her mom and then Lucas. "Wish me luck!" Her mom and grandfather wished her luck. As she headed backstage to wait for her turn, she noticed the judges coming in and walking toward the woman checking in the dancers.

CHAPTER 12

"Wow, she's really good," Stephanie said in a low voice to nobody in particular as she watched the performer from the side of the stage.

When she had finished, the girl walked toward Stephanie taking her hairband off and letting her black curly hair down. She noticed Stephanie looking at her as she passed. "What are you looking at blondie?"

Stephanie scowled at her and then turned her attention to the next performer. The judges made notes and would thank each performer. Sometimes they would ask a question, but usually not. As it got closer to her turn, Stephanie could almost feel tingling in her hands and feet. She closed her eyes and took a few deep breaths in an effort to calm herself.

"Stephanie Starr." The lead judge's tenor voice was easily heard as he called her onto the stage.

Stephanie opened her eyes and put on a smile as she walked over to the sound manager and handed her mix tape to him. She glided to the middle of the stage, got into her starting pose and nodded to the man on the side of the stage. She smiled at the judges and held still as the music began. On the beat of her musical queue, she turned and instantly moved in sync with the music. The upbeat tempo proved perfect for her jazzy dance style. This portion only lasted for a minute before the music slowed down and she shifted into the ballet style she preferred. She slowly changed her face to a somber expression that matched the music.

With the stage lights shining on her, the three judges were in shadow. Stephanie could see them sitting there about a third of the way back, but could not make out their faces. As she turned and glanced out at them, she could have sworn one of them looked like her father. The way he held his head and the shape of his body. She frowned a little deeper as that observation struck her. She ignored it and kept dancing, but when she looked out at the judges again, she could not ignore the similarity.

'Show business is not a good life.' The pained expression on her father's face as he said those words were as clear to her as the day he said them. Staying with the routine, she extended her arm and pulled her hand up. She grimaced as a sharp pain shot through her wrist, but she softened her face with the original somber look and finished her routine. Stephanie remained still the last few seconds until the music stopped. She stood, smiled, and bowed.

Stephanie walked away when the lead judge spoke up. "Miss Starr, did you recently injure your wrist?"

She stopped and glanced down at her wrist and then looked out at the judges. "I broke it in a car accident when I was younger."

"I see. Thank you."

Lucas smiled as he watched each dancer perform on the stage. Audience members were kept in the last half of the auditorium and were asked to remain silent. Still, after each performance, a light applause was tolerated. When Stephanie came forward he leaned in and whispered into Rose's ear. "You can see how nervous she is."

Rose leaned into Lucas. "Poor thing. I hope she does okay."

"I'm sure she'll be fine." His face lit up as Stephanie started her routine. When she frowned on stage his smile disappeared and he made a small grunt when she grimaced. There were several other auditions they needed to sit through before they would see Stephanie. He got up and stood with Rose as they waited for her to come join them. When she approached, her make-up had been wiped off and her eyes were red and puffy. She had obviously been crying.

"I should have never come." Stephanie walked past the two of them and out the door.

Rose looked at Lucas with a scowl. He shrugged and they followed Stephanie out of the building. When they got outside she had already gotten into the car. Rose opened the passenger door and peered inside. "Don't you want to look around?"

"No, I just want to go home."

Rose sighed and looked at Lucas who again shrugged and climbed in the driver's side.

Stephanie sat behind her mom and stared out the window as they drove on the highway toward home. The setting sun made the car's shadow stretch out past the road and onto a large field they were driving past. It got distorted as it would pass different patches of trees and bushes. The shadows of passing cars and trucks would blend in with theirs before moving past. She imagined each one colliding into their car, killing her father. After an hour of silent driving, her father had died a hundred times in her mind. She sniffed and wiped her face of the tears that had been streaming down and tore her face away from the virtually brutal scene.

Lucas had apparently been watching her in the rear-view mirror for the moment she turned away from the window he spoke up. "Your wrist was hurting you as you danced?"

She nodded. "Yeah."

"I thought it had stopped hurting several years ago."

"Well it hurt today. It hurt like hell!"

"Stephanie!" Rose turned in her seat. "Please don't talk like that."

"Sorry." She looked down at her shoes.

"When we get home, I'm going to make a doctor appointment and we'll see if we can get your wrist fixed."

Stephanie nodded.

Lucas sat his suitcase by the back door in the kitchen. "I'll give you a call when I touchdown." He turned to find Mary right next to him. He brought his head back in surprise. "Whoa. There you are."

Mary smiled. "As always." She leaned in and kissed him. "One of my students says she has tickets to your next show..." She paused as the phone rang. She walked over to the phone hanging on the wall and picked it up. "Hello?... Sure Honey, just a moment." She held the phone out to Lucas.

He walked over and grabbed the phone. "Hello?... Yes, in a couple of hours." He looked down at his watch. "Well, I suppose I could take a later flight... You're welcome... Yes, I love you too... Okay I'll see you in a few." He put the handset back onto the cradle on the wall and turned to Mary. "She wants me to go with to her doctor appointment. They'll drop me off at the airport after that."

Mary smiled at Lucas.

"What?"

She came up to him and put her arms around him and put her head against his chest. "You. It wasn't too long ago you would rush off to your flight. Stephanie is lucky to have you around."

Lucas hugged her back. "I guess I've learned to appreciate family more."

Stephanie sat on the examination table as the doctor squeezed on her wrist with his finger and thumb at various points. Rose and Lucas sat in chairs nearby and watched.

"No pain?" The doctor let her hand down onto her leg.

Stephanie shook her head. "Uh uh."

The doctor held his hands out in front of him and made loose fists. "Can you move them up and down like this?" He demonstrated the movement with his own hands, moving the fists up and down while keeping the rest of the arm still. When Stephanie had mirrored that for a few seconds he moved his hands from side to side. Stephanie did the same. The doctor then rolled his hands in small circles while still keeping his forearm still. "Nothing?"

"No." Stephanie put her hands down.

"Hmmm. And this pain happens often?"

"Oh no, it happened a few times when I was eight after I got my cast off and then stopped. But then it happened again a couple days ago while auditioning for school and it really hurt." She glanced at her mom as she said the last part.

The doctor directed his attention to Rose and Lucas. "We can take an x-ray of the area, see if anything shows up; go from there." He stood up from the small stool. "We have a machine here so I'll... wait..." He turned to Stephanie. "How did you break your wrist at the age of eight?"

Stephanie opened her mouth and then closed it. After swallowing she answered his question. "My dad and I got into a car crash. He died."

"I'm so sorry. That's a terrible thing to go through at any age." He paused. "This might sound like a strange question, but were you thinking of that the other day when your wrist hurt?"

Stephanie's eyes went wide. "Yes!" She leaned forward. "I was thinking about how one of the judges looked just like my dad and then thinking about how my dad didn't want me to do ballet. He said show business wasn't a good life." She took in a breath. "How... ?"

The doctor sat back down. "I think you have a psychosomatic injury."

Rose scowled. "I've never heard of it."

The doctor looked at Rose. "It's a case where the mind is determined that a pain or other symptom is real and because of that you actually feel it." He turned back to Stephanie. "Your accident was a very traumatic event. Thinking of it caused your mind to believe that your wrist should hurt. So it did."

Rose stood and put her hand onto Stephanie's back. "So what do we do?"

"Psychosomatic pain is usually associated with stress. In this case, the memory of the accident. A painful memory is hard to deal with and sometimes requires therapy. I think, however, that since this hasn't happened in so long you need to look at what it is about the memory that was so stressful at this time of your life." He patted her leg. "You seem like a smart girl. You get that figured out and I think you'll be fine." He stood. "I'll have the nurse give you some good places if you want to get another professional involved."

Lucas followed Rose and Stephanie out of the doctor's office, his gaze not on anything in particular. With his head down, he walked in the general direction of where they had parked and stopped next to a car as he waited for Rose to unlock the doors.

"Dad. We're over here."

Lucas looked around to see Rose and Stephanie standing next to their car. He had walked up to the wrong one.

"You okay, dad?"

He walked over. "Yeah. Just thinking about what Ray said to Stephanie and why he said it." He got into the passenger side of the car. He remained silent for a minute as Rose drove before turning his head back toward Stephanie. "I am so sorry. This is my fault."

"Papa?"

"While there is some truth to what your dad said, the way I behaved made it much worse. There were many times I should have come home and didn't. A birthday party, a baseball game. Ray was my son and I didn't take the time out to show him that I loved him. I didn't take the time to learn what made him tick or who his friends were. So we were like strangers to each other." He sighed and turned in his seat so he could see Stephanie. "So of course he would tell you that it's not a good life. But it doesn't have to be. You see Ray would just keep it all bottled up if I missed something. Sure Mary would say something to me, but I guess I didn't take it seriously. Remember when you were younger how upset you would get if I missed your birthday and you would call me and tell me how you missed me? That was good, really good. I would like to think it helped me be a better person." He paused. "Know what I mean?"

Stephanie listened as Lucas talked. When he had finished she slowly nodded. "I think so."

Rose chimed in. "Remember, your father bought the lessons and he would want you to be happy. I think that he had a fear of you making the same mistakes your Papa did; putting your career ahead of your family. Just make sure you make your family a priority and I know your dad would be very proud of you. Think you can do that?"

Stephanie smiled and nodded. "Yes, I can."

CHAPTER 13

Stephanie grabbed the few items from the mailbox and walked toward the house as she flipped through them. Her eyes grew big and she ran into the house as she pulled one of the envelopes away from the rest. She discarded the unwanted mail onto the counter and opened the envelope.

"Oh please. Oh please." She pulled the letter out and read it. After scanning for a few seconds she screamed and did a little dance. She went to the phone and dialed. "Papa? I got accepted!... Yeah, I don't even think it's a form letter because there's a comment about my audition... Mhmm that's it. They said I clearly had the training and the skill, but I was a bit out of practice... Oh thank you! I love you too!"

Stephanie hung up the phone and screamed again and as she left the kitchen the phone rang. She ran back to pick it up. "Hello?... No she isn't here, may I take a message?... Okay. Mark. Wait. Dr. Phelps?" Stephanie smiled. "I will definitely give her the message. Bye."

Rose came into Stephanie's room with two matching suitcases. "Here, you can use these. Yours is too small."

Stephanie looked at the set and then up at her mother. "Daddy's?"

Rose nodded as she teared up. "I wish he could be here to see this."

Together they packed the suitcases with the required clothing. When they were full, Stephanie went to her closet and took down a shoebox from the shelf and set it on the bed by the suitcases and opened it. Inside lay the pair of slippers given to her by Mrs. Parker.

"I know she would be proud of you too. Is it wise to take them with you? Won't someone steal them?"

"I have to. She gave them to me to be my inspiration."

"Well tomorrow's the big day. Did you get in touch with your Papa?"

Stephanie smiled. "He's landing tonight so he can drive with us."

"How can we be lost? We were just there a few months ago." Stephanie leaned forward from the back seat to look down at the map Lucas had spread out between himself and Rose.

Lucas placed his finger down on the map. "Okay, I see it." He slide his finger along the line. "Back here we were supposed to turn and I missed it."

"How far is that? We're going to be late."

Rose looked up at Stephanie. "Stephanie. Calm down. We'll be fine." She looked over at Lucas. "How far back is that?"

Lucas folded up the map and handed it to Rose. "It looks like about an hour drive back to the turn off."

"An hour!? That's two hours of lost time!"

"We'll be fine Sweetie." Lucas pulled the car back onto the road. "Just a little later than expected. Why don't you read that book I gave you?"

Stephanie sat back. "I already finished it. This trip is taking forever."

Several students walked on the campus with their parents in tow carrying luggage to the dorm buildings. Some exchanged simple pleasantries while others hugged each other in delight. Stephanie looked down at her paper to verify the building and room number. "This is it. This is the building."

Rose set down the suitcase. "I need a break." She looked at the cars parked along the street and an open space in front of the building. "Oh sure, now there's space to park. Who's your roommate?"

Stephanie looked at her paper. "Julie Olson."

Lucas picked up the other suitcase. "Okay, break's over. Lets go see this room."

They all entered the building after waiting for a handful of adults to leave. The hall extended forwarded where students and parents and siblings were walking or standing around. They worked their way up the side staircase just inside the entrance to the second floor and went to Stephanie's room where a girl stood by the dresser unpacking her own suitcases with the help of her parents.

The girl looked up. "Stephanie? Hi, I'm Julie." She walked over and shook Stephanie's hand, her dark skin a dramatic contrast to Stephanie's own. Her mom cleared her throat. "Oh yeah, and these are my parents, Ron and LaSandra."

Stephanie smiled as she shook her hand. "I'm Stephanie. Oh, I guess you already know that." She laughed. "And this is my mom and Papa. Rose and Lucas."

Julie's parents maneuvered in the tight quarters around her and shook the hands of Rose and Lucas as Julie continued talking. "Do you have a preference for top or bottom bunk?"

Stephanie looked at the bunk bed. "I've never had a top bunk. Do you mind?"

"Not at all. Relieved, in fact. I would probably be afraid of falling off. Have you gotten your schedule yet?"

"No. I wanted to unpack first."

"We tried when we got here, but they closed an hour ago. We can go together in the morning. I was thinking…" She looked at her parents and shut her mouth.

"Oh, thank you." Stephanie opened her suitcase and found a wrapped package inside. She looked at her mom with her eyes wide and a grin on her face. "What's this?"

"Open it and see."

Stephanie unwrapped the box and found a cell phone. She gasped. "My own phone!? Oh thank you!" She stood and hugged her mom.

"This is so you can call me on the weekends and for emergencies. We only get 100 minutes a month on that phone."

"I'll be careful. I promise." She sat down on one of the desk chairs and pulled it out of the box. "What's the number?"

Rose handed her a piece of paper. "Don't give it out. We only get 100 minutes a month."

"Mom, I'm 18. You don't have to repeat yourself."

Rose rolled her eyes and looked at Lucas who watched the interaction and chuckled to himself. "Steph, why don't we get the rest of your stuff unpacked and look around. Your Papa and I have to go soon."

"I can unpack on my own. Let's go look at the rest and then you guys can leave." She picked up the phone and put it into her clutch.

After the trio looked at the bathrooms and the common room with the public refrigerator and microwave, Stephanie gave each of them a kiss on the cheek and a hug. She held on to Lucas and took a deep breath.

Lucas patted her on the back. "You'll do fine Sweetie. You just call one of us if you need anything. Okay?" Stephanie nodded and let go as she sniffed.

Rose handed her a tissue as she wiped her own eyes and then hugged Stephanie again. "I love you. Call me this weekend."

"Okay. I love you too." She watched as Rose and Lucas went to the front door, looked back and waved, and then walk out of sight.

When Stephanie returned to her own room, Julie's parent had also departed and she was laying on the bottom bed leafing through a magazine. She sat up. "Want me to help you unpack? I cleaned out the drawers for you when I did mine. You never know what people put into them."

"Um, okay."

"I couldn't believe how long it took to get here. I think my parents did it deliberately. First we had to go out to breakfast. Being my first year in college, you know. Then we had to drive my brother to his school and then we had to stay there for a while. I mean, c'mon, this isn't his first year. He knows what he's doing. You know?. Then we had to drive around here for a while. They were driving me nuts. I'm so glad they finally left. You know?"

Stephanie blinked. "So you have a brother?" She unpacked her clothes and put them into the drawers set aside for her.

"Yeah, he's two years older than me. He's on the football team, a special player that they recruited from high school. He even got a scholarship. He's only an hour away so we should go watch him play. You know? He has a bunch of friends on the team too. They're nice. I think my parents want me to go here so that he can keep an eye on me. Gosh those are old."

Stephanie had pulled out the ballet slippers given to her by Mrs. Parker. The slippers were tied together by the laces and she hang them on a nail protruding out of the wall. "They were a gift by my ballet teacher to inspire me. They're the slippers of Anna Pavlova."

Julie's eyes grew wide. "Seriously? You're joking. Seriously?"

Stephanie nodded.

"You are so lucky. First the cell phone and now the slippers. I am so glad to be your roommate. I think you're going to be the most popular girl here. Everyone's going to want to see the slippers. You know? How long have you had them?"

Stephanie backed up a couple steps and stared at them. "Two years now. I haven't done much dancing since I got them. I looked at another school, but it just didn't feel right."

"You haven't danced in two years and they accepted you? You must be really good. I don't think I could stop for a couple months and remember how to dance. You know? My dad says that it's all in my head that after you do it for a long time you have muscle memory, but I think my muscles don't have good memory." She took in a breath and laughed a little.

Stephanie chuckled. "I didn't go completely without dancing. I just did it in my house when I had free time. Think we'll have any classes together?"

"I'm sure we will since we're both freshman. Probably those other classes that they make us take. I don't know why they make us take all of those classes. Why do I need History when I'm dancing? You know? I just don't understand it. We can compare schedules when we get them tomorrow. They open at eight. I want to be there first thing so we can get it done."

"Eight?" Stephanie sighed. "Want to go look around campus?"

"Okay."

"Where do we get our schedules?" Stephanie stopped to look at a large school map prominently placed near their dorm.

"Didn't you do the tour?"

"I was going to, but my mom suddenly had to work over the weekend and Papa didn't have enough notice to help out so I didn't make it."

"Oh! Well let's see, this is obviously where we are." She pointed to the dot on the map. "And… oh where is it?" She pulled her hand away. "Ah! Here it is." She put her finger on a building outline. "This is where we can get food."

Stephanie laughed. "I can see your top priority."

Julie grinned at her. "Ya gotta take care of the basics first." She looked at the map again. "Okay, here is where we we will get our schedule. It's also the same building where we do financial aid and where you can look at some job postings."

Stephanie nodded and then looked around and then back at the map. "I'm not very good with maps. Where is it?"

"C'mon. I'll show you."

CHAPTER 14

Julie turned the light on. "C'mon or we're going to be late."

With her eyes squinted, Stephanie looked at the digital clock sitting on one of the tiny desks. "It's only 5:30. Why are you up so early? Our first class isn't until 10."

Julie handed a sheet of paper up to Stephanie. "I picked this up when we were getting our schedules. I was going to show it to you, but we were doing other things for the past few days and then I just forgot to show it to you. Sorry."

"Let's see. 'Ballet Dancers. All dance majors with a focus on ballet are expected to be in the dance studio daily at 6 am as assigned below.'" Her lips moved as she continued to read to herself. Stephanie fell back against her pillow and sighed. "School is going to kill me."

Stephanie walked in to the assigned dance studio with her bag over her shoulder and sat down on the floor as she held her hand up against her yawning mouth. After putting her slippers on, she went over to the bar and stretched.

"You really aren't a morning person are you?" Julie stretched next to her. "We had to get up every morning at 5:30 so Jerome could go to football practice. All year round he was either in football camp or spring practice or general practice. And because my dad had to go to work very early, my mom would be the one to take him to practice and she didn't want me to stay home alone so I would have to go with."

Stephanie yawned again as she turned toward Julie and held her leg up to her face with her toes pointed toward the ceiling. "Yeah, I don't think I would have survived. What does your dad do that he has to be up so early?"

"You know those high voltage power lines? They're called transmission lines. He works on those. He says he likes to get out early before the heat of the day expands the lines making them drop up to seven feet. How about your dad?"

Stephanie lowered her voice. "Daddy died when I was eight. Car crash."

"I am so sorry. I shouldn't have brought it up. My mom and dad are always saying that I talk too much."

Stephanie swallowed. "No, you're okay. It's okay. He…" She stopped as the dance instructor appeared next to her. She looked at Stephanie for five seconds and then moved on to Julie and observed her in the same way before moving on again. After she had gone down the line and observed each girl or boy she went to the center of the room.

"Good. Everyone here is taking this…" Two girls walked in and quickly changed into their slippers and went to the bar while the teacher watched them.

Stephanie stared at the girls as they quickly got to the open spot next to her.

One girl had curly black hair up with a hair band. "What are you staring at blondie?" She narrowed her eyes and curled her lip a little as she spoke.

Stephanie's eyes went wide and she looked back to the teacher.

"That is the last time you are late." The teacher's gaze swept across the room. "You're either here on time or not here at all. And if you are not here, then you may as well go home. It's time to grow up ladies and gentlemen. If this isn't what you want to do for the rest of your life, then you should not be here." She paused and stared at the two girls that had walked in late for a few seconds before breaking her stare and addressing the entire class. "Now, let's see what we got to work with this year."

"Oh my goodness, I thought for sure I was going to pee my pants when those two girls walked in late and what was that girl's problem? Here will you hold this?" Julie handed Stephanie her bag and hopped on one foot while adjusting her raised shoe. "Who was that teacher? She scares me."

Stephanie stopped walking and looked at Julie. "I don't think she ever introduced herself. You know, I saw that girl at auditions. She wasn't very nice then either."

Julie took her bag back and continued walking. "Really? What's her name?"

"Marilyn."

"Ah. She's going to be trouble. Let's go get some breakfast. I'm starving. At least we get a chance to eat before classes start. My brother says that his classes start right after his morning practice and he has to eat before practice or he doesn't get to eat at all. Can you imagine…" she kept talking as she walked along beside Stephanie.

When they got to the cafeteria, Julie smiled at the student behind the counter. "Good morning."

"Hey, what can I get you?" He grinned back at her.

"I'll have some scrambled eggs and sausage."

The man got a styrofoam plate and put on the requested items and handed it to her. "Take care." He looked at Stephanie and waited for her order.

"Oh, I'll have some of the mixed fruit and oatmeal."

He handed her bowl and plate to her and focused his attention onto the next customer.

Stephanie scowled at him and then moved in behind Julie at the cash register. "He's rude."

Julie scowled and looked back. "He is? I didn't notice."

Stephanie slowed down as she entered the building to let her eyes adjust from the bright sunshine outside. She and Julie worked their way to the classroom and entered. The class had a larger ratio of boys to girls compared to the morning ballet warmup standing around the sides some recognizable from that morning. She glanced up at the clock on the wall. The red second hand approached the 12.

"Good afternoon and welcome to Jazz dance." The teacher talked exactly at 2pm. "I'm Mrs. Shaw and we're going to have a lot of fun in this class, learn a lot and push ourselves. But be sure, that if I feel you aren't pushing yourself, I will ask you to leave. So, let's get right to it."

After the class, Julie waited outside for Stephanie to come out. "What's next? Aren't we in the same class?"

"Psychology at 3:30."

"With Mr. Randall?"

"Yes."

"That's right! Let's get changed and eat. I'm starving. Why do you think we have to take Psychology?"

"Maybe they can teach us to mesmerize our audience with our dancing."

Julie raised her hands and wiggled her fingers at Stephanie. "Or hypnotize them to give us all their money. Don't we have a singing class at 5:30?"

"Yes. With Mr. Johnson. We're in that together too."

"We gotta make sure we eat before that class."

Stephanie laughed.

Stephanie dropped her bag inside the door of her room and slumped onto the floor. "I don't know how much of this I can take." She sighed and took out a couple of books from her bag and carried them over to the desk that had become hers over the past couple of months and started her homework. When Julie walked in an hour later, she looked up to look at the time. "It's nine o'clock. I was worried about you. Go out on a date without telling me?"

"I wish. Mr. Johnson asked me in for some extra vocal training. He says I have 'the gift' and he wants me to make the most of it. What are you working on?"

"Researching my Psychology midterm paper. I want to get my stuff together before I go to the computer lab and type it up. Between the normal classes, dance, music, and our special ballet practice; I feel like I hardly have time to breathe."

Julie sighed and sat on her bed. "I hate research papers. I never know if I have enough material." She laid back onto her pillow. "I'm too tired to do any more school work. I'll start mine tomorrow after breakfast." Within seconds of laying back, Julie fell asleep. Fully dressed.

"Wow. She's really tired." Stephanie yawned and looked back at her work. "Another hour. Then I'll go to bed." She flipped a page in the book. "Maybe another two. And now I'm sounding like Papa and talking to myself."

Stephanie felt a shake on her shoulder. She opened her eyes long enough to see Julie standing over her before closing them again against the light. "Okay, I'll go to bed."

"No, it's time to get up. You fell asleep at the desk."

Stephanie sat up and looked at the clock through squinted eyes. "No, that can't be right. I just closed my eyes a minute ago."

Julie looked at Stephanie's notes and laughed. "'My id and ego is due to dancing in the grass while singing in colored jazz'?"

"What?" Stephanie looked at her notes. Her entire last paragraph consisted of a nonsensical mixture of singing and dancing and psychology.

"Hurry up. We can't be late."

Stephanie sighed. "I must have been dreaming as I wrote that. School is going to kill me."

Stephanie walked into her dorm room after her last class to find Julie at one of the desks eating a big bag of chips as she studied for her midterms. She changed into her dance clothing. "Aren't you coming?"

Julie looked up. "Coming to what?"

"I got an email from Mrs. Shaw saying to come by the dance studio at eight. Did you check your email?"

"Yes! I checked my email!" Julie closed her eyes and sighed and then opened them again. "Sorry. Tests always get me wound up tight. Once my entire family banished me to my bedroom for the day so I wouldn't yell at them because I normally did my studying in the dining room. Every time one of them walked nearby I would growl. Anyway, I was in the computer lab just an hour ago and I checked my email. Nothing from Mrs. Shaw."

"Huh. I wonder what's going on."

After Stephanie changed into her dance attire and put on a jacket, she walked over to the dance building and went to the studio she went to in the morning. Mrs. Shaw stood in a corner looking at some papers while a few other students, a mixture of boys and girls, stood inside. When Stephanie walked in she looked up and acknowledged her with a nod and continued to look at her papers. After a couple more students arrived, she grabbed a stack of papers and handed them out.

"Thank you for coming. What I'm handing to you could be your future; if you want it. It's an opportunity to perform professionally at an upcoming event next semester." She handed the last packet out. "This is optional. You don't have to do it. However..." She paused and looked at them. "You are the top of your class and this is something that can launch you into your career. Think of it as my early Christmas gift to you. I know it's more work on your already busy schedule with midterms on you and an upcoming performance here at the school, but I know you can do it. Look it over tonight and if you feel it's too much just let me know. Any questions?"

Stephanie looked at the others as they also looked around. Nobody said anything.

"Good. Come here every night at this time for the rest of the semester. Next semester we'll also meet every night until the presentation. I'll see you tomorrow and we'll discuss the roles."

Stephanie found Julie along with several others in the common room studying. She went to their room and sat on the bottom bunk and stared at the slippers that hung on the wall.

Julie followed Stephanie into their room. "What did Mrs. Shaw want?" Stephanie handed her the papers. Julie looked through it. "A ballet?"

"A professional event next semester. We have to practice every night for the rest of the semester."

"A professional..." Julie's eyes got wide. "Professional! This is wonderful! I'm so happy for you! I knew you were the best!"

Stephanie smiled. "Thanks. You know I want to dance more than anything in the whole world. I just hope I can do this along with everything else."

"You'll do fine. You're the best dancer I know. Tell you what, why don't we go to my brother's football game this Saturday. Just the two of us. Take a break from school."

"I have a class in the morning, but I have the afternoon free until seven. What time is it?"

"Two o'clock. You'll love my brother. He's nice, but don't tell him I said so."

Stephanie grinned.

CHAPTER 15

On Saturday, when Stephanie got back from her morning class, Julie sat at her desk with jeans and jacket on, holding a small bag packed with snacks. "Hurry up. Let's go."

Stephanie smiled. "Okay. I'm almost ready. Do I need to bring something?" She dropped her books onto her desk.

Julie's eyebrows furled a little. "No, just yourself and some cash for food."

"I thought we were bringing snacks."

"That's for before the game starts. We'll want to eat something in the middle of the game. One time I forgot to bring money to a game and did I regret it. I kept smelling those hot dogs around me and wishing I could have one."

"Okay, honestly, is there ever a time you're not thinking of food?"

"Of course there is."

"Oh? When is that?"

"Right after I finish eating."

"Hmmmm I'm fairly certain you're just planning your next meal."

When the girls got out off the bus, the stadium lot overflowed with parked cars. Students and alumni walked in clusters toward the entrances. Julie led a curious Stephanie toward the gate. She showed a couple of tickets as she passed the attendant. "Our seats are over this way. They're not the best, but they work. To get the really good seats you gotta pay. Jerome gets a couple of season tickets for being on the team."

Stephanie nodded as she looked around. "Is he going to meet us at the seats?"

"No, we'll be able to see him after the game along with the rest of the team. C'mon, I need to go pee before we sit down." Julie weaved her way through the crowd with practiced ease and disappeared into the bathroom.

Stephanie caught up and went inside too. When she came out, Julie waited for her with two drinks in hand. She held up one and then the other. "Root beer or Coke?"

Stephanie grabbed the root beer. "Thanks."

"This way. They're about to enter the field." Julie led the way past several spectators to their assigned seats and sat down. "Just in time!" She stood again and cheered and jumped up and down with others as the team ran onto the field.

Stephanie stood and clapped and then sat down and drank some of her drink as she grabbed her apple from the snack bag.

"See?" Julie touched her shoulder. "There he is, number 83. He's a wide receiver. Oh! And there's Mike the quarterback. I like him, he's nice." She named several of the other players. After a while, the game got underway and Julie watched intensely as Stephanie looked around the stadium and periodically watched the game with a little interest. She jumped a little as Julie yelled along with the bulk of the stadium. "Wooo! Yes! First down!"

"That's good?" Stephanie had to raise her voice to be heard above the noise of the stadium.

"You really have no clue about football, do you?"

Stephanie shook her head. "My Papa tried to explain it to me when I was little, but I didn't get it."

"Okay. See the large areas on the ends by the giant posts? Those are the end zones. Each team is trying to get the football into those areas."

"For a touchdown. I know that."

"Okay. Well you also have multiple attempts at getting that touchdown. Subgoals, if you will, of 10 yards each. You get four tries to go at least that far. Each try is called a down." She turned her attention to the game as she continued. "Every time you get those 10 yards, you get another four downs. You start over at the first down to get the next 10. If you don't get there by the end of your fourth down, then the other team... No! What down..? Oh now they're going to punt."

"Punt?"

"Yeah. This is their forth down. They don't think they can get to that 10 yard subgoal so they're going to kick the ball so the other team isn't so close to their goal. It's called a punt."

Stephanie nodded her head. "Okay." She watched the game with a little more interest. "So can't you just kick the ball to get the touchdown?"

Julie laughed. "No. For a touchdown, you have to carry the ball. If you're close enough, you can kick the ball through the posts. That's a field goal. It isn't worth... Don't let him... interception! Whooo! Go! Go!" She had jumped up after seeing the interception and sat down again after the the play was over. "What was I saying?"

When everyone else jumped up, Stephanie had jumped up so she could see what was happening and had clapped and cheered too. "You were saying how much you enjoy this game."

"I do. It's fun to watch and see if my brother can make the touchdown. I always tease him when he isn't able to make it. He's a good player, but don't tell him I said so."

"27 to 24. Now that's a good game. I always like it when it's a close game. Too bad Jerome didn't make any touchdowns this game. Did you like it?" Julie turned to Stephanie with a wide grin still on her face.

"I enjoyed it. Maybe I was just too young when Papa tried to explain it to me and we didn't get to watch often. He traveled a lot. Where do we go to meet your brother?"

"You're going to like him. He's nice. I called him earlier this week and told him that we were coming so we can just hang out a little and wait for them to finish up. They'll first talk about the game and what went well and what could have been better, but I don't think it will be a long talk since they won. Then they'll take a shower." She put her hand on Stephanie's shoulder. "Oh my goodness, trust me. You want him to take a shower." Stephanie laughed. "Then we can meet him outside the locker room." She looked into the empty snack bag. "I wish I had gotten an extra hot dog in the 4th."

Julie led Stephanie into the bowels of the stadium until they arrived outside the locker room where they sat on the floor and waited. It wasn't long before some of the players came out and the girls stood. A few of them recognized Julie and greeted her as they passed. Some left while others stood around and talked to each other.

"Hi Mike!" Julie waved to the quarterback, a smile on her face.

"Hey Shortstop. You made it to the game." He walked over to where Julie stood and smiled down to her. "You're looking good."

Julie beamed as he talked to her. "Oh! This is my roommate. Stephanie." She turned to Stephanie. "She's here to meet Jerome. She didn't know anything about football before today, but I taught her." She turned back to Mike "Now she's a fan. We'll be here to watch all of your home games. I'm sorry I missed the last one, but Mr. Johnson has me practicing for a special presentation that's coming up." She looked down for a second and then looked up, her hair falling across her face. "Think you can come hear me sing?"

Mike smiled. "If I can. I would love to hear you sing."

"Jewel, why do you keep bothering Mike?" Jerome walked up and gave his sister a hug. "This the roommate you've been telling me about?"

"Yup. This is Stephanie. Stephanie, this is my brother Jerome."

Stephanie took his offered hand and shook it. "Julie has said some nice things about you."

"She must have been feeling delusional. She never says nice things about me."

Julie punched Jerome in the arm. "I do so."

He rubbed his arm. "Of course, what was I thinking? Jewel is always nice to me."

Stephanie looked past Jerome and saw another football player leave the locker room and start to talk to some of the other players. She watched him for a second then directed her attention back to Jerome. "I wish I had a big brother to look out for me."

"Steph is an only child."

"So no big brother to punch, eh?" Jerome rubbed his arm for emphasis.

Stephanie smiled. "No. Nobody to punch." She looked back at the other football player and when he made eye contact she smiled and then looked back to Jerome. "I would have liked having a brother or a sister. I think Julie feels safer knowing that you're here." She looked back at the other player and saw he was watching her.

Jerome noticed the interaction. "You want to meet Hawk?"

"Hawk." Julie rolled her eyes. "Pfffft. His name is Luke. I don't know why he insists on being called 'Hawk'."

"Hey Hawk!" Jerome gestured with his hand. "C'mere. I got someone you gotta meet."

Hawk ambled over as he looked at Stephanie. "Hello. I'm Hawk." He extended his hand, which Stephanie shook.

"You mean Luke."

Hawk lost his smile and glanced over at Julie then smiled again at Stephanie. "It's a nickname, but I like it. If you watch the game, you'll see it's also printed on my jersey. How do you know Jerome?"

"His sister, Julie, is my roommate. I attend the dance school."

"I should have known. You have the figure of a dancer. How long you been dancing?"

"Since I was eight. Well, actually, in some ways since I could walk. You know, you really look familiar. Have we met before?"

Hawk laughed. "I thought that was my line. But you're right. There is something familiar about you. Did you grow up in Miami?"

"Gosh no."

"Hmmm. No, I can't imagine you did. Nobody can live in Miami and keep such a light skin tone."

Stephanie opened her mouth in mock exasperation. "Are you saying I'm pale?"

Hawk held is hands up below his face. "No, no. I would never say such a thing. I'm just saying people in Miami are normally, um, not so, uh, are usually a little darker."

Stephanie laughed. "I'm teasing you."

Hawk lowered his hands and winked. "Oh good. I wouldn't want to ruin any chances of seeing you again."

Stephanie lowered her head and then looked up a little with her head tilted. "You want to see me again?"

"If I can. You have a phone number I can reach you at?"

"You got a pen?"

Hawk patted his pants and then looked around for his backpack. "Hold on. Don't go anywhere." He ran back to where he left his backpack and then returned with a pen in hand.

Stephanie took the pen and wrote her cell number onto his hand. She smiled up at him. "You're going to call me?"

He looked down at the number on his hand and then back at her. "I will call you tonight."

"Oh, it can't be tonight. I have this practice I gotta go to."

"When does it end?"

"Steph!" Julie called from down the hall. "We gotta go or you'll be late. Jerome is going to drive us back."

Stephanie looked over at Julie and then back at Hawk. "I'll have five minutes at 10 or maybe 10:30. I don't know." She started to walk away and then stopped and looked back. "Okay, maybe you can call me at 10:30, but it can't be for long. Just five minutes." She walked several steps further and then turned around to look back while walking backwards. "I gotta go. It's Mrs. Shaw. If I'm late she'll kill me." She turned back around to meet with Julie. When she looked back she saw Hawk looking down at his hand.

Julie looked back at Hawk and then at Stephanie as they walked away. "Did you write your number on his hand?"

Stephanie giggled. "I did! I can't believe he wants to see me again!"

CHAPTER 16

"Steph!" Julie shook Stephanie awake. "Get up! We're going to be late."

Stephanie opened her eyes and looked at the clock to see a time of 5:45. "Oh no!" She got down and got dressed. "Why didn't you wake me?"

"I've been trying to for the past 10 minutes. When did you finally get off the phone?" Julie grabbed her bag and stood by the door.

"Um, I don't know" Stephanie looked around in her drawer. "Midnight? Have you seen any of my socks?"

"Oh my goodness! Weren't you on the phone with him for a couple of hours Saturday night too? Get some out of my drawer and I'll hold a spot for you. You don't want to walk in after Mrs. Shaw, you know." Julie walked out as Stephanie continued to scrounge around for some socks.

After getting ready, she grabbed her bag and ran out of the room and across the campus green to her class. Once in the building she took off her jacket and dumped it with her bag next to the bags already lying by the wall, slipped out of her gym shoes and into her ballet slippers and got into position next to Julie a couple seconds before Mrs. Shaw walked in.

"You are so lucky." Julia whispered.

"Tonight?" Stephanie sat on the floor eating an apple as she leaned back against the bed. She covered her phone. "Julie, Do we have plans tonight?"

Julie turned in her seat to face Stephanie and pointed at the books on Stephanie's desk.

Stephanie put the phone back to her mouth. "I do need to do some studying for finals… No, I have a class then. It… I think I can, sure. But it can't be for too long." She smiled. "Okay. See you then."

"What are you thinking? You can't go out on a date tonight. You can go out on Saturday!"

"It will only be for an hour."

Julie frowned and looked down at her. "Just like the phone calls were only supposed to be for 10 minutes? You kept me up with your giggling and laughing and you were almost late this morning."

"I couldn't help it! We just get to talking and time slips away from me."

"Yeah, well 'Hawk' should have some consideration for your schedule." Julie finger quoted his name as she emphasized it.

Stephanie scowled. "Yeah? At least I have a date. You're pawing all over Mike and has he ever asked you out even once?"

Julie's mouth dropped open. She stared at her for a second, closed her mouth, turned around and slammed another book open. "Fine. Do what you want with your time. I'm just glad I'm not the one that has to face Mrs. Shaw when you're late for your special practice tonight."

"Fine! I will!" Stephanie got up and walked out.

"Fine! I hope you trip and break something." Julie closed her eyes as tears stung them.

"Was it rough growing up in Miami?" Stephanie slurped on her drink as she looked at Hawk across the table from her.

"I don't know. I guess compared to a place like this. You learned to watch your back. Definitely avoided alleys at night. Took care of my sister. How about you?"

"Oh I don't think so. Sometimes I would ride my bike to Papa's house from mine tho I don't think he liked me doing that."

"I thought your dad died when you were young."

"He did. Oh, Papa is my grandfather."

"That's weird. Calling him 'Papa'."

"Is it? I never thought about it. I've always called him that. For as long as I can remember, when I would visit him and grandma around Christmas, he would watch The Nutcracker with me because he knew my dad wouldn't watch it with me."

"No? Your dad wasn't very nice."

"No, my dad was wonderful. He just didn't like ballet or theater. Papa is a stage actor and traveled a lot for work so he would be gone for long periods of time."

"And you became a ballet dancer?"

"Yeah, I wasn't so sure about that either. When I first started my lessons I felt so guilty because I thought it was my fault he got into the car accident. I had been asking about ballet lessons for Christmas. Then when I actually got lessons for Christmas, I lost it. My mother convinced me that the accident wasn't my fault. She told me that my Dad had been the one to buy the lessons, but I don't think he believed I would have stuck to it. My mom says he would be proud of me and that I should make sure my career doesn't keep me from my family, like it did to Papa."

Hawk munched on another french fry and nodded.

Stephanie blushed. "I'm sorry. I'm just prattling."

"No! I like listening to you talk."

Stephanie smiled. "What time is it?"

"Seven-thirty."

"Oh no! We gotta go. I can't be late."

"Okay. It's only 10 minutes away. You'll be back in time."

Stephanie grabbed her coat and walked toward the door of the restaurant. "Can I ask you a question?"

"Um, yeah? You already did."

"Does Mike like Julie?"

"I think so, yeah. Why?"

"Because he hasn't asked her out on a date." She climbed into his car.

Hawk shrugged and got in. "Some guys aren't very good at asking girls out. I think my dad worked with my mom for almost a year before he got the nerve to ask her out. See you Saturday?"

Stephanie smiled. "Definitely!"

Stephanie ran into her dormitory and saw Julie in the common room watching TV as she ran past. Julie looked over at her and then back to the TV. She ran over to Julie and gave a her a hug around the neck from behind. "I'm sorry for what I said earlier. Also, Mike does like you." She let go and walked toward their room.

Julie perked up and looked around. "Wait, What? He does?"

Stephanie smiled at her and headed off to their room to change. As she ran back through, she yelled out, "Maybe you should call him instead."

When Saturday afternoon came, Hawk parked in front of the dorm and sat in his old car waiting for Stephanie. He changed the station on the radio and it died. "Oh, come on!" He slammed his hand on the dashboard without effect. When the car door opened, he sat back and smiled and greeted her as she got in. "Hi."

Stephanie looked at the dashboard where he had hit it. "Everything okay?"

"Yeah, radio stopped working. I thought I could get it working with a slap, but it didn't help."

"Oh. So what are we doing today?"

He started to drive. "Well just yesterday my coach said we need to work on co-ordination. So how about some Putt-Putt? That counts, right?"

"That sounds fun. I've never played."

"I did once when I was visiting my aunt in Chicago. It's fun."

"Oh yeah? I was in Chicago once too, but I didn't play Putt-Putt. I went to the Chicago Theater to see Papa perform and then I went up the Sears Tower."

"Really? I did too." Hawk chuckled. "Some girl on the elevator complained about suffocating."

Stephanie turned to look at him with her eyes wide and her mouth open. "Wait, when did you say you went?"

"I don't know. Um, let's see I think I was 15 so that would have been six years ago."

"I think that was me!"

"No, seriously? Are you kidding me?"

"Wait a minute. If you heard me on the elevator, then maybe we saw each other at the top." Stephanie gasped. "Were you the boy afraid to look out the window?"

Hawk looked at her and then back to the road and then looked at her again. "That was you? No way!"

"I put my toes…"

"… against the glass and looked down."

"And you nearly fainted." She laughed.

"I don't do so well with heights. I just can't believe that was you, all those years ago. I knew you looked familiar."

Hawk pulled into a parking space at the miniature golf place and ran around to open the door for Stephanie. She smiled as she got out and held his hand. "It's like we were meant to be."

They went inside where not only could you play miniature golf, but could also play arcade games, bowl, or get some pizza. He paid for the clubs and handed one to Stephanie. "You ever visit Miami?"

"No, never been there."

"Oh good. Wouldn't want you to already know something else that could embarrass me. You go first and I'll keep score."

They walked to the first hole. "I always thought these places had large features like windmills and pyramids or faces of presidents. This is just some green and blocks of wood." She frowned when her ball flew past the hole and bounced off in another direction. After another couple of hits, she sunk the ball.

Hawk took his turn. When his ball didn't go in after he had passed Stephanie on the number of tries, he clenched his jaw and took in a deep breath. "This is definitely harder than I remember."

After they finished, Hawk drove Stephanie back to her school. They sat in the car and continued talking for several more minutes before conversation slowed down and grew quiet. Stephanie looked out the window toward her dorm building and then back to him before speaking up again. "Well, I guess I should go inside." Hawk leaned over a little, paused, and then leaned in to kiss Stephanie who responded as he hoped. After kissing for several minutes she backed off. "I really need to go. I can't be late."

"Do you really need to go? We won't see each other until next Semester."

"I do." Hawk leaned forward and kissed her again. After several minutes she pulled back again. "I really do need to go. This is the last practice until we get back and Mrs. Shaw wouldn't forgive me for missing it. Merry Christmas. Call me at my house when you get home." She kissed him again on the lips and left the car.

Hawk sat next to Mike and Julie watching as Stephanie danced and Marilyn took center stage to be lifted by a male dancer. He leaned toward Julie. "Wasn't Stephanie going for lead?"

Julie turned her head a little as she kept watching with her yes. "Marilyn beat her out in the end."

After the show, the three worked their way back to the dressing rooms. Various people were entering and leaving the rooms and walking around. They saw Stephanie as she entered her room and followed her in. Hawk paused at the door and looked over at someone walking away as the other two entered in and congratulated Stephanie on her performance.

"Hawk?" Stephanie stood and walked over to him. "What's wrong?"

"That guy just came out of here."

"I'm sure it's okay. Come on in."

Hawk hugged her and walked in behind her. When they got inside, Stephanie looked around on her dressing table as she held her hand to her neck. "Okay, where is it?"

"Your necklace. I knew something wasn't right." Hawk ran out the door and in the direction the man had travelled. When he got to the exit door he looked around and went through the door. The man neared the end of the block as he walked away. Hawk took pursuit. When his foot splashed in a puddle, the man looked behind to see Hawk coming up fast. The man's eyes went wide and he ran as hard as he could.

Hawk's long legs and constant training were no match and he caught up to the man and shoved him against the wall. He grabbed the man by the coat and jerked him toward himself. Without even hesitating, he punched the man in the face. "Where's the necklace?" His voice grated through his clenched teeth.

The man pulled the necklace out of his pocket and held it up. "I'm sorry. I just wanted to give something to Maggie for her birthday next week and this looked like something that wouldn't be missed."

"And you think it's okay to just take something that doesn't belong to you?" He raised his fist to strike the man in the face, but as he cowered Hawk hesitated. He lowered his fist and let him go. "I better not see you around here again." He turned to see Stephanie, Julie, and Mike standing down the street, outside the door.

Stephanie ran toward him as he walked back along the building. When she got to Hawk, she stopped. "You didn't have to hit him, you know."

Hawk shrugged. "Sometimes that's the only way to make your point. Here you go." He held out his hand with the necklace draping over the side.

Stephanie took it from his hand and hugged him. "Thank you, thank you." She untangled it. "Daddy gave it to me the year he died." She put it around her neck and clasped it. She ran her fingers along the chain. "I know it isn't an expensive necklace, but it means the world to me."

Hawk nodded and took her hand as they walked back to the rest of the group. "We should go out for pizza and celebrate Stephanie's first job."

"Stephanie should pay since she's getting paid for this." Julie quipped.

"Yay, Stephanie's paying!" Mike agreed.

Stephanie raised her hands up. "I'm paying!" Everyone cheered. "As long as it's cheap."

Stephanie slurped her drink when her cell phone rang. She fumbled for her clutch and pulled out her phone. "Hi mom!... No, I haven't been using the phone a lot." She winked at Hawk. "No, I definitely want to keep it... Mhmm" She started to take a bite of pizza when she dropped it onto the plate. "Seriously!?" She stood and spun around to the back of the chair. "Next week? Congratulations! That's awesome! ... Yes, I can come! Can I bring Hawk? ..." She squealed in delight. "Okay, I love you!" She jumped up and down. "My mom's getting married!"

"What's this about me going?"

"Can you come?"

Hawk smiled.

CHAPTER 17

"Think they'll like me?"

Stephanie leaned her head on Hawk's arm as they stood at the terminal. "I'm sure they'll love you." She picked her head up. "I wonder what's taking my mom so long… oh wait, there she is." She ran down the terminal and gave her mom a hug.

Rose held her tightly and then let her go. "I'm sorry I missed your show. There's so much happening here."

"I know! It's so exciting. There will be lots of other shows for you to see."

Rose looked up at Hawk as he came to stand behind Stephanie. "You must be Hawk."

"Pleased to meet you ma'am." He extended his hand.

Rose shook his hand. "We've heard so much about you." She let go walked in front of them. "Let's go get your luggage. Your papa and grandma are anxious to see you. They both wanted to come, but then there wouldn't have been enough room in the car." She glanced back at Hawk. "Definitely wouldn't have been enough room."

"Papa!" Stephanie ran forward and gave her grandfather a hug as he opened the door.

Lucas gave her a firm hug. "Hey Sweetie. It's so good to see you." He kissed her on the cheek.

"Hi Honey." Mary stood next to Lucas. She gave Stephanie a hug, let go and looked up at Hawk. "Who's this?"

"Papa, grandma. This is my boyfriend, Hawk."

Lucas took the extended hand. "Hello, I'm Lucas Starr. You're a big fella, aren't you? How tall are you?

Hawk smiled. "Six–four, sir."

"Welcome to our home, Hawk. Why don't you guys come in. I'm sure Stephanie and her mom have a lot to talk about with the wedding and all." Mary led the way into their home.

"They've been talking non-stop all the way here." Hawk smiled.

Rose stood back and let the others go in. "Stephanie wouldn't hear of going home first. She wanted to come here to see you guys." After everyone else had entered, she came inside.

Mary closed the door. "When do you go back to school?"

"We have go to back Sunday night so I can get to my warm-ups early Monday morning."

Lucas sat down. "You were telling us about that at Christmas. Getting any better at mornings?"

"Some. Not like Julie tho. She's up before the alarm even goes off. I don't know how she does it."

Lucas laughed. "You'd be surprised what you can get used to."

"It's almost lunchtime. You guys hungry?" Mary hovered by the kitchen doorway.

"We had something earlier. Thanks, Mrs. Starr" Hawk trailed off.

Mary smiled. "Don't be shy because you're a guest. I know young men like you are always hungry. How about some sandwiches?"

Hawk glanced at Stephanie who responded. "Thanks grandma, that would be wonderful."

"Stephanie, why don't you and I go help your grandma while Papa gets to know Hawk a little more?"

With a smile to Hawk, Stephanie followed Rose into the kitchen.

Mary opened the refrigerator door. "He seems nice."

"He is. He's really good to me."

Rose got the bread from the breadbox. "You said he's a football player when you were here for Christmas. What's his dad do?"

"He was in construction. He had some kind of accident so now he's on disability. It's sad."

"What about his mom?" Mary put a jar of mayonnaise on the counter along with some lettuce.

"She died when he was young."

Mary smiled. "Ah, okay. Now I see it."

"See what, Grandma?"

"The connection. Not always, but usually people have common hobbies or a shared experience or a common hurt that draws them together." Mary made some sandwiches. "You lost your father at a young age and he lost his mother."

Stephanie scowled. "I don't see what that has to do with anything. He's nice to me, attractive, and he has a good future ahead of him. I like him."

Rose patted Stephanie's shoulder. "It's okay. I'm sure you have your eyes wide open and you're making sure his values and life goals match yours. Let's talk about this weekend instead. How do you feel about being in the bridal party?"

Stephanie turned with her eyes wide open. "I would love to, but isn't it too late?"

"I took a recent dress of yours to the store when picking out the bridal party dresses. All we have to do is get there this afternoon for final adjustments."

"That would be wonderful!" Stephanie hugged her mother. "How many people are going to be there?"

"It's last minute, obviously, but we're expecting between 30 and 40 people to be there."

"That many? I didn't realize." Mary poured some chips into a large bowl. "Where are you having the reception?"

"Well at first Mark thought we could have it at the Lakeside Banquet Hall."

Mary put her hand to her mouth. "No."

"Isn't that where you and daddy had yours?"

"Yes." Rose sighed. "Once I told him that, he understood why we couldn't have it there so we're having it at the Oasis Hotel."

Mary smiled. "Oh, that's a beautiful place. I'm surprised you were able to get it on such short notice."

"Me too. A case of perfect timing. They don't keep a waiting list and someone had just cancelled a reception of their own. It not only made the reception hall available, but several rooms. Which reminds me Steph. I kept meaning to tell you in the car, but kept forgetting to. We won't be staying at the house."

"So, Hawk. That's an unusual name these days. I'm sure there's a story there."

Hawk smiled. "Actually, it's just a nickname that I chose. My last name is Buteo, which is the genus name for hawks. I learned that just a couple years ago, so I got my friends to call me that."

Lucas nodded. "That's clever. So I guess if someone says your whole name they're really saying 'Hawk Hawk'." He smiled. "What's your major?"

"Oh, I'm going pro. My coach says so and I even have some scouts looking at me. I think I'll probably get an offer at the beginning of the next year."

"That's good. I'm sure you'll be an asset to any team. I'm sure the school is making you pick a major isn't it?"

Hawk sighed. "My dad made me pick one. Said you never know what might happen, so I was thinking Sports Medicine, but that was too much. So I'm in Business Management now."

"Sounds like your dad's a smart man. What position do you play?"

"Offensive lineman. Though I do act as receiver sometimes."

"How many fumbles this past season?"

Hawk frowned. "One."

"Oh, that's not bad at all. So I guess you and I are going to be roomies this weekend."

"Sir?"

"Rose was able to get a block of rooms at the hotel for wedding guests. Stephanie and Mary will be staying in one room while you and I stay in another. Is that a problem?"

"Uh, no sir. No problem at all."

Mary popped her head into the living room. "Lunch is ready."

Stephanie watched as Hawk pulled the suitcases out of the trunk, a frown on his face. "Everything okay?"

"Huh? Oh, yeah. Just not what I had in mind. But this is nice." He looked at the hotel after he put the luggage onto the luggage cart. "It's a nice place."

"It is." She put her arm through his. "They have a beautiful garden out back we can walk through tonight."

Hawk leaned down and kissed her. "I look forward to it."

"Let's go you two. We have a rehearsal dinner we gotta get ready for." Rose dropped her small bag onto the cart.

Stephanie looked up at Hawk. "I'm sorry. I didn't know about that."

"Maybe we can still get some time in after the dinner." He pushed the cart into the hotel as Stephanie followed.

"Stephanie. It's so good to see you." Mark came over and put his hand out to shake hers then put both arms out. "I guess a hug is appropriate for this occasion."

She laughed. "Yes it is." She hugged him. "Dr. Phelps, this is my boyfriend, Hawk Buteo."

"Really?" Mark extended his hand. "Your folks must have a sense of humor. It's good to meet you."

Hawk blushed as he shook hands. "It's just a nickname."

"Ah, okay. That makes sense. I'll see you two at the dinner." He turned to greet someone else as she came into the door.

Stephanie followed Hawk as he pushed the cart to their adjoining rooms. "Wow! Look at how red you got. Were you embarrassed about your nickname?"

"I just... I don't know. Somehow I felt... I did. I felt embarrassed."

"I think it's great. No need to be embarrassed about it. How many people are going to know how you came up with it? And even if they did, it's a clever play of words."

Hawk smiled. "You sound just like your grandfather."

"I'll take that as a compliment, thank you very much."

"Rose, this is my aunt, Ruth." Mark and Rose stood in the middle of the small hall welcoming family members and close friends as they arrived, introducing them to each other.

"Oh, I am so happy for you." Ruth hugged Mark. "I was so surprised when I got your phone call." She hugged Rose. "Welcome to the family. We never thought Mark would get married. How did you two meet?"

Mark and Rose looked at each other. "Well, actually I went to high school with his little sister, Janie."

Ruth raised her eyebrows and looked at Mark. "Is that right?"

"Yes it is. When Mr. Starr was in the hospital a few years ago, Rose and I met while I was checking in on him."

"Of course, he and your dad were old friends. I had forgotten about that."

Stephanie sat at a nearby table with Hawk, Lucas, and Mary. "Papa, I didn't know mom went to school with Dr. Phelps' little sister."

"At the time, I didn't know it either, but apparently she did."

"I wonder what it would have been like if Mom had married Dr. Phelps instead of my dad. Maybe then I could have had a dad."

"Well if she had married him instead of Ray, then I wouldn't be your grandfather. Would I?"

"Oh, I didn't think of that."

"And, of course, who's the one that introduced you to The Nutcracker and ballet dancing?"

Stephanie smiled and leaned against Lucas. "You. I'm sorry, Papa." She sighed. "Sometimes I miss my dad. It would've been nice if he could have walked me down the aisle." Her eyes got wide and she looked up. "Not that I don't appreciate you walking me down the aisle, Papa."

Lucas kissed her on the forehead. "I understand. Either way, I would have had the last dance, right?"

"Of course." She kissed him on the cheek.

"Stephanie! Oh my goodness, look how big you've gotten!"

Stephanie looked over. "Maggie!" She stood and hugged her.

Maggie looked at Stephanie as she stood in front of her. "I guess you're still dancing? You have an impeccable posture."

Stephanie blushed. "Yes, I'm going to school to become a professional." She turned toward Hawk. "Hawk, this is my aunt Maggie. Maggie, my boyfriend Hawk."

Hawk stood, towering over her. "It's good to meet you."

Maggie took a step back. "Oh." She stepped forward again and shook his hand. "It's good to meet you too. You go to school with Stephanie?"

"No, I go to a different school in the same area."

"He's on the football team there, Maggie."

"I bet he is." Her eyes swept his entire frame. "So how did you two meet then?"

Stephanie laughed and followed Hawk's example in sitting down. "Well formally, we met when my roommate introduced me to her brother who introduced me to Hawk."

"Formally?"

"Well, we did sort of meet when we were teenagers." Stephanie looked at Hawk who sighed and closed his eyes. "When I was up in Chicago to see Papa's performance, we saw each other up in the Sears Tower."

"Really?" Maggie looked between Stephanie and Hawk. "Wow. It's almost like you were meant to be together."

"I know, right? Hawk is just his nickname. His real name is Luke which is very close to Lucas. See, Hawk?" Stephanie put her hand on his arm. "We met early in life and your name is almost like my Papa's. You can't ignore the signs."

Maggie laughed. "Right. Well I wish you both the best. I'll talk to you later."

Stephanie watched Maggie walk off before turning to Lucas. "Papa, you should tell Hawk how you and grandma met." She looked at Hawk. "It's a good story."

"I don't want to bore Hawk with that."

Stephanie looked at her grandfather. "Don't be silly." She turned back to Hawk. "He was actually dating someone else and the F.B.I. approached him to help on a case."

"Oh?" Hawk looked at Lucas. "The F.B.I.?"

Stephanie tapped his arm a few times. "Yes! There was this guy who's parents were immigrants from Russia…"

Lucas laughed. "Sweetie. Are you going to tell the story or am I?"

Stephanie smiled, bowed her head and gestured with her hand for him to continue.

"Let's see… I had just started out, barely 20 years old. I was dating a girl named Penny and we had been in Chicago for six months doing a new play under this tyrannical man named James…"

Hawk listened as Lucas told his story. "Wow, weren't you nervous at all? What if he had a gun?"

"Oh, I wasn't nervous." Lucas waved it off. "The agents were down in the basement so I knew I was safe."

"But what if he had a gun?"

Lucas shrugged. "I never even thought about it. Just reacted."

Stephanie beamed. "I love that story."

Mary rubbed his cheekbone. "Poor Lucas had a bad bruise for over a week. But that didn't stop his boss. He just changed the script."

"Whatever happened to Penny? Did she make it big?" Hawk looked between Mary and Lucas.

Mary pulled her hand away. "Poor Penny. She didn't do well at all. She was so broken up about it she ended up jumping off the Hollywood sign itself."

"She was quite the theatrical girl." Lucas sighed. "I'm not sure if she knew of Peg or it was just a coincidence."

Mary drew herself back a little as she looked at Lucas. "Who's Peg?"

"Peg Entwistle or 'The Hollywood Sign Girl'. Apparently she didn't do so well either. Back in the early thirties, she had climbed up a ladder left behind by some workmen onto the 'H' and jumped to her death. According to legend, she received a letter the very next day with an offer for a role."

Mary shook her head. "Where you get this stuff is beyond me."

"The captain has turned off the seatbelt sign. Feel free to move about the cabin, but do please keep your seatbelt fastened while at your seat." The stewardess put the microphone back into its place and walked to the back of the plane to retrieve the drink cart.

"Finally." Hawk undid his seatbelt and made a show of taking in a deep breath.

"Do you need to use the lavatory?" Stephanie put her hand by the buckle.

"Oh, no. I'm fine. Just don't like to feel so constrained. That was some story your grandpa told. Can you imagine meeting someone and he turns out to be a spy? Or what about those F.B.I. agents? I bet they had interesting lives."

"I'm sure they did, but I gotta go pee. Be right back." She undid her seatbelt and went to use the lavatory. When she got back, Hawk was looking at the flight catalog. "Anything interesting?"

"There's a lot of interesting, but not a lot of affordable. Look at this floor lamp. Sure it looks nice, but who would pay 200 dollars for it?"

"Not me." She pulled her cloth beach bag out from under the seat in front of her and got out a pad of paper and a pencil. After stowing the bag back under the seat, she put down her tray and laid the pad onto it and wrote her name in different styles.

Hawk watched as she did this. After she had written her name in block letters, cursive, and a combination of the two in five different ways he pointed to one where she had written two large interlaced cursive S's on top of each other and the rest of her name next to them in smaller cursive. "I like that one. What's with the need to write your name over and over?"

"Well…" Stephanie tried another variation of her name. "… it occurred to me that I might want some business cards. And I definitely need a résumé." She scribbled out what she was working on and started over. "Wouldn't it be cool if I had a signature look? Something that draws attention to my name in a unique way?"

He nodded and watched some more as she went through two other variations. "You know, most girls I know would write their name a different way."

"Oh?" She looked at him. "How?"

"Well… most girls would try to picture how their name would look with a different last name."

She looked down at her name. "Oh, well I couldn't do that. I'm never changing my name." She started on another variation of flowing script.

"Never? What if we got married? You wouldn't change your last name?"

"Of course not, silly. If I did that then I would have to call myself Hawk too and that would just get confusing." She grinned and chuckled at her own joke.

"No, I'm serious. You would never change your name?"

She looked at him, her grin fading into a slight smile. "No. Why would I want to change my name?" She went back to work on writing her name in different styles, the smile fading from her face.

Hawk stared at her for a second with a frown on his face. "There are lots of famous ladies who have changed their name. It's the traditional thing to do when you get married. It's a show of love and respect."

Stephanie looked at him. "Look, I'm Stephanie Starr. Starr. And someday I'm going to be a star, just like my papa. How could I possibly give up my name? That would be insane."

"Here, let me carry that for you." Hawk reached for Stephanie's suitcase as it came around the carousel.

"Thank you." She looked at him as they walked through the airport. "You've been quiet." Hawk's face remained impassive. "Are you mad at me?"

"No." He set the suitcases down, showed the claim tickets to the security agent and then picked them up and carried the suitcases through the doors to the shuttle stop before setting them down again. They waited for the bus and got on it. The 10 minute ride was spent in silence. When they got to his car, he put the suitcases into the trunk and drove them to her school. After he parked in front of her dorm, he got out and got her suitcase from the trunk and set it on the sidewalk.

"Will I see you this week?"

He looked at her. "I don't know yet. We'll see." He kissed her cheek and got into the car and drove off.

Stephanie blinked as tears stung her eyes. She picked up her suitcase and carried it to the building. As she got closer, the tears rolled down her cheeks.

Julie smiled and looked up as Stephanie came into their room. "Hey! How was… what's wrong?" She stood and took the suitcase from Stephanie and set it down next to the bed. "What happened?"

"Is it me?" Stephanie sat down on the lower bed. "Is it wrong for me to want to keep my name?"

Julie sat down next to her on the bed and put her hand onto Stephanie's back. "No, there's nothing wrong with that." Her eyes went wide for a second. "Especially with your name. I would kill for a name like yours. Why? What happened?"

"You know how I've been talking about making a business card using my name as a logo?" She paused as Julie nodded. "Well I was trying to figure out what it should look like on the plane and Hawk said that if we ever got married that I should change my name. Of course I told him that I couldn't do that." She held her hands out at her beach bag which held her paper. "Starr. How can I change that name?"

Julie nodded. "I think… well it's okay to keep your name."

Stephanie looked over at Julie. "But?"

"Well… " Julie grimaced and looked away from Stephanie toward the doorway for a second before looking back. "I just think that, for me, it's a sign of love and respect to change my name. But some very famous people didn't and I totally understand you not wanting to with your name."

Stephanie looked past Julie toward the door and frowned. "Where are the ballet slippers?"

CHAPTER 18

Julie looked to where the slippers had hung. "What?"

"Anna's ballet slippers. Where are they?" She stood and looked at Julie, her eyes getting larger.

"You didn't put them away? I thought that you had put them away before you left. After your necklace was stolen, I just figured you were worried about them being stolen."

Stephanie looked back at the place where the slippers had been hanging. "Oh no!" She swallowed, her breath becoming quick and shallow. She sat down next to Julie and put her hands up to her face as fresh tears streamed. "What am I going to do?"

Julie stood, her lips drawn into a straight line. "We're going to find those slippers."

"You think he'll help us?" Stephanie asked Julie as they walked to class.

"Well we reported them stolen to the school authorities ..."

"They wouldn't know them from any other pair of ballet slippers."

Julie rolled her eyes. "They didn't even know what ballet slippers were. So we're both agreed that we think it was Marilyn?"

"She was the one most interested in them. Even asked if she could wear them!"

Julie chuckled. "Sorry, but the look on your face when she asked. You'd have thought she asked you to sell your first born child."

Stephanie sighed. "Can't believe she asked that."

"Most of the girls think he's cute."

"He is really cute even if he is a bit nerdy."

Julie looked at Stephanie. "Oh? I didn't think you even noticed."

"I noticed. It's just that I already have a boyfriend." She paused. "Had a boyfriend."

"Still no call?"

Stephanie shook her head. "Mmm mmm. I think I'll call him."

"No, you shouldn't do that. Men should be the hunters."

"Well you called Mike."

"Actually I asked Jerome to get him to call me." Julie blushed enough that Stephanie could see it in her dark skin.

Stephanie's mouth dropped open. "You're blushing."

Julie put her hand to her face. "I am?"

"You didn't tell me you asked Jerome to have Mike call you." She held the door open for Julie and they both entered the classroom. Inside were a handful of students already sitting and a steady stream came in behind the girls.

Julie shrugged it off. "Obviously I'm embarrassed by it, but it worked. Hi Daniel." She sat down next to Daniel who sat in the middle of the the third row. A seat he called the most advantageous spot. "Stephanie and I are hoping you can help us with something."

Daniel grinned, exposing a set of brilliantly white teeth. "Sure." He opened his book to the chapter they were coving. "What do you need to know?"

"Actually, this isn't for class."

Daniel set his glass down on the table. The three were at a nearby restaurant so they could talk without other students hearing. He sat across from Julie and Stephanie as he listened to their proposal. "So let me get this straight. You want me to date this girl and find out if she stole some ballet slippers?"

"Not just ballet slippers." Stephanie blurted out. "Anna Pavlova's ballet slippers."

Daniel looked at Stephanie and nodded. "Right. Anna Pav... something-or-other's slippers."

"Pavlova. She was a famous ballerina and they belonged to her. Mrs. Parker gave them to me before she closed down the dance studio. They're very special."

"I feel like James Bond. Date the girl to extract information."

"Well don't get too cozy with her." Stephanie picked up a french fry and dipped it into the pile of ketchup on her plate. "She's pretty popular with the boys if you catch my drift." She ate the fry.

The students lined the wall along the hallway waiting for class as the morning sun poured in from the glass doorway at the end. Daniel pointed with his finger as he held his hand down by his waist, his eyes on Stephanie who stood a little distance away. After she nodded he directed his attention to Marilyn who stood with her shoulder near the wall talking to another girl facing her. He walked toward her and dropped a book next to her feet and bumped into her as he bent down to pick it up.

"Watch it!" Marilyn backed up and steadied her styrofoam cup. "Making me spill my coffee!"

"I am so sorry." Daniel stood.

She looked at Daniel and then down into her cup. "Well, no harm done. I still have my coffee." She took a sip. "I've seen you before. You're in my lit class aren't you?"

Daniel scowled for a second and then his face brightened. "Yes! How do you feel about A Tale of Two Cities?"

Marilyn rolled her eyes. "I love it! We need more beheadings. Guillotine!"

Daniel barked out a short laugh. "Okay. Hey how would you feel about a study session tomorrow night for the test on Friday? I have some study materials we could go over…" He trailed off.

The corner of Marilyn's mouth twisted up. "Okay."

"Great. I'll see you later. I gotta get to my class." He walked off as Marilyn watched him go.

Daniel walked into the cafeteria and looked for an empty booth. In one of the booths, a girl looked at him and pointed. Opposite her, Marilyn peeked around the high back of the bench and smiled and waved him over. He walked over and stood next to the booth.

"Hi Daniel, this is Stacey. She was just leaving."

Stacey scooted across to the end of the red cushioned seat and stood. "I was just leaving."

He smiled and started to sit in the vacated spot when Marilyn patted the place next to her. "Sit here. That way I don't have to read upside down."

"Um, okay." He hesitated and then sat down and put his books onto the table. "So I bought some study guides for the three books we'll be tested on. I also talked to a friend of mine who had this professor a couple years ago and he told me what he could remember." He looked up from the materials to find Marilyn staring at him.

"Are you a senior? I heard you're a senior."

"Yeah, I graduate at the end of this semester."

"So why are you taking this class now? Everyone else in the class is a freshman or sophomore."

Daniel cleared his throat. "Well, I didn't do so well in high school lit' so I put it off along with a couple of other classes. Guess I was excited about doing the fun stuff."

Marilyn nodded. "You know when you suggested that we get together I thought it would be at your place. You know, someplace without a lot of distraction." She gestured to the rest of the cafeteria with groups of students talking and laughing or walking by.

"My roommate is a constant distraction. Always has friends over playing video games. So let's see what we got here." He pulled the first book from the top of his stack.

After they had studied for thirty minutes she put her hand on his arm. "Can we stop? I'm getting tired."

"Sure."

"I need to get up early for ballet practice."

"Oh? You're in ballet?"

She nodded. "Let's do this tomorrow at my place. You know, less distraction."

"Well? Did she take them?" Stephanie ran up to Daniel as he walked across the parking lot and walked with him.

Daniel glanced at her. "I don't know yet. We're seeing each other again tonight in her room. Maybe I can get her to show them to me."

Stephanie faltered in her step. "Her room?"

"Yeah which is good because that makes it easier to get her to show them to me."

"In her room."

"Yeah." He scowled and looked at her. "Is that a problem?"

"No! Of course not. Why would it be a problem?"

Daniel knocked on the open door. Inside he could see Marilyn talking to Stacey on the bed. They both looked over at him and smiled as they stood.

"Hi Daniel." Stacey walked over to him as she talked. "I was just leaving." She smiled back at Marilyn and walked down to the common area of the dorm and plopped into a chair to watch the television.

"Don't just stand there, come on in." Marilyn gestured with her hand and then adjusted her necklace against the tight t-shirt. "Oh, close the door. Fewer distractions." She smiled as he first scowled and then complied.

"I thought we could cover Emma today." Daniel set the book and a sheet of paper onto the single desk in the room.

"What's this?" Marilyn picked up the paper. "'How is the setting important to the story?' Oh boy. This is going to be intense." She leaned against the edge of the desk and fanned herself with the paper.

"Yeah, not my favorite subject. Give me business law classes any day." He came up beside her and looked at the questions. "So what question do you want to do first? Let's discuss."

Marilyn looked over the list and looked at Daniel. "Where are you going after you graduate?"

"20 questions? Okay. I did an internship last summer in Chicago with a firm that is willing to take me on when I graduate."

"That's awesome."

"My turn. Um… how many different outfits do you have for ballet?"

Marilyn's eyes got big. "Want me to model them?"

"Well…"

"Okay, hold on." She went to the dresser and pulled out three different outfits. "Turn around and close your eyes."

"I wasn't expecting..."

She did a spinning gesture with her finger pointed up. "It will only take a minute." After he turned she continued talking while she changed. "When you're a dancer you learn how to change your clothes very quickly. Different scenes could require different outfits and you don't want to keep the audience waiting. Okay. You can turn around."

Daniel turned around. "That was fast. Oh, that's nice." He made a show of looking at her white outfit as she twirled around. "I thought girls wore pink."

"Not always. It can be different colors depending on what is wanted by the director."

"What about shoes?"

"Yes." She pointed to one of the pairs of slippers at the base of the dresser.

"How can you tell one pair from any other?"

"They're different sizes. Mine are the smaller ones." She smiled.

Daniel nodded. "What else might tell them apart? Say you have a few pairs in a pile."

"Oh. Well some are satin and some are leather. These days you might even have some nude colored slippers." She dropped her voice to a whisper and Daniel had to come closer to hear her. "Sometimes it's the age of the slippers. Look at these." Her conspiratorial voice dropped even lower at the end as she opened a drawer to reveal a pair of old slippers.

"Those look pretty old. Why do you have them in the drawer?"

She pulled them out. "These are very special as they once belonged to a famous ballerina. I'm thinking of wearing them tomorrow." She put them back into the drawer and turned to Daniel. She moved her face in close to his and paused. After another second she pulled her head back a few inches. "Want to see another outfit?"

"Maybe we should study some." Seeing her shoulders sag, he continued. "Not sure about you, but I really need to get a good grade on this test."

Marilyn sighed. "I guess you're right."

"I honestly thought she was going to kiss me." Daniel pulled out a chair and sat down next to Stephanie as she and Julie ate breakfast. "Don't know what I would have done."

Julie smiled as she took a bite of her omelet. "Probably would've kissed her back."

Stephanie held on to her half eaten apple as she looked at Daniel. "I don't like her."

"Well I think you will like this; she definitely has those slippers. They were in a drawer. I gotta run." He stood. "Good luck, I'll see you guys later."

Stephanie watched Daniel leave. When she looked back, she found Julie staring at her. Blushing, she looked down and tucked her hair behind her ear before looking up again. "What?"

Julie smiled. "Nothing. Now we just gotta figure out how to get those slippers back without getting caught. We better get going ourselves." She picked up her tray and waited for Stephanie before dropping it off. They both headed to morning practice.

Stephanie sat on the floor putting on her slippers as Marilyn walked into the room carrying her duffle bag. Ignoring her, she focused on her shoes and after putting them on, walked over to the bar to start doing some stretches. As she turned to focus on her other leg, she saw Marilyn walking across the room toward the bar. Her eyes got big. "You're wearing them!?"

CHAPTER 19

Everyone watched Stephanie as she let go of the bar and walked up to Marilyn. "You can't wear those! Take 'em off."

Marilyn snorted. "Excuse me?"

"Take them off! They're not yours!"

Marilyn rolled her eyes and stretched. Stephanie stood frozen as she watched this. Suddenly she ran forward and yanked Marilyn by the hair, pulling her down and causing her to yell out in pain. Marilyn pushed at Stephanie's face trying to get her away, but Stephanie wouldn't let go. Giving up on that, Marilyn scratched at Stephanie's arms causing her to let go of her hair. They both stood and glowered at each other. Marilyn taunted Stephanie. "You don't deserve them. You don't even have the courage to put them on your own feet."

Stephanie gasped and slapped Marilyn.

Marilyn sneered at her. "Is that all you got?"

With a scream, Stephanie launched herself at Marilyn, grabbing her hair and pulling her down again.

"What in God's name is going on in here!?" The voice of Mrs. Shaw boomed out as she entered the room. She went over to the two girls and pulled Stephanie off of Marilyn. "What has gotten into you two?"

Breathing heavily, Stephanie stepped back. "She stole those slippers and won't give them back."

Mrs. Shaw scowled at Stephanie. "You're fighting over a pair of ballet slippers? I have a dozen pairs you could have."

"They belonged to Anna Pavlova. They were a gift and I had them in my room and she stole them."

Mrs. Shaw stared at Stephanie for a second absorbing what she said and then looked over at Marilyn who had stood. "Is this true?"

Marilyn slipped them off and threw them at Stephanie's feet. "They're too old anyway. Likely to fall apart."

"Both of you, out." Mrs. Shaw pointed to the door. "Come back when you can behave like ladies."

Stephanie stayed crouched by the bed with her hands folded on it as she lifted her head up off the mattress and opened her eyes for a second. After sighing, she unfolded her hands and got up off her knees and turned around to see Julie standing in the doorway looking at her.

"You okay?"

"Yeah, just praying."

"Obviously, but that was longer than normal." Julie pointed to the wall where the slippers had previously hung and raised her eyebrows.

Stephanie nodded. "I put them away where they'll be safe. What time is it?" She looked at the clock. "Nine? The day has gone so fast. Mrs. Shaw saw me in the hallway. She said she expects to see me tomorrow morning. How's Mike?"

Julie grinned. "I'm going to marry that boy. Julie Travers. Has a nice ring to it, don't you think?" She saw the look of sadness overcome Stephanie's face. "I'm sorry. I'm so sorry, I wasn't thinking." She walked over and hugged Stephanie. "You know me, my mouth gets going and doesn't know when to stop. Still no word from Lu... uh, Hawk?"

Stephanie shook her head. "It's been five days since we got back. You think I should call him again?"

"No! You already called two..."

"Three."

"Three? You called him again? Girl..." She shook her head.

"I know. I know. Boys are supposed to be the hunters."

"Of course after you're married then the hunt is over and it's all fair game." She moved her eyebrows up and down.

Stephanie smiled and shook her head. "Julie."

Julie laughed. "Well, it's true!" She hugged Stephanie again and backed up toward the door. "Give him a chance to miss you. I'm going to get a snack before bed. You want something?"

"No. I'm going to get some sleep."

The alarm beeped twice and stopped. Stephanie opened her eyes to see Julie in the middle of the room already dressed and packing her bag. "Do you ever sleep?"

Julie grinned up at her. "C'mon sleepyhead. I want to get some breakfast."

Stephanie plopped back onto her pillow. "Someday, but definitely not today, I'm going to get up before you."

"You do that and I'll go without eating for an entire day."

"That..." Stephanie turned on her bed and sat up. "... would be impossible." She hopped down.

"Exactly my point. I can't imagine you ever getting up early. Just like I can't imagine going a full day without eating. I would faint from hunger. My mom says that she was just like me and that I should appreciate it while I can."

Stephanie looked to Julie. "Yeah, my mom said the same thing. I guess we'll have to worry about that when we get old. Like in our 30s. Be right back, I gotta go pee." She grabbed her practice clothes and left. When she got back, her cell phone could be heard ringing. She ran to her purse and pulled it out. "It's Hawk! Should I answer it?" Without waiting for a response, she opened it and answered. "Hello?"

Julie gasped and grabbed Stephanie's sleeve and pulled her toward the door, shoving her bag into her arms as they walked.

"Hi Hawk." Stephanie smiled as she got led along. "I only have a couple of minutes... oh, you too?" She listened as she walked beside Julie toward their classroom. "Apology accepted... Ummm I think I can. I'll have to double-check my schedule... Okay! I'm at class so I gotta go. I'll let you know." She walked past Marilyn, ignoring her gaze and set her bag down and hung up the phone and put it into her bag. "He called to apologize and says we should come to a practice game this Saturday."

"That would be fun. Do you have time? You've been awfully busy and mid-terms are coming up."

"He just apologized, so I gotta make time for him. We can go and come right back after the game." She changed her street shoes for slippers alongside Julie and went to the bar to start her stretches, yawning as she did.

Stephanie sniffed in quickly as she opened her eyes and looked at the clock. Four o'clock. She sighed and went back to sleep. Twenty minutes later she did the same thing. She pursed her lips and laid back down. When she awoke again to look at the clock, it was five. She stared at the clock for a minute and started to close her eyes when she jerked her head up. She sat up and got down from the top bunk and turned to look at the bottom bunk. Empty.

"Wow, you're up early." Julie whispered as she opened the door, light streaming in from the hallway..

Stephanie sighed and kept her voice low. "For the past three hours I've been waking up every 20 minutes hoping that I could get up before you. When did you get up?"

"About 10 minutes ago." She came into the room and turned on the light as she closed the door.

"Aw man! I was up at... oh, I think it was past four thirty and then it was five. I must have just missed you."

Julie smiled. "At least I won't have to hear you gripe today. On Saturdays you're normally dragging your sorry self out of bed crying about the time of day."

"I do not."

Julie chuckled. "Yes, you do."

After Stephanie got dressed, the two girls got some breakfast, put on their jackets, and walked toward the dance studio. Like little islands, the lamp posts lit up the sidewalk and ground at points along the way. A student jogger would pass them occasionally and in the distance they could see some students gathered for morning exercises in a parking lot. The girls were talking about the practice game as Daniel snuck up behind them and tailed them.

"Jerome says he can't come get us because before the game they have some warm-ups."

"Yeah, that's what Hawk said. That our practice…"

"Boo!" Daniel grabbed Stephanie's waist. Stephanie and Julie both screamed. He laughed and came around to their front and walked backward.

"Daniel!" Stephanie put her hand up to her chest. "You scared me to death."

He continued to laugh. "I can't believe how easy it is to sneak up on you two. You should be more aware of your surroundings."

Julie hit Daniel. "And you shouldn't be sneaking up on people."

"So where are you two going today that you need a ride?"

"Football game." Both girls replied in unison.

Daniel looked between one girl and the other. "You two like football? Huh. Well I can give you a ride."

Stephanie perked up. "That would be great. It wouldn't be a bother?"

He smiled. "Not at all. I have my business law class this morning and then I am available. Should I just stop by the dance studio to get you?"

"No, we gotta get some snacks first. Just pick Steph and me up at dorm D."

"Stephanie?" Mrs. Shaw glided up next to Stephanie as she changed from her slippers into a pair of gym shoes. "Would you mind staying behind a moment?"

"I'll just be…" Julie motioned her head toward the hall and walked out along with the other dancers.

Stephanie tied her shoe laces and stood. "Yes, Mrs. Shaw?"

"Is everything okay? This past week you've been, ah, distracted. While your form is impeccable, it feels your heart just isn't in it. I can understand the theft affecting you, but it was even before that. "

"Everything's perfect." Stephanie smiled. "My boyfriend and I had a bit of a falling out, but everything's okay now."

Mrs. Shaw nodded and bit her lip. "May I give you a piece of advice? Boys may come and go. At this age, they're never quite sure of what they want. Don't let it keep you from enjoying what you do."

The smile faded from Stephanie's face. "Okay."

"I'll see you tomorrow for the new program rehearsal?"

"Four o'clock."

"Good." She smiled. "See you then." Mrs. Shaw turned and walked away leaving Stephanie to go.

"Why the sour face?" Julie picked up her bag and walked alongside Stephanie as she exited the studio.

"Just someone else trying to tell me what's important in my life." They walked in silence until they got to their room where Stephanie dropped her bag. "You think Anna had everyone telling her what she could or couldn't do?"

Julie looked up from where she packed the snacks. "She was a teenage Russian girl in the late 1800s. Of course everyone was telling her what she could or couldn't do." She paused. "But didn't she also buck trends and make a new standard for what it meant to be a ballerina? Endured the taunting of her classmates and practiced long hours to perfect new techniques she learned from various instructors?"

Stephanie looked at Julie with a softened face. "I guess you're right."

"Darn, we missed the kick-off." Julie moved down the row and sat down. Choice seats were easily available with only a few dozen spectators present.

"Who are they playing? I thought football was over." Stephanie sat down next to Julie.

"It's a scrimmage game, so it's just themselves. They split the team up and do a practice game. You see, the coaches have reviewed what went right last season and what went wrong. Then they come up with different ways do better and they practice the different plays to see how they work."

"I'm impressed at how much you know Julie." Daniel slid down the row and sat next to Stephanie.

Stephanie grinned at him. "What do you expect? She has both a brother and a boyfriend on the team."

"And Stephanie has a boyfriend on the team too." Julie replied without looking away from the game.

"I should have known." He huffed. "Two cutest girls on campus and you're both dating football players from a different school."

"Awww. Aren't you sweet." Stephanie turned her attention to the game. "They're always so rough."

"Especially that guy. The ball isn't even in play anymore and he's still slamming that guy like it is. Who is that anyway?"

Stephanie's mouth fell open. "That's Hawk."

The spectators watched as the other player and Hawk got into a heated exchange. The coach and assistant coach ran out and directed the players to the sidelines.

"I like 'em tough." The voice came from behind them.

Stephanie looked back and saw Marilyn and Stacey sitting five rows up. Marilyn gave a mocking grin and then looked back to the field. Stephanie gasped and looked forward. "What is she doing here?"

Julie glanced back. "Oh, she is evil."

"Who we talking about?" Daniel looked back and saw a smug look on Marilyn's face. She blew him a kiss and smiled.

"You're boyfriend's cute." Marilyn came down to where Stephanie and the others were sitting after the game. "I can see why you like him. Man like that can make you feel good."

"Why are you here Marilyn?"

She feigned surprise. "Why, the same as you. To watch a bunch of hunks battle it out on the field."

Stephanie huffed and narrowed her eyes. "My boyfriend is playing. That's why I'm here."

"Sure honey. You keep telling yourself that." She looked Stephanie up and down. "And maybe you can keep that little hot bod of yours out of trouble. C'mon Stacey." She continued down the stairs with Stacey in tow and worked her way toward the exit.

"She makes me so mad."

Hawk walked out of the locker room and up to Stephanie as she waited with Julie and Daniel. "Hey Steph." He kissed her. "I didn't think you were going to make it."

"What was that?"

"It's called a kiss. I guess we're out of practice and need more?"

Stephanie grinned. "I can always use more kisses. No, on the field. You were so rough."

"Oh, that. I was just in the moment. Didn't have time to do my pre-game ritual." He looked at Daniel. "Hi, I'm Hawk."

Daniel nodded. "Daniel. Girls needed a ride."

"Where's Mike?" Julie looked around Hawk toward the locker room. As she looked, several players came out including Mike. She ran over to him and kissed him.

"I'm starving. Anyone want to get some pizza?" Hawk looked between Stephanie and Julie and Mike.

Stephanie took Hawk's hand. "Sounds good to me."

Hawk and Stephanie arrived in his car before everyone else who rode with Daniel. The gaming and pizza place had a handful of customers as they walked inside and up to the counter.

"Can I help you?" The young man behind the counter stood from his stool.

"What do you guys want on your pizza?" Hawk turned to everyone as they walked in.

"Mushrooms and onion." Daniel piped.

"With sausage." Mike suggested.

Julie looked at Mike. "No, I prefer pepperoni."

Stephanie curled her nose. "I can't stand pepperoni. What about bacon?"

"Okay, I can do that."

The man scratched pepperoni off his paper and wrote down bacon. "Have a seat and I'll bring it out in about 20 minutes."

"Oh look, they have PacMan here. I haven't played that since I was little." Mike walked over to the arcade game and dropped in a quarter. Everyone huddled around him and watched as he played. "I used to be the best at this game. Nobody could beat me." He progressed several levels before losing. "Guess I'm out of practice."

"Hey, where do you guys want your pizza?" The employee walked up holding their pizza with oven mitts on his hands. He accidentally dropped a bundle of napkins.

"Oh, let me get those for you." Stephanie bent down from the waist and in a fluid movement pulled the napkins up off the floor and held them out for him.

"Well look at you, little miss graceful with the perfect posture."

Hawk frowned. "You have a problem with her posture? Of course she has perfect posture. She spends hours every day practicing it." He poked the man on the shoulder and raised his voice a little. "Maybe you could use some lessons on posture yourself."

The man grimaced as Hawk poked him and backed away. "I didn't mean anything by it."

Stephanie stepped toward Hawk. "Hawk, it's okay."

Hawk's face grew red and his eyes narrowed as his voice grew even louder. "Didn't mean anything by it? Then why did you say it? Huh? She's already sensitive about this."

"Hawk!" Stephanie put her hand on his shoulder. "It's okay!"

He jerked his head toward Stephanie who backed up a step. After staring at her for half a second he blinked and looked back at the employee who had taken several steps back.

Julie walked over to the employee and took the pizza. "Thanks." She handed him some cash and looked at everyone else. "Maybe it would be best if we eat this someplace else."

Hawk walked toward the door. "We can go to my place."

CHAPTER 20

"What were you so angry about?"

Hawk glanced at Stephanie and then back to the road. "What? I know how you're sensitive to how people look at you. You even told me once that people have teased you and called you snooty because of your posture."

"No, it's more than that. Even at the game you were so rough that you had to be pulled off the field." He continued to drive as she looked at him. "Why are you so angry?"

He continued to look ahead. "I just… I don't know. I just get mad. Everyone gets mad."

"Yeah, but you get, like, really mad." Her eyes went wide as she expressed her observation. She lowered her voice. "You scared me."

"I'm sorry." He glanced over at her and put his hand on her leg. "I didn't mean to scare you. I normally have a pre-game routine that helps and I didn't do it because I thought I would be seeing you."

Stephanie stared ahead. "It's okay. Obviously you can't miss your routine if this happens."

Hawk made sure everyone was following him properly and drove into the parking lot of an apartment building. "Here we are." He got out of his car.

Stephanie got out and looked up at the building. "You live here? This is nice."

"Well I share it with a another player so it's a lot cheaper, but yeah. This is where I live."

Hawk led everyone up to the fourth floor and into his apartment.

Julie dropped the pizza onto the coffee table. "This is nice. How do I get on this plan?"

"Letter in football four years straight and be a star lineman." Hawk looked up a second. "Yeah, that should do it. If my dad needed a job, they could have gotten one for him too."

Stephanie looked back from the window where she stood looking out. "I didn't know schools can do that."

"Well, not the school exactly. The alumni were willing to do it. They approached us on behalf of the university. They're the ones that put me up here. I'm really not supposed to talk about it."

Julie looked at Stephanie and mouthed 'wow' to her as she grabbed a slice of pizza.

Hawk sighed aloud. "Guys, I'm sorry."

Mike stopped as his hand hovered over a slice of pizza to look at Hawk. "What?"

Hawk rubbed his temples as he looked down. "I'm sorry that I ruined the afternoon with my outburst." He sighed again.

Stephanie walked over to him and leaned her head onto his upper arm as she put her arm around his back. "We forgive you."

Daniel took a big bite of his slice and talked with his mouth full. "Yeah, forget about it man." He set his slice down. "Excuse me, where's the bathroom?" After Hawk pointed it out, he left the group. When he came out he found Hawk waiting there. "Oh, excuse me."

"I've seen the way you look at Stephanie." He kept his voice low. "You better watch yourself." He walked back into the living room. "Hey, guess what Mike and I are doing next weekend?"

Daniel walked back into the living room and picked up his pizza.

Julie looked at Mike. "What are you doing?"

He grinned. "We're going hunting."

"Oh! I love venison." Stephanie beamed at Hawk.

Hawk put his arm around her waist. "Not deer, wild pigs."

Mike laughed. "It's going to be a lot of fun."

Daniel wiped his mouth with a napkin. "I've never been hunting."

Still grinning, Mike looked at him. "You should come with us then! It'll be great."

Daniel looked at Hawk and then Mike. "Wish I could, but I have to study for some exams."

"Thanks for the ride Danny." Julie opened the back door and got out of the car.

"Yes, thanks." Stephanie followed her out and closed the door.

Daniel rolled down the passenger window. "I never thought of going to a scrimmage game before. It was fun, but your boyfriend is scary."

Stephanie grinned back at him as she walked toward the dorm. "Keeps the wrong kind of boys at bay." She continued on toward the dorm with Julie.

Julie looked back to see that Daniel had left then looked at Stephanie as she opened the door to the building. "What's with Hawk today? He was worse than normal."

Stephanie looked at Julie with an open mouth. Closed it and then opened it again. "Worse than normal?"

"Girl, where have you been? The boy is always angry about something. Today he was just out of control." She continued half-way up the stairs before realizing Stephanie wasn't following. She looked back to see Stephanie standing at the bottom of the stairs with her mouth open again. "Don't tell me you never noticed."

Stephanie climbed up the stairs narrowing the gap to Julie. "He gets upset sometimes, but don't we all?"

Julie shook her head. "You have got to open your eyes. Don't be love blind. Remember, I know him from last year too. I've seen him get kicked from games because of that temper of his."

"I've never seen him get so angry like he did today. Maybe he was just having a bad day." She looked at the clock as they passed through the common area. "I should get to the studio and get some practice in. You coming?"

Julie slowed down and looked back at Stephanie. "Um, no. You know how Mr. Johnson has been taking up more of my time with singing?" Stephanie nodded. "Well, I'm thinking I want to focus on that more. I really like it. After this semester, I won't be doing ballet anymore." She headed toward their room.

"Oh." Stephanie kept walking toward their room behind Julie. "When were you going to tell me?"

"I just made up my mind today about it." She stopped and turned around. "You're the first person to know."

Stephanie hugged her. "I'm sure you'll do great. You have a beautiful voice."

"Thank you. I'm glad you understand. Do you have a quarter or two I can borrow?"

"Payphone?"

"Payphone."

Stephanie dug into her pocket and pulled out some pennies and a nickel. "Hold on, I think I have some in my purse." She opened up her purse and pushed some things around inside. "Here we go. I thought I had some." She pulled out two quarters and handed them to Julie.

"Thanks! I gotta call Mike and then I'm going to go do some practicing of my own." She hugged Stephanie again and walked out.

Stephanie watched her go and then pulled out her phone and dialed before putting it to her ear to listen. She sat down at her desk and sighed as she waited. "Hi Papa… No, everything's fine. I just wanted to call and hear your voice."

Over the next couple of weeks, Stephanie's day fell into a constant routine. Get up for ballet practice. Take classes. Ignore the taunts of Marilyn. Talk to Hawk during lunch. Take more classes. Practice ballet. Eat dinner and maybe talk to Hawk. Practice for the upcoming ballet program. Study for midterms. Collapse into bed. Get up for ballet practice. Take the offered apple from Julie on the way. Take classes. Roll her eyes at Marilyn. Talk to Hawk during lunch. Take more classes. Practice ballet. Eat dinner and maybe, no definitely, talk to Hawk. Practice for the upcoming ballet program. Study for midterms. Collapse into bed while worrying about midterms. The days were long and tedious and starting to take their toll.

"What day is it?" Stephanie came in to the room after getting her shower and getting dressed.

"Ummm… Wednesday. Why?" Julie looked up from her desk.

"That's what I thought. I feel like I'm supposed to be doing something today, but can't remember."

"Well midterms start today."

"No, I know about that."

"Somebody's birthday?"

"No, that's not it either."

"Well I don't know. You think you're ready for your history test?"

Stephanie made a rude sound in her throat. "I hate history. But I think I'll do okay."

Julie closed her book and took a deep breath. "I think I'm ready too." She grabbed her bag and joined Stephanie in heading out the door. "So I was thinking of taking classes over the summer. If I do that my course work in the fall and spring would be less and I can focus more on my singing. Of course then I have to make sure I keep my grades up and to do that I'll need some sleep…"

"Since when do you need sleep? You get, what? Three or four hours a night?"

Julie scoffed. "As if! I normally get seven, though sometimes I have to get by on six because I have to get up early and resume my stud…"

"Résumé! That's what I'm forgetting!" Stephanie sighed and shook her head.

"Oh, that's right, I remember you saying something about that. You didn't work on it?"

"No. I completely forgot. Mrs. Shaw is going to kill me."

Mrs. Shaw stood outside the door to the studio. Her face lost it's usual passive expression and almost became a smile until she saw Stephanie shaking her head. "What happened? You said you would have it for me today."

"I know Mrs. Shaw and I'm so sorry. I got so busy with studying for midterms and everything it slipped my mind." Stephanie furled her eyebrows. "I might have time tonight?"

"I have five students to recommend to two different companies. If you don't give me something by tomorrow, it will be four."

"I'll have it, I promise."

"See that you do. I would hate for you to miss out on this opportunity."

Stephanie swapped out her shoes and joined Julie at the bar and stretched, sighing deeply as she did.

"Can't bring a simple sheet of paper? It's not like you have much to put on it." Marilyn's voice followed Stephanie as she walked past.

"You know what I don't understand?" Julie put her foot up on the bar and leaned into it. "Why would she ask for your résumé now?"

"If you're good enough, they'll practically guarantee a job at graduation time."

The next morning, Mrs. Shaw stood ready at the studio door and accepted the paper from Stephanie. She took some time to look at it. "Good, you included all that we discussed." She looked up and smiled. "We'll have to wait to see what they say, but I think it will go well. There will be representatives from a few companies at this next performance too, so be on your tip toes." She turned and entered the studio.

Stephanie walked from heel to toe, pushing up on her toes until she arrived at her usual warm-up spot.

Julie grinned at her. "You're so silly sometimes."

"Hawk says they're having another scrimmage game on Saturday afternoon. Want to go?"

Julie smiled. "What do you think?"

"Well…" Daniel sighed and leaned back in his chair.

"Don't you like going to the games?" Stephanie scowled.

"No it isn't that. I actually enjoy it more than I thought I would. I, um, just need to do some homework."

"There's all day tomorrow for that."

Daniel opened his mouth and then closed it. "I don't know."

"Please?" Stephanie put her hand on his arm. "It would mean a lot."

Daniel looked at the hand on his arm and then at her face and sighed again. "Yeah, I can take you, but I gotta get some gas on the way. Hope you don't mind."

"I don't mind at all."

"I'm just glad we can go at all." Julie responded. "Normally we could get Mike or Hawk to come get us, but these last few weeks we've been unable to coordinate between schedules. Taking the bus takes so long."

Daniel pulled into a gas station. "Be right back."

Stephanie turned to Julie. "Hawk said that they have warm-ups in the morning and then a break before the practice game. It isn't enough time to come get us, but he said he often goes to his place for a bit to study and stuff. Would you mind if I go to his place and meet you at the game?"

"What if he isn't home?"

"It's only a few blocks away. I can walk."

"Okay with me. See if Daniel will do it."

Stephanie waited as Daniel came back from paying inside the station. "Hey Daniel, you remember where Hawk lives?"

"Sure. Just a few blocks from the stadium on the edge of campus."

"Can you drop me off there? I'm going to surprise him."

Daniel nodded. "I can do that. I'm sure he'll enjoy the surprise."

After they arrived 30 minutes later, Stephanie got out of the car. "Thanks. See you guys at the game." She watched them drive off and went into the building. She took the stairs up to the fourth floor and knocked on the apartment door. She waited several seconds and knocked again. "Hmmm, he must not be here." As she turned to leave, the door opened a few inches.

"Oh, hey Steph. I wasn't expecting you here." Hawk quickly opened the door and stepped out into the hall, closing the door behind himself leaving an inch opening. "What are you doing here?"

Stephanie scowled and peered around him to see inside. "I came to surprise you. Who's in there?"

He shifted himself to block the view. "Just a couple of guys from the team."

"Oh yeah? Who?" She craned her neck to see past him. When he didn't answer, she stepped past him and pushed the door open.

"Honest Steph, it's just…"

Stephanie stepped inside to see a couple of the players sitting around in the living room.

"It's just Todd and Chris like I said. You ready to go to the game?"

Stephanie turned to face Hawk, her eyes narrowed. "What's that smell?"

Hawk reached out for her hand. "C'mon, let's go to the game."

Stephanie stepped back, her eyes wide. "You've been smoking pot!?" She glanced at the other two players who looked down, avoiding eye contact. "How could you do that?"

"Look, it's nothing. Just a way of relaxing before the game. It takes the tension off."

She glared at Hawk. "So this is what you do to help with your anger? Smoke some weed?" She walked toward the door. "I gotta get out of here. I can't take this."

"Steph. It's no big deal. A lot of players do it."

Stephanie turned to face him. "Oh! So that makes it okay? Lots of people use illegal drugs, so that makes it okay?" Her nostrils flared as she took in several quick breaths. "I can't be dating a pot head." She yanked the door open and stormed out.

"Steph…" Hawk watched as she walked out the door.

CHAPTER 21

"Stephanie." Hawk drove alongside Stephanie as she walked on the sidewalk. "Let me drive you to the game." He braked when the car got ahead of her. "There's no reason for you to walk. Get in the car."

Chris reached up from the back seat next to Todd and tapped him on the shoulder. "We're going to be late."

"C'mon Steph. Let me drive you to the game."

Stephanie stopped and looked at him. "Do you honestly think I'm going to get into that car knowing what you've done?" She continued walking at a faster pace.

"Let's go Hawk. We don't want to be late."

Hawk sighed and accelerated, leaving Stephanie behind.

"Oh, there you are. I thought you were going to miss the kickoff." Julie turned her attention back to the field as the players arranged themselves.

Stephanie stopped as she got near Julie and Daniel. "Can we go home?"

Julie scowled and looked at Stephanie's tear-streaked face. "Why? What happened?"

Stephanie looked around and lowered her voice. "He was smoking pot."

Daniel's mouth fell open. "What?"

Julie's eyes went wide. "He can get suspended for that."

"I just… I just gotta go. Can we go?"

Julie glanced at the field and then looked back at Stephanie. "Of course." She turned toward Daniel.

"Yeah, of course. We can go. What happened?"

Stephanie told them what happened as they worked their way to Daniel's car. "I just can't believe he would do that."

Julie let Stephanie get into Daniel's car and then followed her in. "Actually it makes sense. Jerome said that some players do that and that some have been suspended from the school."

"But he was so nice when I met him. He never treats me badly."

"Eventually it would come out. You can't hide who you are forever."

When they got back, Stephanie and Julie decided to spend time watching some television in the common room. Stephanie sighed.

"You gonna be okay?"

"Yeah. No. I don't know. I guess I will be. I thought he might be the one."

Julie nodded. "I know." She waited for Stephanie to say something else, but didn't hear anything. "You want to get something to eat?"

Stephanie tried to smile. "I'm not hungry, but I'll go with you."

The two girls went to the school's food court with Julie in the lead. Stephanie mostly kept up, looking down at the shoes of Julie as she followed. Now and then, she would need to look up to see where Julie went and then move again in her direction.

"Whoa, careful Steph."

Stephanie stopped and looked up to see she had almost run into Daniel who had a tray laden down with various items. "Oh, sorry Daniel."

"Hey Danny, want to sit with us?" Julie had turned around when she heard his exclamation.

"Sure, I can do that. Where you sitting?"

Julie looked around the crowded room. "There's a place. You two sit there and I'll get some food."

"Aren't you eating Steph?"

Stephanie shook her head and headed off toward the indicated table.

Daniel turned to Julie. "She going to be okay?"

Julie watched as Stephanie plodded away. "I hope so."

Stephanie's eyes opened. Normally she would be getting up in another hour on a Sunday. As she laid there, she saw Julie quietly come into the room. "Good morning."

"Hey sleepyhead. How you feeling?" Julie turned on the light.

Stephanie squinted and took in a deep breath. "I'm okay. A little sad, but okay." She put her hand over her eyes as she got adjusted to the light.

"That's good. I was a little worried about you. What are you doing today?"

"My final production is next weekend so after church I need to practice for that. Not sure what else I'm doing. Just relaxing I guess."

Julie opened her mouth to say something then paused. "You know your phone was ringing last night."

"Yeah. I was ignoring it. How about you? What are you doing today?"

"After church?" She sat down on the chair and looked up at Stephanie. "Well, if you're feeling okay, I thought I might go out for the day."

"It's okay." Stephanie smiled. "You can say you're going with Mike."

Julie smiled. "Oh good. Yeah, Mike is coming over early this afternoon and we're going to go hang out for a while before going to their scrimmage game. You might even be back from practice when he comes."

"They have another game today?" She sat up in her bed "I didn't realize."

"If you don't want me to go, I'll just hang with Mike around here for a while and then come home."

Stephanie hopped down to the floor. "Don't be silly. You're going to marry that boy, you should be with him. Ready for some breakfast?"

"I never thought you'd ask."

Julie sat on the front step of their dormitory watching the street. She smiled as she saw Mike's car coming toward her and stood. As she walked toward the street her smile faded when she realized that Hawk sat in the passenger seat. The car came to a stop next to her and they both got out. She ignored Mike and looked at Hawk. "What are you doing here?"

"I need to talk to Stephanie."

"Well she's not here. She's practicing for her show next weekend." She looked at Mike and widened her eyes for a second before looking back at Hawk. "I don't think she wants to talk to you."

"Yeah, she made that obvious last night. I just... I just want to try to make it right."

"Make it right? I don't think this is just something you can make right."

"I gotta try."

Mrs. Shaw watched as the cast finished the last scene and applauded. "Bravo. That was beautiful. Just beautiful. Tiffany, make sure you're smiling. Tracy, I'll need one extra spin there next time. You all did a great job, go enjoy the rest of your day. I'll see you tomorrow morning." As everyone left, she called Stephanie to her.

"Yes? Did I do something wrong?"

"No. In fact, you were flawless. The best I've seen you do in over a month. You seem... centered, for lack of a better word. Both companies are keen on seeing you perform next weekend. Keep this up and you'll have a tough choice to make."

Stephanie grinned. "Thank you Mrs. Shaw. See you tomorrow." She ran on the balls of her feet across the stage and to the dressing room where she changed. When she walked out of the building she squinted against the bright sunlight. "I really need to get me some sunglasses." As she walked toward her dorm, she saw Julie walking toward Mike's car. She slowed down and came to a stop when she saw Hawk get out of the car. Other students, including Marilyn, walked by her as she listened to Julie confront him. She listened for a second, closed her eyes and sighed. She opened her eyes and walked forward.

Hawk saw her. "Stephanie." He took a step toward her and stopped. He glanced at Julie and Mike and then looked back to Stephanie. "Can we talk?" He paused for the un-given response. "Please, just let me talk."

Stephanie stared at him tight-lipped. "Fine Hawk. You can talk."

"Alone?"

Stephanie started to walk away and then looked back. "Well come on."

Hawk caught up to her. "You're right. I shouldn't be smoking marijuana. But see? You're helping me be a better person. This is something you can help me with. Don't we all have problems that we need to fix?"

She took a deep breath and let it out. "True."

"See? So if you come visit me before the games, you keep me from doing it."

"But what about the times I'm not there? What if I can't come to a game?"

"Hmmm. I could call you."

"I don't know."

"C'mon. Am I that bad of a person?"

"No, you're not. Okay, I'm willing to try, but if you do it one more time…"

"Great! That's great!" Hawk hugged her and she hugged him back. "What are you doing today? Can you come to the game?"

"Yes, I can."

They walked back toward Julie and Mike who were sitting on the hood of the car and talking. When Julie saw them coming back, she looked back and forth between them and scowled at Stephanie.

Stephanie watched as the players gathered on the field ignoring Julie as she stared at her. After several seconds she turned to Julie. "What?"

Julie shook her head and looked back on the field. "Love blind."

"Don't you see? He's my only chance."

Julie turned back to Stephanie "Your only chance?"

"Yes. My only chance at getting married and having the last dance with Papa."

"When I was in high school, my friend Allison had a boyfriend with anger issues. Then one day he hit her. She gave him a second chance, and a third, and a forth. Know what happened when she gave him a fifth chance?"

"What?"

"He put her in the hospital." She put her hand onto Stephanie's shoulder. "I don't want to see you in the hospital."

"He's never hit me."

Julie stared into her eyes. "Don't let him. You hear me?"

"I won't."

They both turned their attention to the field in time for the kickoff. A player caught the ball and knelt down on one knee to end the play. Julie gestured with her hand. "He had time. He could have gotten 15 on that easy."

"I don't know. They were coming pretty fast."

The players lined up against each other. When the ball snapped, Hawk blocked the defensive player while the quarterback looked around for a receiver. Not seeing one, he ran. A defensive player hit him on the side causing him to drop the ball. Hawk saw the ball hit the ground and jumped onto it while other players clamored for the ball. Eventually the whistle blew and players peeled themselves off the pile. At the bottom Hawk laid on the ground, holding the ball. He held the ball up for the referee and stayed on the ground.

Stephanie put her hand to her mouth and stood. "Oh! He's hurt!"

Julie grabbed at Stephanie's arm, keeping her from running down. "I'm sure he'll be fine. Players are always knocked around a little. Honest. It's okay, sit down."

Stephanie looked at Julie, back to the field, and then back to Julie again before sitting down and turning her attention back to the field.

The coach ran out onto the field and talked to Hawk. A couple of other players gathered around and helped him up. He put his arms around their necks and limped toward the bench on the sideline. When he got there he took his helmet off and gave a slight smile back toward Stephanie. Someone brought him an ice pack and he watched the rest of the game from that position, changing out ice packs periodically.

After the game, the coach came over and talked with Hawk who then stood and tried to apply some weight to his injured leg. He immediately picked it up and shook his head and sat down again. The coach and Hawk talked for a minute before the coach looked up to see Stephanie and Julie standing there. "It looks like Hawk has a serious knee injury. We're going to take him to the hospital and have it examined. Would you like to follow?"

"I'll drive them." Mike had come up beside Julie and put his arm around her waist, pulling her close to himself.

Julie put her arms up and pulled away as she made a face. "You're all stinky. Get a shower first."

Stephanie came up to Hawk. "How bad is it?"

"I've had worse."

"Really?"

He grimaced. "Actually no, I haven't." He stood onto his right leg with the assistance of a couple other players and limped away. "I'll see you at the hospital."

Stephanie, Julie, and Mike all entered the hospital's emergency room. They saw Hawk sitting in a wheel chair. Nearby the coach and the players that had helped him were seated. Hawk waved at them and they came over and sat by him.

"I really don't like hospitals." Stephanie took his hand as she sat down. As always, she had perfect posture.

"I wouldn't either if I went through what you did."

"Mr. Buteo, we're ready for you now." The nurse came over and undid the locks of the wheelchair.

"It's okay if my girlfriend comes too, right?"

"Sure. C'mon honey." The woman looked briefly at Stephanie and then looked back and watched as Stephanie stood. "You can keep him company. Sure wish I had your posture."

Hawk closed his eyes and took a deep breath before opening them again.

"You okay?" The woman put her hand onto his shoulder as she pushed him along.

"Yeah, I'll be okay."

They went to a room where the nurse took Hawk's vitals and wrote them down onto a chart. "Heart rate is 62, and your blood pressure is 100 over 70."

"Is that good?"

The nurse smiled. "I wish mine was so good. The doctor will be here in a moment." She walked past the open door and put the chart onto a hook outside.

After a few minutes a doctor came inside looking at the chart. "Luke Buteo?"

"Yes."

The doctor sat on a small swivel stool near him and shook his hand. "I'm Dr. Patel. Says here you injured your knee during a game. Why don't you tell me about it."

Hawk told how he had jumped onto the ball and several people also jumped for the ball and someone had landed on his knee and how he heard a snap and a felt shock of pain through his body.

The doctor nodded. "Okay. Let's get you setup for an x-ray and we'll see what's happening inside of that joint." He stood. "Someone will come by in a couple of minutes to take you." He shook Hawk's hand and left.

Stephanie shifted in her seat. "I hate the waiting."

Hawk nodded. After several minutes an orderly came into the room. They went to the radiology department and waited until they were ready for him. Stephanie needed to wait while he went inside for the x-rays. After another 20 minutes, the orderly pushed Hawk out into the hallway. He frowned at Stephanie. "We have to wait for the x-rays to be developed and then wait for someone else to look at them."

"Yeah, I know. He's called a Radiologist." She fell in behind as the orderly pushed Hawk back to the waiting room.

"Probably just a bruised cartilage. Take a week off and I'm sure you'll be as good as new."

Hawk shifted in his wheelchair. "Thanks coach." He grinned at Stephanie. "I'll probably need someone to help me get better."

"Oh really? Have someone in mind?"

"Maybe." He winked at her.

Doctor Patel came to the group in the waiting room and sat down across from Hawk and nodded toward the coach. "I assume this is your coach?"

"Yes sir."

"Okay, then he'll want to hear this too. What you have is a torn ACL along with some bruised cartilage."

"How bad is it?"

The doctor looked between Hawk and the coach. "I'm sorry. This is a career ending injury."

CHAPTER 22

Hawk stared at the doctor. "No, there's gotta be something I can do. Or something you can do?"

"What about surgery?" The coach leaned forward.

The doctor shook his head. "We need to perform surgery, but the damage is so severe that normal knee function won't be possible for a long time. If ever. There is some research into this kind of thing, but that's some years off before it can be used." He handed Hawk a few sheets of paper. "That first one is a prescription for pain medication. The second is the list of orthopedic surgeons that work out of this hospital that can do the surgery. You need to contact one to do a proper consult and schedule the surgery. I would've had one come and talk to you directly, but none are in today. The third one is information on the immediate care for your injury. The nurse will take you back to a room and wrap it. I've instructed her to also give you a pain killer so you won't be in pain much longer." He stood. "I am sorry." He shook Hawk's hand and then the coach's hand and left.

Hawk stared after the doctor until he disappeared out of sight and then turned to the coach. "What am I supposed to do now? I was going pro."

"Sorry son. What you need to do now is get better and focus on your studies." He put his hand on Hawk's shoulder as he stood. "You gotta figure out a new plan." He turned to Mike. "You taking him home?" When Mike nodded he started toward the doors.

"Tough break Hawk." One of the other players said as he stood to follow the coach. "I don't know what I would do."

The other player followed. "Yeah, sorry Hawk."

A few minutes later the nurse returned and wheeled Hawk to the same examination room. There she gave him a dose of the prescribed pain killer then wrapped his knee. When all was done, Hawk sighed and looked at Stephanie. "Let's get out of here. I'm beginning to see why you don't like hospitals."

They rode on in silence toward Hawk's apartment for a while before he finally spoke up. "That pain killer is starting to kicking in. I can't feel anything at all."

"That's good." Stephanie smiled at him. "Have you thought about what you're going to do now with college?"

"No." He grinned. "Who knows? Maybe I'll become an F.B.I. agent."

Stephanie smiled back at him. "I'm sure Papa would like that."

"I'm serious. His story inspired me."

When they got to his apartment building, he carefully got out of the car with the help of Stephanie and Mike and used his crutches as he made his way to his apartment. Once he got inside, he looked around. "I suppose I'll have to move into a normal dorm. I don't think I'll be allowed to stay here."

Mike looked over from the kitchen as he got some water. "I didn't think of that. Maybe if you can pay for your portion, they won't mind that you stay."

Hawk nodded. "I guess I'll have to ask my dad."

Stephanie hovered near him. "I need to get going soon."

Julie caught Mike's attention and nodded toward the door with her head. "Just come down when you're ready Steph. Mike and I need to catch up anyway."

Stephanie smiled at her. "Okay." She watched as they left and turned her attention to Hawk. "Do you need anything before I go?"

He smirked. "How about a kiss?"

She leaned forward to kiss him and he put his arm around her waist to pull her closer. As they kissed, she felt his hand go under her shirt and she jumped back. "What are you doing!?"

"I thought we were having a moment."

"Well the moment is over!" She pulled her shirt firmly down. "Do you need anything before I go?"

"No, I guess not. Will I see you this week?"

"I'm not sure. I'll be practicing a lot for my show next weekend, but I'll try." She stepped up to him and kissed him briefly on the lips. "I'll try." She walked to the door and when she opened it looked back and smiled before leaving.

After Stephanie and Julie got dropped off at their dorm, Stephanie went ahead into the dorm while Julie said goodbye to Mike. She waited for Julie to come inside and grinned at Julie. "You won't believe what Hawk tried to do."

"Let me guess. He tried to feel you up?"

Stephanie's eyes went wide. "How did you know?"

"He's a guy. That's what guys do. Now and then I have to smack Mike's hand away and tell him he has to wait and that I'm worth it."

Stephanie laughed. "I hope he's going to be okay. I don't know what I would do if someone told me I couldn't dance anymore."

Julie nodded. "Yeah, that would be hard."

Marilyn sat in the common area and saw them as they walked toward their room. "Too bad about your boyfriend. Guess he won't be going pro after all."

Stephanie stopped. "How did you hear about it?"

She looked at her leg and ran her finger in little circles on it. "Oh, I know a couple of the players."

Julie scoffed. "I bet you do."

Marilyn glared at Julie and then directed her attention to Stephanie. "Guess he'll need some extra special attention."

Stephanie's eyes narrowed. "What's that supposed to mean?"

Marilyn looked back toward the television. "You know what I mean."

"Yeah, it's my last performance before summer break. There's supposed to be a company recruiter there! Think you can make it?" Her smile disappeared as she listened on the phone. "I understand. I wish I could come and see… Okay, love you too." She pressed the button to end the call and dialed again. "Hi mom… I'm doing okay. I just wanted to remind you of my performance this Saturday at two. Think you can make it?" She smiled. "Good!… No, I just talked to Papa and he can't make it… Yes, I'll call grandma and tell her. Okay, see you then." She repeated the process to call her grandmother. Eventually, she got an automated greeting and a beep. "Hi grandma. I'm just calling to remind you of my performance this weekend. Mom says she can drive you both here. Saturday at two. Bye. Love you."

Julie walked into their room and waited for Stephanie to get off the phone. "I thought you had practice tonight."

"It got canceled. Mrs. Shaw left a note and said she would see us in the morning."

"Huh. Wonder what happened. Mike is taking me out for dinner. Tacos. Want to come?"

"Let me see." Stephanie looked into her purse and looked to see how much cash she had. "I think I'll be okay. Sure, I would love to come."

The girls went outside to wait for Mike and found him already there walking toward the dormitory. He smiled when he saw them. "Hey Shortstop. I was just coming to see if you're ready to go."

"You mind if Stephanie comes with?"

"Not at all. You like tacos? It's taco Tuesday, only 50 cents a taco."

"Love 'em."

Mike got into the car. "You talk to Hawk lately?"

"No, not really. I've been busy and when I tried to call there was no answer or he said he was busy and couldn't talk. Why?"

Mike glanced at Julie. "No reason."

"What? What is it?" She climbed into the back seat as Julie got into the front passenger seat. "What's wrong?"

Mike sighed as he started to drive. "Well I'm sure he's fine. He's a little moody, even for Hawk and avoiding us." He focused his attention to Julie. "Thursday night is half-off at the movie theater. Want to go?"

"What's playing?"

"They have True Lies, Forrest Gump, and Shawshank Redemption."

"Oh, that Redemption movie looks good. I saw a commercial on T.V. yesterday."

Stephanie quietly ate while Mike and Julie chatted about their plans for the summer. Mike's family had plans for a trip to see some relatives in New Jersey and after that he wanted to get a job. Julie planned to get a job where she could sing, but could only think of a jazz bar near her home that might allow that opportunity.

Mike scowled. "I don't like the idea of you singing at a bar. You could get hurt."

"I can take care of myself."

"I know you can, but... " He sighed and looked at her. "Please don't do that."

Julie saw the look of concern in his eyes. "Okay. I won't. Maybe there will be a musical at the play theater. It's a bit out of the way, but I can check it out."

He smiled and hugged her. "Thanks."

"I can see why you want to marry him. The way he looks after you." Stephanie went up the stairs in the dorm ahead of Julie.

"You said that Hawk is nice to you. Isn't he?"

"He is, but it's… different. I can't quite name it. I'm thinking I should go see how he's doing tomorrow afternoon."

"Do you have time?"

"I should have time. Think you and Mike can drop me off and then pick me up after?" Stephanie dropped her purse onto her desk in their room.

"It's kind of out of the way. Maybe you can get Danny to drive you."

Stephanie's eyes went wide. "It's an hour drive. I can't ask him to do that."

"He's always looking to make a buck. Maybe you can pay him." Julie plopped down onto her bed and laid back. "I am stuffed. I don't think I've ever had so many tacos."

"I've never seen anyone eat so many tacos! How many was that? Five?"

Julie patted her stomach and grinned. "Six!"

Stephanie giggled. "Better be careful. You don't want to become a fat Mrs. Travers."

Julie made a sound of disgust. "I will do no such thing. So you going to see about Danny taking you?"

"You really think he'll do it?"

"Not if you don't ask."

Stephanie grabbed her purse reached in for her phone. "I don't have his number. Do you?"

"Hold on." Julie got up and rummaged through some papers on her desk. "He gave it to us a few weeks ago, remember? Here it is." She picked up a small piece of paper that had been torn off something bigger and handed it to Stephanie.

Stephanie dialed the number. "Hello... Daniel? Hi, this is Stephanie. Starr... Oh, okay. I wasn't sure you would recognize my voice... What's up? Well..." She looked to Julie who prompted her on. "I was wondering if you could do me a favor. I would pay you... Well, I was wondering if you could drive me over to Hawk's place on Thursday. If it's a problem... You can?" She smiled. "That's great. How much would you... Are you sure?... Oh, okay. That's great. Thanks!... Um, about six?... Okay. Thanks!" She closed the phone and looked at Julie. "He said he was going to a book store over that way anyway. Talk about lucky."

Julie smiled. "Yes, lucky."

"Well don't you look all dolled up." Daniel smiled at Stephanie as she approached him and his car.

"Do I look okay? I wanted to look nice for Hawk."

"Oh, I'm sure he'll appreciate it. You look very nice. Get in and we can go."

Stephanie noticed a few books piled onto the back seat as she got into the front. "What are you doing with your school books?"

Daniel got in and started to drive. "There's a book exchange that will buy and sell used college books about half-way between the two schools. I won't be using these for the rest of the semester."

"Doesn't the bookstore do that too?"

"It does, but this place will pay you more. You have to do it early because they will only take so many. If you wait too long then they won't buy anymore."

"Oh. That's smart."

"If you like, I can drive you when I return the rest of mine."

"Sure." They drove on in silence for minute before Stephanie spoke up again. "What you doing for the summer?"

"Last summer I did an internship at a company. It didn't pay anything, but they liked me so I'll be going to work for them."

"You're real smart Daniel. I bet you're going to do great."

"Thanks. That means a lot coming from you."

Stephanie looked at him. "How do you mean?"

"Well look at you. You're beautiful and smart. Always particular about the people you hang out with. Your opinion means something to me."

Stephanie blushed. "Thank you."

They pulled up to Hawk's apartment building. "Thanks Daniel."

"No problem. How much time do you need? An hour?"

"That should be good. I just want to surprise him and make sure he's okay."

"Okay. See you then."

Stephanie watched as he drove off and looked up to toward Hawk's apartment. She saw movement and smiled to herself. "He is going to be so surprised!" She walked into the building and took the elevator up, careful to step over the gap so she didn't get her thin heels caught in it.

When she got off the elevator, Stephanie heard a door close in the direction of Hawk's apartment. She walked to his apartment and stopped in front of his door. She adjusted her dress and hair and went to knock, but paused. She tried the doorknob and found it unlocked. Smiling to herself, she slowly pushed the door open and snuck inside.

A quick look around showed an empty room. She quietly closed the apartment door and walked a few steps in when she heard a girl's laughter coming from the direction of Hawk's bedroom. She furled her eyebrows and crept toward his open door. She peeked inside his bedroom and her eyes went wide. Standing in the middle of the room, she saw the back of a girl and Hawk kissing her as his hands caressed her arms.

CHAPTER 23

Hawk caught sight of Stephanie and jerked himself upright. "Stephanie!"

The girl turned her head. It was Marilyn! Stephanie didn't say a word. She turned and stomped toward the door.

"Stephanie, wait. It isn't what it looks like." Hawk hobbled out of his bedroom using a crutch and went after Stephanie. "Stephanie."

When she got to the elevator, she paused and looked at the doorway to the stairs and then down at her shoes. She made a fist and pounded the down button with the bottom of it. She grunted and hit it two more times before looking up at Hawk who had caught up to her.

"Stephanie… what you saw. It was nothing." She raised her eyebrows and took a half step back, but remained silent. "Honest. She's just a friend who came by to see how I was doing." He took a step toward her.

"Don't you come near me." Her voice became a near growl. "Don't you dare."

"She's just a friend. It didn't mean anything… C'mon Steph. You know I love you."

"I know? I know!?" Her voice rose in volume "I'll tell you what I know! I know that you have issues and you need to get some help! Professional help! You smoke pot to help with anger, which doesn't help by the way. You're dating me and you invite Marilyn into your bedroom. Marilyn! You're a selfish pig!" She glared at the closed elevator doors and reached down and slipped one shoe off and threw it at Hawk. He flinched as the shoe hit him. She then took the other off and threw it at him and opened the doorway to the stairs. "I never want to see you again!"

When she reached the bottom of the steps, she had to blink to see clearly. "Stupid tears." She wiped the wetness from her eyes with the back of her hands, smearing the makeup across her cheeks and onto her temples. She walked out to the street and sat down on the curb to wait for Daniel. Stephanie squirmed and looked behind her, but didn't see anything and continued to look down the street.

After another minute she looked up and saw Hawk staring out his window at her. Next to him she could see Marilyn with that stupid grin on her face. She stood and walked away, careful to not step on anything sharp. Why did she throw her shoes at him? When she felt she had moved out of view, she sat down again and waited.

Daniel almost passed Stephanie. It wasn't until she stood and waved at him did he recognize her. He slammed on his brakes and stopped a short distance past her. She walked toward the car on the sidewalk as he backed up. Once he reached her he stopped and waited for her to get in. "What happened? Are you okay?"

"Yeah, let's just go home."

Daniel started to drive and glanced at Stephanie. "Do you want to talk about it? Did he hit you?"

"No, he didn't hit me."

He slowed down a little and looked at her for several seconds before looking back to the road. "Did he, um, do anything else?"

Stephanie looked at him for a second with a her mouth slightly open and her brows furled and then in an instant, she jerked her head back and her eyes went wide. "No! No, not that. I caught him kissing Marilyn!"

"Really? Marilyn? That's terrible. I'm sorry."

"I really don't want to talk about it." Her phone rang. She opened her purse, pulled out the phone and opened it. But instead of putting it to her ear, she turned it off and put it back into her purse.

The rode in silence. When they got to her dorm, Daniel pulled slowly up by Stephanie's dorm and put the car into park. "If you need anything or just want to talk, just call me. Okay?"

Stephanie sighed. "Thanks Daniel. I'll be okay." She went inside, ignored the students as they stared at her make-up streaked face, and got a hot shower. When Julie came in she told her all that had happened.

Julie stared at Stephanie with her eyes wide and her mouth hanging open. "That pig! How dare he! Are you okay?"

"Yeah. I should have listened to you. I'm sorry."

"Don't be sorry! It isn't your fault he cheated on you."

Stephanie sighed. "I'm tired. I think I'll go to bed."

"Stephanie?" Julie stood by the bed and pushed the blonde hair from Stephanie's face. "C'mon, you gotta get up."

"No I don't." She kept her eyes closed. "There's no point."

"We need to go to practice."

"I'm not going." Stephanie rolled over. When she didn't hear a response, she rolled back over and opened her eyes to an empty room. "Figures. Nobody really cares." She closed her eyes as tears stared to fall and wet her pillow.

"Here."

Stephanie felt something plop down onto her pillow. She opened her eyes to see an apple sitting there with Julie standing beside her. "You're not going to practice?"

"Girl, you just got your heart ripped out of your chest. How could I leave you alone at a time like this?"

The tears poured out as she stared at Julie. "How could he do this to me? And with Marilyn?" She heaved.

"Because he's scum and you deserve better. Someday you'll find the right guy."

Stephanie got her breathing under control. "I don't know. I'm beginning to think that maybe I won't be able to get married."

"Because of one boy? Don't say that."

"It isn't just Hawk. Boys never get me. All through high school the boys avoided me or barely talked to me." She shook her head. "Nobody asked me to the dances, I didn't even get to go to prom. I really wanted to go to the prom. They had the cutest dresses at the store."

"Well Hawk took a quick liking to you so I think others will too."

Stephanie sat up and swung her legs off the bed to let them dangle and shrugged. "I guess."

"When you go to your practice later you can say the alarm broke."

Stephanie stared at the floor for several seconds before saying something. "Don't think it's worth it. Marilyn or someone else will always do better than me. Surprised I even made it into the program."

Julie's mouth dropped open. "Okay. Where's your phone?"

"In my purse."

Julie turned around and stepped the one step necessary to get to the desk and opened Stephanie's purse. After pulling out the phone she opened it and pressed and held the number three button.

"What are you doing?"

"Calling your grandpa. He'll talk some sense into you." She held the phone out to Stephanie. "Talk to him."

Stephanie accepted the phone and put it to her ear while Julie sat on one of the chairs and faced her. "Hi Papa... not so good." She sighed and told her grandfather what had happened with Hawk. "You did? How could you tell?" She looked at Julie. "That's what Julie said, that he was always mad... I guess I did. I don't know. Maybe I was hoping I could change him."

Julie chuckled to herself and shook her head.

"Yeah, I know." She clicked her tongue and rolled her eyes. "Okay, I promise... No. I don't think I'm going to do it..." She sat upright and waved her arm. "Because I don't think Mrs. Shaw even likes me! She's always complaining about my attention or attitude..." She listened for several minutes and slumped her shoulders. "Yeah they're here... Okay, hold on." She hopped off the top bunk and pulled a suitcase out from under the bed. Unlocking and opening it revealed the worn ballet slippers.

Stephanie put the phone back to her ear. "Okay, I'm looking at them…" She nodded and pulled them out and set them on the floor. "Okay… What!?" She stood, her eyes going wide.

Julie jerked back at the outburst and then leaned forward trying to hear the full conversation.

"I can't wear them. They're Anna's slippers…" She closed her eyes for a second and took a breath. "They're not Anna's anymore. They belong to me. But they…" She sighed. "They're not Anna's anymore. They belong to me. I know they belong to me, but… Papa… Fine. They're not Anna's anymore. They belong to me." She said the last repetition in a rush.

Julie laughed and put her hand over her mouth.

With the corner of her mouth curled up a little, Stephanie looked at Julie and waved her hand down at her. "Stop it." She redirected her attention to the phone. "Papa… I've never worn them." She sat down on the bed and put her feet on each side of the slippers. Listening to her grandfather on the phone, she picked up her right foot and hovered it over the slipper for an agonizing 10 seconds. "Okay, I'm wearing them."

"You are so not wearing them!"

Stephanie squeezed her eyes closed. "… No." She opened her eyes and sighed. She slipped her toes into the slipper and then reached down and pulled the back around her heel. "That's one…" She held the phone up to face Julie. "He wants to know if I really have it on."

Julie grinned. "Yes, Mr. Starr, she has one of them on."

Stephanie twisted her lips and brought the phone back to her ear. "Good enough?…" She mouthed something without sound and put on the other slipper and then held the phone up to Julie again.

"Now she has on the other one."

"Okay. I have on both slippers… Again?… They're not Anna's anymore. They belong to me… Yes, I cherish them very much… No, she didn't give them to me in vain." Stephanie swallowed and looked at her feet and nodded. "Okay. Okay. I will… Yes… I love you too Papa. Bye." She closed the phone and looked up at Julie. "Happy?"

"Yes. Now let's go get some breakfast. I still haven't eaten."

"I gotta go apologize to Mrs. Shaw and make things right." She handed her apple to Julie. "You can have it. I feel more sick than hungry right now."

Stephanie knocked on the door of Mrs. Shaw's office and waited. After a few seconds she heard Mrs. Shaw invite her inside. A small desk occupied most of the space in the eight by ten foot room. Stacks of music sheets and CDs lined one wall and boxes of costumes lined the other. Several other papers cluttered the desk.

"Miss Starr, how may I help you?" Her tone was flat and her face revealed no emotion.

Stephanie pulled her eyes from the stacks of items along the wall and looked at Mrs. Shaw. "I, um, wanted to apologize for missing class this morning." She paused and waited for a response and then continued. "I will definitely put in some extra time tonight." Mrs. Shaw stared at Stephanie without saying anything so Stephanie continued. "You see I caught my boyfriend with someone else, not that it should matter. I should have definitely been there this morning and I promise I will be there for every practice and even some more."

Mrs. Shaw took in a deep breath. "I see. Well I am sorry that happened to you and I am glad you will be at every practice until the show, but I think it is only fair to tell you that I have pulled you from the recommendation list."

"What!?"

"There's only a couple of days left and I can only recommend those that I believe to be resolute in their path. You are an incredibly talented woman, but with your lack of focus I am not sure about your commitment to the art."

Stephanie stepped forward. "But I am committed. I have been at every practice up until now."

"I am sorry, but it is done. The set went out after this morning's practice."

As Stephanie turned to leave, a man walked up to the office door. He smiled and politely waited for her to leave before entering. She could hear Mrs. Shaw getting out of her chair to welcome him. "Tom, how are you? What are you doing in town?"

CHAPTER 24

The girl from the next room stepped into the doorway of Stephanie's room. "Stephanie! You gotta get him to stop calling. I'm not answering it again." As she spoke, the payphone in the hallway rang. "Take care of it!" She turned and left.

Stephanie walked out into the hallway and picked up the phone. "Hello?" She winced and pulled the handset away from her ear as Hawk's voice boomed out.

"Stephanie, we gotta talk!... Stephanie?"

She put the handset back to her ear and talked with a low tone. "Look, I'm done. We're done. Don't call again. Someone's threatened to call the police on you. Just..." She pulled the handset away and closed her eyes as his voice boomed out again.

"I want to make it up to you. I'm not seeing Marilyn."

Stephanie waited until he finished talking before putting it back to her ear. "Goodbye Hawk." She hung up the phone.

"Hawk again?" Julie paused in the hallway as she headed toward their room.

"Yeah." Stephanie joined Julie and headed back toward their room. "Hopefully he gets the message."

"So, big performance today. Excited?"

Stephanie shrugged. "I really messed up."

"Well maybe one of them will be very impressed and will ask about you. When's your mom getting in?"

"I'm expecting her any time now. She's better about getting up early than I am, but grandma likes to sleep in some. Guess I'm like her in that regard."

Julie laughed. As they were about to turn into their room, she pointed down the hall. "Isn't that your mom now?"

Stephanie looked down the hall and saw her mom, her grandmother, and her grandfather all smiling and walking their way. "Yes! And my Papa too!" She ran down the hall and hugged her grandfather and continued to hold onto him. "I'm so glad you're here."

Lucas hugged her back. "Well, it sounded like you needed the support so I said I had a family emergency." He patted her back. "It will be okay."

Stephanie finally pulled away and hugged her mom followed by her grandmother. "I really messed up. Mrs. Shaw pulled me from the recommendation list. She said I wasn't committed."

"Oh, I'm sorry." Rose put her hand onto Stephanie's shoulder.

"The question is…" He put his finger onto her other shoulder. "how do you feel about it?"

"I feel I am totally committed."

He dropped his hand. "Then show them you're committed. Show them that you have the skill and the passion to be truly great. It doesn't matter that you're not on the list. It's you, not a piece of paper, that will impress them. Focus on the dance and put your heart into it." He smiled. "Make Anna proud of the ballerina that now owns those slippers."

Stephanie nodded. "I can do that. Let me get my bag and we can walk over to the auditorium." She ran to her room and grabbed her bag and ran back out to her family.

"I'm surprised you had the nerve to come." Marilyn glared at Stephanie as they gathered backstage. "I heard Mrs. Shaw pulled your résumé." She leaned forward and pursed her lips. "Poor Stephanie couldn't give her man what he wanted and she got all sad and had to miss an important practice."

Stephanie stepped back and raised her voice. "What is your problem with me? From the moment we met at auditions you have taunted me."

Marilyn narrowed her eyes. "I don't like your kind. You make me sick."

Stephanie tilted her head and scowled. "My *kind?*"

"Yes, your kind. Thin little blonde girls that come from the perfect little home and have the perfect little body. Your little attitude of being perfect. I had to work hard to get here and I'm not going to let someone like you take away my chance." She turned and walked away with her chin held high.

"Perfect?" Stephanie scoffed. "If she only knew."

"Everyone!" Mrs. Shaw stepped into the middle of the gathering. "As you know, this is a special presentation with a recruiter watching. All of you are exceptional dancers and deserve to be here." She focused her attention on Stephanie. "Don't think that the one recruiter is your only chance at making an impression." She let her gaze sweep the group. "As my students, I expect you to always do your best."

"Heart and passion. Make Anna proud." Stephanie whispered this to herself and said a quick prayer as she held her opening pose. When the music started, she gasped in surprise as tingles went up her spine and to her fingers and toes. As she danced, the music danced inside of her. Each movement in perfect sync with the music. Each chord reflected on her face. After the performance, she walked to the side of the stage, collapsed onto the floor and leaned back against the wall with her eyes closed. Never before had she felt so exhausted.

After changing, Stephanie found her family waiting for her near the back of the auditorium. She smiled when she saw them and was about to walk out with them when Mrs. Shaw approached with Tom walking alongside her.

"Stephanie, I'm glad I caught you." Mrs. Shaw turned her head toward the man near her. "This is Mr. Cabrel of the New York City Ballet. He insisted that I introduce you."

Stephanie's eyes went wide as she slowly extended her hand. "Hello."

He shook Stephanie's hand. "Hello. We sort of met the other day at Mrs. Shaw's office. I was most impressed with your performance. Do you have a minute to talk?"

Stephanie nodded before finding her voice. "Yes."

Mrs. Shaw smiled. "I will leave you two. It's good to see you again Tom. We must have dinner tonight while you're in town."

He turned and smiled. "Oh, you know I would love to, but I have a plane to catch in a couple of hours. Maybe next time?"

"Of course." She hugged him and walked away.

Tom turned back to Stephanie. "Have you heard of the New York City Ballet?"

"Of course. It's one of the most prestigious ballet companies in the world."

He smiled. "We take pride in our work and always strive to be the best at what we do. Today, as I watched you dance, I could see that you share in those values. Your dancing is exceptional. A true work of art that's breathtaking."

Stephanie blushed. "Thank you."

"As you may know, we normally train our own dancers." Stephanie nodded. "Well today, I would like to make an exception and offer you a job with our company."

Stephanie turned toward her family with her eyes wide and looked back at Tom. "I... " She put her hand up to her face and then dropped it back down. "I have to finish school. Don't I? How would that work? When would I start?"

"That would be up to you. Think about it and get back to me tomorrow." He handed a business card to Stephanie.

She looked at it. "Mrs. Shaw didn't say anything about giving my résumé to you."

"No, my presence here is coincidental. I needed to be in town for a wedding and decided to visit an old friend. After watching the performance, I asked about you." He glanced at his watch. "I need to go." He shook Stephanie's hand. "It was truly my pleasure to meet you."

Stephanie watched him turn and leave and then looked down at the card in her hand.

Rose nearly knocked the card out of her daughter's hand as she hugged her. "I'm so proud of you! So what are you going to do?"

"I don't know." She looked at her grandfather. "What do you think I should do?"

"It's an amazing opportunity, but you can't underestimate the value of a good education either. I would say you finish your schooling and then take the job."

Julie looked at the card as she and Stephanie stood in their room. "So what are you going to do?"

"I don't…"

"Hey blondie." Marilyn stood outside the open door with Stacey behind her. "If dancing makes you that tired, maybe you should give it up." She grinned and walked on.

Stephanie grabbed the card out of Julie's hand. "I think maybe I'll see about starting this summer."

"Mom! We gotta go!" Stephanie shouted out loud and shook the keys as she stood by the door leading to the garage of her mother's new house.

"We have time." Rose walked in from the other room and stopped to look at Stephanie. "Well, let's go. I don't even know why you're having me come with. You can drive just fine."

"I don't know the way to the Miami Airport from here." She handed the keys to her mom.

They got into the car and Rose started driving. "So you're all ready for tomorrow? How many suitcases are you taking?"

"I think so. Papa said I can stay with him for as long as I need to."

"So how many suitcases?"

"I think two."

Rose glanced at Stephanie and then back to the road. "Have you even started packing yet?"

"I'll have time tonight."

Rose sighed and shook her head. "You're going to be scrambling in the morning. Mark said he would help you with directions. He even got a couple of maps for you."

"Oh good."

"I wish you would let me drive up with you. I would feel a lot better."

"Mom, we'll be fine."

"I can't help but worry. You have to call me when you get there."

Stephanie smiled. "I will."

Rose pulled into the parking lot. "Remember where we parked. Last time here I somehow managed to confuse the north and south terminals."

"That was on your honeymoon mom. I'm pretty sure you had other things on your mind." They went inside and looked at the flight arrival board. "There it is. Gate F-3. C'mon, it already landed!"

"The sign just changed Steph. They still have to get to the gate." Rose smiled and shook her head as she followed Stephanie to the gate.

Stephanie paced back and forth as they waited for 15 minutes. Finally the door to the jetway opened. She craned her neck to look past the initial rush of people coming through until her face lit up and she ran forward. "Julie!"

With a grin on her face, Julie waved and worked her way past the others, dropped her duffel bag and hugged Stephanie. "It's so good to see you! You wouldn't believe my flight." She looked at Rose. "Hi Mrs. um..." She glanced at Stephanie.

Rose smiled. "Phelps."

"I'm sorry. I couldn't remember."

Stephanie grabbed Julie's hand. "Let me see!"

Julie beamed as she held her hand out and prominently showed her engagement ring. "We're getting married on New Year's Day."

"New beginnings, I love it! It's beautiful." Stephanie grinned at Julie. "I'm so jealous!"

They worked their way to the luggage claim area. Rose grabbed one of the suitcases Julie pointed out. "How long are you staying in New York with Stephanie?" She started to walk away.

"I have another one. I don't know yet. I haven't decided."

Stephanie grabbed the other suitcase. "You can stay as long as you like."

The next morning Stephanie dumped a couple boxes of clothing onto the floor consisting of her stuff from the old house that had been boxed for the move to Miami Beach and never put away. "Here, help me find some decent clothes."

Julie sat on the floor and sorted through the clothes. She held up a black dress with three sequin stars across the top. "This is beautiful! Too small for you now though."

Stephanie looked up from her clothes pile. "Oh yeah, I got that when I went to Chicago to see Papa's play. I can't bring myself to get rid of it."

"Who knows? Maybe someday you'll have a daughter and she can wear it." She set it carefully aside and went through the rest of the clothes in her pile. "How did your mom and Dr. Phelps end up here?"

"He got some position at a hospital in Miami."

"Can't say I would complain living here."

Stephanie looked around the room and smiled. "It is nice."

After they finished the piles, they had a couple suitcases full and some extra clothes sitting on the bed. "Looks like we can't bring it all."

"But I really like this outfit." Stephanie held up a pair of shorts and a t-shirt. "Let's see what we can leave behind." She looked through one suitcase, pulling items to the side and looking at the items of clothing while Julie looked through the other. When she finished she looked at Julie. "I can't decide."

"Then take it all." Stephanie and Julie looked up to see Mark carrying a wooden trunk into the bedroom. "I actually used this for my stuff when I moved out on my own. A present from my dad."

Stephanie jumped up. "It's perfect! Thank you so much Mark!"

"My pleasure. Just put what you can into it and we'll load it up into the car. Maybe you won't need both suitcases."

Rose and Mark loaded the trunk into the back seat while Stephanie and Julie put Julie's suitcases into the car trunk. They piled both of Stephanie's suitcases onto the wooden trunk.

Rose hugged Stephanie as tears streamed down her face. "You understand the directions?"

"I do."

"You call me the moment you get there. Promise?"

Stephanie pulled back and wiped the tears from her own face. "I promise."

CHAPTER 25

Lucas entered his apartment when he heard the phone ringing. He went over to the end table next to the couch and picked it up. "Hello?... Hey Rose... No, I haven't heard anything yet, but I'm sure I will soon... It is a long trip. I'm sure they're fine, honest. She's not one to do something crazy." As he talked his cell phone rang. "This is probably her. I'll call you back in a bit... Okay. Love you." He pulled his mobile phone out of his pants pocket, looked at the number and scowled. "Now who is this? He answered it. "Hello?... Yes, I'll accept the charges. Sweetie? What's... Slow down I can't... Stephanie... Stephanie! Where are you?... Look for a street sign on the corner and tell me the names on it." He left the apartment as he waited and locked the door behind himself. "Okay, I'm on my way. Don't move."

Lucas got out of the cab and looked around. Stephanie and Julie ran over to him from a nearby doorway and threw their arms around him and started to cry nearly knocking him down. He put his arms around them both. "What happened?" They both talked at once and made wild gestures with their hands, nearly knocking him in the face. He put his hands up. "Hold on, hold on. Let's get into the cab and get out of here first." He glanced around. "Then you can tell me how you ended up in such an unsavory neighborhood."

Stephanie climbed into the cab after Julie. "They have everything! What am I going to do?"

"Take us to the local police station." After telling the cab driver where to go, Lucas reached his arm around the two girls and held onto them. "It will be okay. At least you're not hurt. Now tell me what happened."

Julie wiped her eyes. "We didn't want to go through the tunnel. All that water above us, what if it caved in? So we were going to take the bridge..."

"But the exit we wanted to take was closed." Stephanie sat up. "So we ended up going through the tunnel and we started to look for a gas station. Julie was trying to tell me where to go, but then she got us lost."

"It's not my fault! How was I to know it was one way? You shouldn't have been going so fast!"

146

Lucas held up his hand. "Shhhhh. There's no need to blame anyone. So then what happened?"

"He came out of nowhere." Stephanie looked to Julie for affirmation. "And I hit him with the car!" Lucas' eyes went wide. "So I stopped and we got out to make sure he was okay."

"Was he okay?"

Julie scoffed. "Yeah. His friend hopped into the car and drove off and then he got up and ran away. That's when we realized it was a trick."

Stephanie leaned her head onto her grandfather's shoulder and cried again.

Lucas put his arm around both girls. "Shhh Shhh It's okay. We can always replace clothes, but we can't replace you. When we get to the police station, you tell them what happened. Maybe they can at least find the car."

Lucas and the girls got out of the cab at the police station. After paying the driver, Lucas led the girls toward the old building where someone was hosing down the sidewalk. Stephanie crinkled her nose and made a face as the odor of fresh vomit reached her.

"Oh!" Julie pinched her nose. "That is just awful."

Lucas grimaced as he opened the door. "Let's just get inside."

An officer at the front desk spoke on the phone. "Yes ma'am, I know the address... No, we cannot come to get rid of the rats... Yes ma'am we do serve and protect... I'm afraid we just don't do that." He winced at the audible slam of the phone on the other end and put his phone down. He looked at the trio. "Sorry about that. Dispatch put her through to me. How can I help you?"

Lucas looked to Stephanie and Julie as they stood together, but they just looked back at him. He looked back at the police officer. "These young ladies were the victim of a faked car-pedestrian impact."

The officer looked at the girls. "Someone ran into you, pretending that you hit him?" The girls talked at once, trying to explain what happened. The officer held up his hand and waited for them to stop. He pointed to Julie. "Tell me what happened." After listening to the tale, he nodded. "Okay, we'll need to fill out a report." He pointed to a bench nearby. "Wait there until I get an officer that can take the report."

After waiting nearly 30 minutes, another officer came up to them. "You need to file an incident report?" After they nodded, he waved them to follow him. They stood and followed him to a desk where he took down the girl's names, contact information to where they were staying and specifics of what happened. When he finished, he handed Lucas a copy of the report. "We'll contact you if we learn anything."

As they were leaving, Stephanie sighed. "Welcome to New York City, Stephanie."

147

The next morning, Lucas's roommate came out of his bedroom to get some breakfast and found Julie and Stephanie sitting at the kitchen table eating breakfast. "Hello Stephanie, you're up early. From what Lucas told me, I didn't expect to see you until after he and I got back from work."

"Hi Steve." Stephanie set her apple down onto a napkin. "I couldn't sleep last night."

"I'm sorry. I hope they can give you some news soon." He grabbed a bag of bagels and cream cheese from the refrigerator and sat down at the table with them. "How long you staying here Julie?"

"Well, maybe a week or so. Now I gotta call my mom and ask for money so I can buy the plane ticket because mine was stolen along with my purse and my license. I think you need a license to get money from Western Union. Not sure how I'm going to get money to get my ticket home." She sighed and leaned her head against her hand.

"Lucas or I can always receive money and give it to you."

Julie nodded her head. "Okay. Thanks."

Lucas came out of the bathroom, freshly showered. He walked over to Stephanie and kissed her on the head. "Hey Sweetie. You doing okay?"

Stephanie shrugged as she chewed on another bite of her apple. "I can't believe I left the engine running."

"How could you know? It's not your fault." Lucas patted her on the shoulder. "When are you due at the NYCB?"

"Two days."

Lucas nodded. "How about you, Julie? You doing okay?"

"As best as can be expected I guess. I gotta call my mom today to ask for some money. She is going to freak."

"You? If Papa didn't talk to my mom, I think she would have been on the next flight here…" She stopped as the phone rang. "That's probably her saying she's arrived."

Lucas went to phone and picked it up. "Hello?… This is he… Mhmm…" He looked at his watch. "Sure, I have time… Great, see you soon." He hung up and turned to the girls. "The police have found your car. We have to go claim it."

The officer that met them led them back through the building and into a fenced car lot. "Someone upstairs has your back because this never happens. The guy driving your car ran a red light right after he had stolen it and a black and white was right there. Driver ditched the car and ran. Here it is."

Stephanie ran forward. "My car!" She looked inside as Julie came up behind her. "Everything's here!"

Julie peered inside. "I don't see my purse."

"What?" Stephanie looked for hers too.

"Both purses are inside." The officer explained. "While we can generally keep someone from removing something the size of that trunk you have there in the

148

back seat, we can't guarantee someone won't jump the fence and steal something as small as a purse. Let's go inside and fill out the release papers."

After filling out the appropriate paperwork, Stephanie and Julie drove to Lucas's apartment while he took a cab. They didn't dare stop for gas until Lucas could go with them. Once there, he and Steve helped the girls move everything upstairs to the apartment.

"This is a nice trunk." Lucas admired it as he set it down. "Mark gave it to you?"

"Yeah. You should see their new place down in Miami Beach. It is very nice."

"I look forward to seeing it. Maybe we can go visit the beach." He winked at Stephanie. "So who's heart did you break moving up here?"

Stephanie looked down. "Nobody. I don't... " She sighed and looked up. "I don't think I'll ever get married, Papa."

He put his arm around her shoulders. "Don't say that. Why do you say that? Because of that Hawk fella?"

"No. I tried to date a couple of other guys too. I just don't think I can do it."

Julie shook her head. "They were awful to her. One even stalked and harassed her after they broke up."

Stephanie looked at her grandfather. "I'm sorry. I don't think we're ever going to get that dance."

"Welcome to your new office, Mr. Clark." Susan opened the door and preceded Daniel into the office. He looked at his name on the door before following her inside. "Of course the latest computer system the company has. Someone from IT should stop by later today to make sure you're properly set up. You all set for Thanksgiving next week?"

Daniel nodded. "I think so. How about you?"

"Going to my husband's family so maybe not as good as yours." She chuckled and pointed to a gift basket on his desk. "The CEO always welcomes his new executives with the same items. You can just give the ballet tickets away."

"Actually I like ballet."

"Really?" She raised her eyebrow in skepticism.

"I had a serious crush on a ballerina back in college, but she was into the football player type." He picked up the two tickets from the basket. "They're for tonight. Performing on Broadway. Not sure if I can find someone to take with me on such short notice."

She looked at him with a smile. "Oh, I'm sure you'll have no shortage of ladies willing to join you."

He looked down and smiled before looking up again. "So where do you sit in case I need anything?"

"Go down two doors to your left and I'm in the cubicle across from there." She walked to the door and paused in the doorway. "You want it open or closed?"

"Open is fine. Thanks." She nodded and walked off. Daniel glanced at the computer and then looked through the basket. Inside it had an envelope with the ballet tickets, recent editions of Money and Fortune magazines, some fruit, a gift certificate to a local bar & grill, and a brochure to the in-house gym. He looked down at his slim figure and tossed the brochure into the trash before picking up the gift certificate. "Guess I could get something to eat and go to the ballet by myself."

Daniel stepped into the darkened interior of the bar & grill. Barstools remained mostly available and only a few of the tables were in use. Daniel went over to the bar and asked for a menu before ordering a beer and some buffalo chicken wings. It only took 20 minutes before other seats became occupied as local businesses emptied out. A slender redhead caught Daniel's eye as she sat next to him.

"You going to drink that water? I am so thirsty." She flipped her hair back and looked at him.

Daniel raised his eyebrows and scowled a little. "Help yourself."

"Thanks." She lifted the glass and took a sip. "It's so hot today. So what are you doing tonight?"

"Actually I have plans to see the ballet."

"Oh. You're one of those." She got up and went to the other end of the bar and sat next to another guy.

Daniel chuckled and shook his head. He ordered a second beer and focused on eating his chicken wings.

"Are those any good?"

Daniel jerked his head up and to his left to see a dark haired woman sitting there with a drink in front of her. He hadn't noticed her sit down. "Actually they aren't too bad. I got the mild."

"I'm thinking of getting an order for myself, but not sure if I should get the mild or hot."

"I like to get the mild at a new place. If it's too hot, it's hard to eat, but you can always ask for hotter sauce."

The woman smiled. "That's a good idea." She ordered a plate of wings.

Daniel extended his hand. "My name is Daniel."

"Oh, I'm sorry. Jennifer." She shook his hand. "Sometimes not sure where my head is. You must think I'm a complete head case."

He chuckled. "Not at all. If anyone here is crazy, it's me."

"Oh? Why is that?"

He pulled the tickets out of his back pocket. "I have a pair of tickets to see The Nutcracker on Broadway and was thinking about going by myself. I bet I could sell 'em."

Jennifer looked at the tickets, back to him, back to the tickets, and then back to him again. "May I...?" She held out her hand.

"Sure. Knock yourself out." He handed the tickets to her. "They're for tonight. A gift at my new job. Don't know what I was thinking."

"I'll go with you, if you don't mind."

"You will? You don't even know me."

She grinned. "I figure any guy that walks into a place like this with ballet tickets is probably safe." She handed the tickets back to him. "What if I meet you at the entrance? Then we can both get changed."

He looked down at his clothes. "I didn't even think about that. Sure, I'll meet you there." He stood and looked at her. "Front entrance. Six thirty?"

She looked up at the clock on the wall. "Maybe closer to six fifty?"

"Sounds good. I look forward to it." Daniel turned to leave with a grin on his face.

Daniel stood on the sidewalk with his hands in his pockets. A cab pulled up, splashing water up near him as it hit the pothole near the curb. He moved back, but once he recognized Jennifer, he ran up and opened the door for her.

"Thank you." She smiled at him as she climbed out.

"Here, let me get that." He looked at the meter and handed the driver some cash. Once he got the change, he looked at Jennifer who stood just a little shorter than himself. "Wow, you look great."

"Thanks. You don't look so bad yourself." She reached out for his arm and walked with him, her heels clicking on the sidewalk as they went to the building. They quickly discovered that the tickets were for box seats near the stage. The lights were already dim with dancers on the stage when they got there. Jennifer leaned over to Daniel and whispered, "Wow, I'm liking this company you work for."

"I think I am too." His eyes swept the interior of the theater and then toward Jennifer. She noticed him looking at her and smiled and then redirected her focus back to the dancers. He watched and soon his head started to move to the rhythm of the music. Suddenly he sat up straight.

"You okay?"

Daniel leaned forward. "I think I know her."

CHAPTER 26

Daniel paused as he reached the backstage area and scanned the clumps of dancers as they stood around talking to each other. When he saw Stephanie he watched for several seconds as she smiled and laughed with the other dancers. Eventually he walked toward her. "Stephanie?"

Stephanie looked over and grinned. "Daniel!" She ran over to him and hugged him. "What are you doing here? You came to see me?"

"Actually, I didn't even know you were in New York. How long have you been here?"

"Two years. I share an apartment with a couple of other girls here. How about you? How long you been in New York?" Stephanie held onto Daniel's hands with her own as she listened to him talk.

"Just this week. I was working in Chicago and got a promotion that required me to move here. The CEO gave me a welcome basket and there were tickets to tonight's show in it. "

Jennifer watched the exchange and the way Daniel looked at Stephanie and sighed. "Daniel, perhaps I…"

"Oh! Where are my manners?" Daniel let go of Stephanie's hands and held his hand out toward Jennifer. "Stephanie, this is Jennifer."

Stephanie noticed Jennifer for the first time and the excitement left her voice. "Oh."

Jennifer smiled. "We…" She nodded toward Daniel as she looked at Stephanie. "We just met. He had an extra ballet ticket and I wanted to see the ballet. Beautiful performance."

"Oh." Stephanie shook Jennifer's hand briefly. "Thank you." She smiled at Jennifer. "Thank you."

"Someone's in a good mood." Susan looked up from her desk as she heard Daniel walking by, humming to himself. "Found someone to join you at the ballet?"

Daniel paused at her desk. "Yes I did. It was a beautiful performance."

"Who did you get to go with you?" She leaned forward and put her head into her hands.

"Her name was Jennifer."

Susan sat up. "Was? I thought it went well. Aren't you planning on seeing her again?"

"Remember how I said I had a crush on someone in College? Well she's here. In New York. She's a ballerina. When I saw her..."

"Old emotions came to the surface eh? How did Jennifer take it?"

"I don't think she knew anything. To her, I was just introducing her to one of the dancers."

"Trust me. She knew."

"You think so? I didn't want to hurt her feelings."

"What did she say when you took her home?"

Daniel looked upward as he recalled the incident. "Um... well I held the cab and walked her up to her building's door. She was saying how she had a nice night and she hugged me and said to take care." He looked at Susan.

"Oh yeah, she knew. But I don't think you hurt her feelings."

"Well that's good. Talk to you later." Daniel headed to his office. After unlocking the door he disappeared inside and closed the door behind himself before making a call. "Good morning. Is Stephanie there?"

Daniel watched as Stephanie looked around the restaurant. "Nice place, isn't it?" She looked back at him and nodded, putting a slight smile on her face and then looked at the menu. He watched her for a second and then looked at his own menu.

"Welcome to Le Bernardin, are you ready to place your order?" The waiter appeared from nowhere, his French accent catching them by surprise.

"I'm ready, how about you?" Daniel looked over at Stephanie.

"Um... can I have some more time?" Stephanie looked up at the waiter.

"But of course, madam." He gave a slight nod of the head and left.

Stephanie looked back at the menu. "Everything's so expensive."

"Pick anything you like. It's on me."

Stephanie looked up and smiled and then back to the menu, her smile quickly disappearing. She turned the page and sighed. "Maybe the salad."

Daniel scowled and picked up the menu to find the item. "That's the cheapest thing on the menu."

"Well it's what I want."

He sighed. "Okay." Turning in his chair he was able to catch the eye of the waiter and motion with his head.

"You are ready to order?"

"Yes, the lady will have the mesclun salad and I'll have the tuna." He looked at Stephanie. "Would you like some wine?"

She leaned forward and whispered, "Is it expensive?"

He gave a slight shake of the head and looked to the waiter. "We'll have a bottle of white wine."

"Very well sir." The waiter took their menus and left.

"I can't believe my luck in seeing you perform the other night. I almost didn't go."

"Oh? Why not?"

He shrugged. "Felt strange to be going by myself. Then Jennifer offered to go with me."

"She seems nice. When are you going to see her again?"

"We're not seeing each other, it was just a one time thing."

"Oh." She started to put her hands onto the brilliant white table cloth and then hesitated and put her hands back into her lap. "I'm afraid to touch anything for fear I might mess it up."

Daniel chuckled. "Yeah, I had no idea it was this nice. I just asked someone at the office for a nice place to take you to dinner."

"So you just got here this week? Where were you before?"

"Chicago."

"I've been there. I went there to see Papa's play once."

"I remember."

"You do?"

"You had mentioned it once."

She scowled. "I didn't realize I told you."

The waiter presented a bottle of wine to Daniel. "How is this sir?" Daniel looked at it for a second and nodded. The waiter proceeded to pull the cork and pour two goblets of wine before leaving.

Daniel took a sip of his and set the goblet down and waited for Stephanie to try it.

She picked it up and sniffed at it and took a sip. "Not bad."

"Not bad? It's good. You know what that cost?"

Stephanie gasped. "I didn't ask you to buy it."

He held up his hands above the table. "No, you're right. I'm sorry. Um, so how's the ballet going?"

She sat up and leaned forward. "It's going great. I get along with everyone and we're doing some great stuff. We went to Washington, D.C. a few months ago and had the time of our lives. I never saw the Washington Monument before. Well, you know, in person. There was so much to see, but I only had a couple of hours so Karen and I just did some things around there."

"Karen?"

"She's also with the company and one of my roommates. The other..." She was interrupted by the introduction of their food. After the waiter set before her, she took the upright fan folded napkin and set it on her lap.

Daniel looked at the mountain of greens on the plate before Stephanie with wide eyes. "Wow, that's a lot of salad."

"There's no way I'll be able to eat all of this." She looked at the plate before him. "That looks good too."

"Give me a moment and I'll let you know." He pulled a bite-sized chunk of the fish off and stabbed his fork into it. "So I gather you're not seeing anyone?" When he put the fish into his mouth he closed his eyes as he chewed. "Oh yeah, this is good."

"No, and I don't intend to. I just want to focus on my ballet for a while." She took another bite of her salad and looked up at him with a small smile as she chewed.

"Oh." His voice was flat and the smile went away from his face. He looked down at his plate. "I was rather hoping we could start seeing each other."

"Daniel, it's been good to see you…"

"But you just want to be friends."

She put her fork onto her plate and reached her right hand out and laid it onto his left hand. "I'm sorry. I'm just not ready to date."

He nodded his head and looked down at his plate. With his fork, he pulled off one piece of meat and then another and then another until scattered pieces of meat were all that remained on his plate along with the strips of asparagus and rice.

"The 'I just want to be friends' speech. I hate that." Brad shook his head as he, Rick, and Susan sat in chairs and listened to Daniel tell about his evening. "So what are you going to do?"

"I don't know." Daniel shrugged as he leaned against his desk facing them. "I really like her."

Susan rolled her eyes. "You guys. Look Daniel, what you want to do is be there as a friend. Don't lose the connection. You've only been back in her life for a day. Give her some time and then ask her out on a date again."

Daniel nodded. "I can do that." He sighed. "I guess my weekend is open. What are you guys doing?"

Rick shrugged. "Just doing laundry."

Brad looked at Rick and then back to Daniel. "You know, my family owns some land upstate. My grandfather built a cabin right next to the lake. Good for fishing and hunting. I've been thinking about going up there to do some hunting. Maybe the three of us could go together. If you don't mind the snow. Supposed to snow this weekend."

Rick looked down at his empty coffee cup and then over to Daniel. "Well I gotta get some more coffee and get to work." He stood and looked at Brad as he turned. "Count me in, sounds like fun." He left the office.

"I should get going too. I need to get ready for a meeting." Susan stood and followed Rick out the door.

"I've never been hunting." Daniel walked around his desk and sat in his chair. "Sounds like it could be fun."

"Ever shoot a gun?"

"Nope, never did that either."

"Then I guess I'll have to teach you."

Rick watched out the windshield as the wipers pushed the falling snow to the side. They were driving through another long stretch of snow covered trees. "How far did you say this place was?"

Brad smiled as he drove. "Bored already? Growing up, my dad would bring me and my brother up here and we would spend an entire week or two just swimming, fishing, hunting, exploring." He paused. "Hasn't really been used much since my dad died last year. I think he was the only one of his generation that really appreciated the place. Once he died, I couldn't bring myself to come up here."

"So how long since you been there?"

"Went with my dad just a month before he died. He wanted to go hunting one last time. I think he knew he was dying."

Daniel looked at Brad from the back seat. "How did he die?"

"Brain tumor. He went pretty quick."

"Well it's nice of you to bring us. Mind if we stop soon? All that coffee from this morning is catching up to me. Maybe just pull over and I can use a tree."

"Can you wait two more minutes? There's a small gas station and store up ahead. I gotta get some supplies."

Daniel nodded and sat back.

The store looked more of an old wood planked cabin then any gas station Daniel had seen. He got out of the car and walked to the side, crunching the snow under his shoes, to look for the bathroom. What he found instead, was an old outhouse. When he finished his business, he went inside the store and found Rick and Brad listening to the old proprietor.

"The idiots running the place don't understand people at all. What they needed was proper medication and some therapy, not a 'commune with nature.'" He saw Daniel and lifted his head in an upward nod. "What can I do for ya?"

"I'm with them. What's going on?"

Brad handed over his credit card. "John here's telling us about a couple of guys that ran away from the, um, happy house."

"You mean the nut house." John handed back the credit card. "Knifed two of the attendants on their way out, so be careful."

Brad picked up the boxes of bullets and other items he had purchased. "We will, thanks. Don't forget, that's 20 for gas."

"Oh yeah, let me turn that pump on." John turned and entered some numbers onto a button panel that had the numbers worn off and flipped a switch. "You fellas are good to go. It's good to see you again Bradley. Regular time?"

Brad waved as he walked out the door. "Yup."

"Don't think I've ever seen such an old gas station before. I swear, if he had a pickle barrel in there it would have fit in just fine." Daniel grinned as he bit into the venison jerky he had purchased. "Mmmm this is really good. He made this himself?"

"He did. John's owned that place for as long as I can remember, though I have no idea how he stays in business. I hardly ever saw anyone else there while growing up."

"You know I bet Stephanie would like this. She likes venison. Would probably like the idea of me hunting."

Brad smiled. "So you've said." He drove on and talked about how he had once kept a turtle at the cabin as a pet. After a while he turned off the paved road and drove through the trees.

"You sure this is a road?" Rick peered ahead.

Brad smiled. "Well, more of a path than a road. A little further in and we'll be at the cabin."

Daniel looked around at the trees. "How much of this belongs to your family?"

"All of it. It's almost 20,000 acres."

Rick whistled in appreciation. "You could get lost in that."

CHAPTER 27

As they rolled up next to the cabin, Brad saw that the door was open and swore. He quickly got out and went to the doorway. Snow had blown in, leaving a snow dune on the floor just inside the door. Snow dusted the sparse furniture. Someone had left some trash on the floor along with a busted glass oil lamp. A frying pan lay upside down on the floor next to the fireplace. Two doors at the back of the main room were closed.

Brad went to one of the doors and opened it to reveal a couple of bare beds. He disappeared inside and a couple minutes later came out of the other door where there were more beds. "Looks like everything in storage is still here. Saves us a trip."

Daniel looked around and found a broom in the corner near the single entrance. He swept the snow out of the cabin and off the porch and steps while Rick picked up the trash and broken lamp. After some effort, they had it all cleaned up and ready for occupancy. Brad got a fire burning in the fireplace and found another oil lamp to light. Soon they were able to take off their coats.

The next morning Daniel and Rick woke up to the smell of bacon. Daniel got up first and went to the main room to find Brad near the fireplace cooking over the fire. "Bathroom?"

Brad smiled and pointed out the window. "Outhouse."

"Ugh. No electricity. No plumbing. And you spent weeks at a time here?" He went outside.

"How deep is the lake?" Rick stood in the doorway to the bedroom.

"Pretty deep. I wouldn't know exactly. Why?"

"Is it any good for ice fishing?"

"Oh yeah. I've done my share of that too. Not sure how much time we have for that this weekend."

"Time for what?" Daniel stepped back into the cabin, without a coat, and shivered as he closed the door.

"Rick was wondering about ice fishing in the lake."

Daniel shrugged. "If that's what you guys want to do. I don't mind either way."

"No, no." Brad grabbed some metal plates that were on the mantle over the fireplace. He pointed at the forks as he piled some food onto the plates. "I promised a weekend of hunting and that's what we'll do. I owe it to my dad."

The men washed their dishes in the lake after using a pickaxe to make a hole through the ice. Rick looked around as he headed back into the cabin. "Okay, Daniel here may not know anything about hunting, but I do and I have some questions. One, we came here in a car. Two, where are the guns?"

Brad laughed. "Makes you wonder how we're going to do this. Or, maybe, why did I really bring you out here?" He gave an evil laugh and rubbed his hands together.

Daniel shook his head and rolled his eyes.

"You're going to love this." Brad led them back to the bedroom and opened the door that led to the shared closet between the bedrooms. He pulled back the rug on the floor to reveal a trap door. When he opened the door, a short flight of steps could be seen. "My dad got tired of dragging our gear back and forth so he and I dug this out one summer."

Daniel peered into the dark hole. "How big is it?"

"For all the effort I wish it was bigger. It's about 10 by 12 feet. Plenty of room to store hunting and fishing gear, canned goods, etc."

"That is so cool. Too bad you didn't put in a generator too." Daniel stepped back to let Brad go first, lighting the way with a lamp. In the holding area, metal shelves and cabinets had been set up to hold some rifles, rope, a pulley mechanism, extra linens, canned goods, and some lamp oil. There were some other items he couldn't identify. "Wow. I would have never guessed."

Brad opened the lid of a chest and pulled out some grey camouflage outfits and handed them out. "Deer don't have the best eyesight, but they're quick to detect movement." He gave Rick a couple of rifles and held the rope out for Daniel.

"What's the rope for?" Daniel took the rope.

"So we can drag it back. Won't walk here on it's own after we've killed it." Brad smiled and headed up the stairs.

Rick looked over his shoulder, his eyes darting back and forth into the trees and then back to the space ahead where they had spotted some bark scraped from a tree.

Brad looked back and then at Rick. His voice was nearly a hiss. "Why do you keep doing that?"

"I don't know. Keep feeling like we're being watched."

Daniel glanced back. "I don't see anything. I think you're just spooked."

Brad put his hand onto Daniel's shoulder. Up ahead, a deer with small antlers had come into the small clearing.

Rick slowly stood and brought the gun up to his shoulder, took aim, and fired. The deer ran off. "I'm pretty sure I hit it."

Brad stood from his crouch. "Let's go look." He led the way to where the deer had been standing and looked at some drops of blood on the ground.

"You definitely hit it." Daniel's eyes followed the trail of frothy red blood.

"Looks like you probably hit the lungs. Not bad. He must be nearby, let's go find him." Brad led the trio through the trees until they could see the deer laying on its side. Brad walked up to the head of the deer and tapped the shoulders with the end of his gun. "Okay, he's dead. Now comes the fun part." He rolled the deer onto its back and pulled out a knife. He headed to the tail end and started cutting.

After they buried the entrails in a shallow grave, Brad instructed Daniel and Rick on how to tie the rope around the deer so they could half carry and half drag him to the cabin. The snow made this a little easier, but they soon had to open their coats as they grew hot from the work. Once they got to the cabin, they used the pulley mechanism to hoist the deer up to hang from a branch so the blood could drain.

Rick wiped his forehead and took off his gear, steam rising from his body. He, along with the others, had already unzipped their tops as they brought the deer to the cabin. "Well Daniel, tomorrow it's your turn."

Rick grinned as he ran his finger over the hole in the tree level with his face. "At least you hit something."

"When you pull the trigger, don't make the mistake of jerking the gun up." Brad held his own gun up to his shoulder and pointed it away from the group. "Some people anticipate the kickback and jerk the gun. Your gun doesn't have that much kickback, so you should be able to just squeeze the trigger..." He put his finger below the trigger and demonstrated the movement. "... and not have such a violent jerking action." He lowered the gun.

Daniel nodded. "Okay. Let me try again. Didn't we see some, what was it called... oh yes, scat, in that direction earlier?" He pointed.

"We can try that way, but we would need to aim back this way. The road is just a little further on."

Rick looked around. "You sure?"

"You'll see." Brad led the group in the direction that Daniel had indicated. After they had walked a little more than 10 minutes, they came to the road covered in snow like a white blanket. "All the time spent here, I know the wood pretty well. I bet if we walked in just a little bit, you'll have a chance Daniel."

"Sounds good." Daniel followed Brad and Rick followed Daniel to a place where some shrubbery grew.

Brad lowered his voice. "I think that if we wait here for a bit, you'll get another chance before we need to call it a day. Remember, aim for the neck and squeeze the trigger as you keep the gun level."

Daniel sat on the snow, his back against a tree with his legs out in front of him and the gun across his lap as he waited. Brad and Rick were nearby crouching down. Snow was falling again so their tracks were nearly covered. After waiting for 20 minutes, a deer came into the clearing they were watching and ate some grass. Daniel lifted his gun off his lap and, as quietly as he could, swung his legs around behind himself so that he was on his knees. The deer lifted it's head up and appeared to look right at Daniel. He froze and held his breath.

After what felt an eternity of waiting as the deer sniffed the air and shifted its ears, it bent back down and ate more grass. Daniel shifted his weight between his knees as he tried to slowly get his feet under him and get into a crouch. He kept his eyes on the deer as it ate. The deer brought it's head up again and shifted its ears. Daniel froze. The deer bent back down to eat.

Silently letting let out his breath, Daniel continued his upward ascent. He brought his gun up and took aim, shifting his left foot as he did so. His weight came down onto a stick, making it crack. Daniel fired as the deer bounded away.

Brad and Daniel were about to move forward to check the area for traces of a hit when Rick held up his hand. "Wait, I thought I heard something." He tilted his head and listened. The others listened too. Not hearing anything he put his hand down. "Sorry. I thought I heard someone shout. Guess that story of the escapees affected me more than I thought."

When they reached the spot where the deer had been eating, all they found was a bunch of hoof tracks being covered by the falling snow. Rick patted Daniel's back. "You just can't shoot, can you?"

Daniel laughed. "I guess not. I really wanted to impress Stephanie too."

"We can all have some of what I shot yesterday." Rick pointed. "That way to the cabin?"

Brad looked in the direction Rick was pointing. "We could, but it would be faster to just take the road from this point."

The three men quickly found the road and walked along it when an old pick-up truck came along side them and stopped. John, the owner of the gas station, leaned over and rolled down the passenger window. "You fellas want a ride?"

Brad walked up to the truck. "Hey John, you're timing is perfect."

"How'd the hunting go?"

Brad opened his mouth to answer when he saw a sheriff's car approaching from behind the truck. He waited for it to stop and the sheriff to get out and approach the group of men.

"John. Gentlemen." He nodded to everyone standing outside the truck. "Everything okay?"

John rolled down his driver side window, getting the sheriff's attention. "Afternoon, Paul. Just about to give these fellas a ride back to their cabin."

The sheriff looked at Brad and the others. "And you are...?"

"Bradley Thompson. And this is Rick Morris and Daniel Clark. Guys from work that I brought with me to do a little hunting."

"Where you gentlemen from?"

"New York City, sir."

"Long way to travel when there are other places much closer to the city."

"My family owns this land here."

The sheriff looked to John who nodded. Reflexively nodding with John, he relaxed his stance. "I've been looking for a couple of dangerous escapees."

Daniel spoke up. "The owner of the gas station told us about them a couple days ago. Killed a couple of orderlies as they ran away from a mental institution?"

"More than that. Just yesterday they killed someone else hunting alone. Took his gun. Their names are Frank Morris and Jimmy Allen. They're not just mentally disturbed, but violent. You gentlemen watch your backs." The sheriff headed back to his car and drove down the street, peering into the trees as he drove.

"Glad we're leaving this afternoon." Rick got into the back of the truck. "The thought of being knifed or shot is not appealing."

Daniel climbed in. "Good thing you came by John. Saved us a long walk."

"I'm just coming at the scheduled time."

Brad followed the others into the back of the truck. "John's coming by to pick up any deer we shot so he can process them for us."

As they arrived at the cabin, Brad hopped out of the truck followed by Rick and Daniel. John drove under the deer until the the deer hovered over the bed of the truck. Brad lowered it and removed the rope. "Thanks John. We'll be by tomorrow morning."

John waved as he drove off. "See you then."

"Oooh. 'Regular time.'" Daniel headed into the cabin. "I get it now."

Rick looked around into the trees as he followed Daniel. "Let's get everything put away and get out of here. I'll feel safer in New York."

Brad laughed.

Daniel put the wrapped venison onto a small table at the entrance to his apartment and then took off his coat and hung it in the coat closet. Grabbing the package, he went to his kitchen and put it into the freezer. He looked at the phone hanging on the wall.

"Maybe…" He opened a drawer and looked up the number to a local movie theater and called them asking for movies and show times the next day. He wrote the information on the inside cover of the phone book and put his thumb onto the button to hang up the phone. Looking at the paper hanging on the refrigerator, he dialed Stephanie's number.

"Hi Steph, this is Daniel. Are you doing anything next weekend?… I was thinking of going to the movies and thought you might like to join me. Not a

162

date, just a couple of friends enjoying a movie. What do you think?" He nodded and looked at what he wrote.

"They have four movies. There's Deep Impact and Armageddon. Isn't that funny? Two movies about meteors hitting the earth. Surprised they still have Deep Impact. That's been out a while. And then there's Saving Private Ryan... Yeah, Bruce Willis. Um..." He looked at the inside cover again. "Two o'clock?... Sounds great. I'll stop by and get you. I have something I want to give you."

Danial paid the cab driver and walked to the building entrance carrying the wrapped venison. The aged red brick building was soot stained with the door recessed. He moved his finger down the list of names on the buzzer panel until he found Stephanie and her two roommates. He pressed the button to the right of the label and waited. He crinkled his nose as the smell of urine assaulted him.

"Hello?" The female voice crackled and popped through the speaker.

"It's Daniel. I'm here to see Stephanie."

"We're in 4A."

The door buzzed and he pulled to open it, but it wouldn't move. Just as he shifted from a pull to a push the door the buzzing stopped. He sighed and pushed the apartment button again.

"Hello?"

"Sorry, I tried to open the door in the wrong direction. Can we try again?"

The door buzzed again and he pushed it open. Inside the foyer the open elevator faced him with a stairwell to one side and a grid of mail boxes on the other. He crossed the worn linoleum and entered the elevator. After he closed the iron gate and pressed the button for the fourth floor, the elevator lurched upward as the motor whined from overhead. Daniel flinched at the movement, but quickly regained his composure.

When the elevator got to the destination, a loud clang reverberated through the shaft and the elevator stopped with a jerk. He winced at the sound and then opened the gate. He walked half-way down the hall where 4 doors were clustered, two on each side, with the lettered designation on each door. He knocked on the A door.

CHAPTER 28

The door opened and Daniel could see the back of a girl walking away as she yelled across the apartment. "Stephanie, your date is here." She plopped down onto a chair with her leg hanging over the side arm and watched the television.

"He's not my date." Stephanie came out of the bathroom putting in her last earring. "Hi Daniel, this is Karen."

Karen raised her hand for a second and lowered it as she continued to stare at the screen.

Daniel looked back to Stephanie. "This building is old."

"Yeah, isn't it great? What's that?" Her eyes went to the package Daniel held.

"Oh, this is for you. It's venison."

"Venison?"

"Venison?" Karen turned her attention to Daniel.

"Yeah. I went hunting with a couple guys at the office up state last weekend."

Karen pulled her leg off the arm. "Up north? Where those mental patients escaped and were killing people?"

Stephanie turned to Karen. "What?"

"Yeah, didn't you hear?" Karen stood up and walked over toward Stephanie and Daniel. "A couple of psychos got loose and were killing people. She looked at Daniel. "You could have been killed."

Daniel grew flush at the attention. "Well, I don't know that we were in that much danger. We were together."

"Seriously." Karen looked at Stephanie. "They killed a couple of nurses and even a hunter. Daniel put his life on the line to get you this venison, you better be happy. Here I'll put it in the fridge and you two go and have fun." She took the package from Daniel's hands and walked into the kitchen.

After the movie, Daniel talked about what he liked of it as they rode in the cab. He looked over at Stephanie to find her staring at him. "You okay?"

"Mmm hmm." She nodded.

"Well I just knew that the dad would sacrifice himself. How could he let his future son-in-law die? You know? But it was still good. I'm glad you picked it." He stopped and looked at her. She had such kissable lips. "So what did you like?"

"I think… I think I picked the wrong movie."

"What?" The cab pulled up to the curb by Stephanie's building. Daniel paid the cab driver and held the door until Stephanie got out. After closing it he followed her to the entrance.

Stephanie turned and walked along the building, away from the stench, and stopped five feet away. She turned to face Daniel. "I really enjoyed going with you. I don't think we ever got to be together like that when we were in school."

Daniel approached her. "I've been told I shouldn't say this…" He paused.

"Say what?"

He stood with only six inches between his toes and hers. If he wanted to, he could just lean forward a little and kiss her. "Did you know I had the biggest crush on you?

Stephanie smile a little, looked down at the ground as her smile grew and then back at Daniel. "I had no idea. I was…"

Daniel didn't wait for her to finish the sentence. He leaned forward and found her coming forward to kiss him too.

Rick put his hand onto the top of the frame of the door as he looked inside Daniel's office. "TGIF buddy. You joining us for drinks?"

"Not this time. I have plans."

"Oh yeah, that's this weekend isn't it? Still think you're moving too fast. It's only been a few months."

"Ten, actually. But I've known her for a long time."

"Yeah yeah, so you've said before. Well if you come to your senses you know where we'll be."

Daniel grinned and waved him off as he picked up the phone and dialed. "Hello, how long are you open 'til today?… Sounds great. Thanks." He hung up and put some papers away into his desk and logged off the computer. After grabbing his heavy coat, he locked his office door behind himself and walked toward the exit.

Susan came up along side him. "So you're buying it today?"

"Yup. I just hope I saved up enough."

She smiled at him as she turned up her collar against the wind and snow and turned to walk in another direction. "Good luck."

A dozen engagement rings glittered in the glass case. "That ring…" He pointed at one of them. "is that white gold?"

"No, it's titanium."

"Oh. Some of the diamonds are square."

"That's called a princess cut. It's quite popular as is the titanium. Would you like to hold one of them?"

"I honestly don't know what kind she would like."

The woman smiled. "Does she like old furniture, buildings, and styles of clothing or is she more into modern things?"

"Ummm a little of each? She seems to take an interest in old buildings and their history, but prefers more modern clothing."

She nodded. "Okay. I would recommend a princess cut diamond in a titanium setting. The gold is thought of as an older style. Do you know her ring size?"

"I didn't even think about that."

She smiled again. "It's okay. Surprise her with the ring when you're ready and then have her come in to have it sized or even exchanged for something she would prefer. What style of setting would you like?"

Daniel looked at the selection and pointed. "That one's interesting. Can I see that one?"

"That's a nice one." The woman unlocked the cabinet and pulled out the ring. After setting it on the counter she pulled the ring out of it's case and handed it to Daniel. "This one has a matching wedding ring that fits inside the engagement ring."

"Oh, that's cool. Let me see." He handed the engagement ring back and she proceeded to pull out a pair of wedding bands and fit the ladies band into the engagement ring.

"At the wedding ceremony, you would just slip it onto her finger. Then after the ceremony is done, she can take them off and fit them together like this. Should I box this up for you?"

Daniel reached out for the inset pair and stared at the glittering jewelry. After several seconds he nodded and handed them back. "Yes."

The cold wind whipped around Daniel as he approached the apartment building. He pressed the button and waited for a response. "It's Daniel." The door latch buzzed and he pushed the door open. Once inside he stomped his feet to remove the snow took the elevator up to Stephanie's apartment. When he lifted his fist to knock, the door opened to reveal Karen.

"You're early. She's still getting ready." She walked away from the door.

He stepped inside. "Okay." He lowered his voice to a loud whisper. "Karen" She turned around and he waved her over. She scowled and approached. He waited until she came closer. "Do you have her mom's phone number?"

"No, why?" She kept her voice at a normal volume.

"I need to talk to her. And her grandfather too."

Karen's scowl deepened. "Why?"

"I just… do." He raised his eyebrows on the last word to emphasize it and then smiled.

She gasped and put her hand to her mouth as she glanced behind herself and then leaned in to him and brought her voice down quieter than his. "Really? You're going to ask her to marry you?"

"A lady at work said I should ask her parents first, but don't you think it's kind of old fashioned?"

"It's tradition. And Stephanie would feel a lot better knowing you have their blessing."

"Yeah, I guess so. Have you met them? Are they nice?"

"Yes, they're very nice. Hold on. I'll get their numbers." She walked toward Stephanie's bedroom and knocked. "Hey Steph! Lover Boy is here."

Stephanie's voice came out of her bedroom. "I'm still getting ready."

"I need your address book. Where is it?"

"In here on my dresser." The door opened to let Karen inside while Stephanie kept herself behind the door. She popped her head around it and smiled at Daniel as Karen went inside and grabbed the small book and returned. She looked at Karen. "Why do you need it?"

"It's almost Christmas. I gotta talk to some people about gift ideas."

Stephanie looked at Daniel again. "I need 10 more minutes."

"Take your time."

She smiled and closed the door.

Karen disappeared into the kitchen and came out with an old envelope and a pen. "Here, write down what you need on this."

After he had finished, Daniel sat down on a chair and waited. When Stephanie came out he stood. "You look amazing."

Stephanie turned around for him. "You like? You said I should dress up."

He smiled. "Very much. I've noticed you don't wear your necklace at all anymore. Back in college you wore it sometimes."

"Oh I still have it, just have to be careful with it. Wearing it all the time took it's toll. I had to get it repaired twice."

Daniel nodded. "I'm glad you're willing to go to a museum on a cold day like this. I thought you might want to stay inside and play a game or something before we go out to eat."

She frowned. "I've been cooped up inside for a week while they fix the heating at work. I need to get out."

"Well then, let me take you."

Daniel waited until Stephanie disappeared into the museum's bathroom before pulling out the paper from his pocket with the numbers on it. He stared at it until he heard the click of heels and he stuffed it back into his pocket. He looked up to see Stephanie walking up to him. "Where to next?"

"Wherever you want to go, I just gotta get some lunch first. Can we go to the cafeteria?"

"Sure."

They took the stairs down to the lower level and found their way to the cafeteria. Daniel grabbed a tray and walked it along the various food items where he grabbed a wrapped sandwich and an apple. He looked at Stephanie and smiled. "Now I gotta figure out what I want." She smiled back and they continued to walk along until he grabbed a hoagie for himself. After they had put a couple of drinks onto the tray and Daniel paid for the meal they sat down to eat.

"You know what would be cool?" Stephanie took a bite of her apple and chewed. "Is if they made a full size Titanic as accurate as possible and put inside of it of things from the real Titanic. Then you could get a real feel... what?"

"Oh, nothing. I'm just surprised you're chewing with your mouth open. You normally don't do that."

"Sorry. My nose is clogged and it's hard to breathe."

"I'm sorry. I didn't realize you weren't feeling well."

Stephanie waved it off and took another bite. "Don't you think that would be cool?"

"That's a good idea."

They continued to eat and discuss the various things they saw at the museum so far and their plans for Christmas. After they had finished, Stephanie excused herself to use the 'powder room' and withdrew. Daniel pulled the paper out again and stared at it. Stephanie came up behind him. "What's that?"

Daniel jumped. "Oh, you scared me." He shoved the paper into his pocket.

"Are you hiding something from me?" She grinned and grabbed at his arm. "What is it? I gotta see." She laughed and kept pulling at his arm. He relented and showed her the paper. She looked at it and then looked up at him. "They're my mom and Papa's numbers. Why do you have them?" She looked down at the numbers again and then looked up and swallowed.

Daniel fidgeted and rubbed his thumb across his fingertips. "I know we never talked about, you now, getting married and maybe this is too soon, but I've known for a long time. I wanted to talk to them first, and it's almost Christmas and I know how you sometimes get sad because of your dad and I wanted you to have a nice memory for Christmas." He started to reach into his coat pocket.

"Wait."

He dropped his hand and looked away. "It's too soon. I'm sorry. I don't know what I was thinking."

"It isn't that."

Daniel looked back. "It isn't?"

"I..." She looked away. "I never thought I would get married because of my name."

"What?" He scowled. "What does your name have to do with it?"

168

She looked at Daniel again. "I thought that if I ever did get married, I would have to change it."

"Why would you do that? Your name is perfect for what you do. You can't change it."

Stephanie took in a shuddering breath as her eyes welled up with tears and she hugged him. "I'm so glad you understand because I would love to marry you."

"You would?"

"Yes!" She stopped hugging him and looked him in the eyes. "I can't imagine it being any other way."

Daniel laughed and took in a deep breath. "I think I'm supposed to call your mom and grandfather first. This isn't at all how I planned it." He took another breath and grinned. "Want to see the ring?"

"Of course!"

He pulled the ring out of his coat pocket and opened the case. As she reached for it he pulled it back. "Wait."

Stephanie's hand paused mid-air as she blinked and looked at him. "What? Why?"

"I gotta make this official." He kept grinning as he got down on one knee and held the ring up. "Stephanie Starr, will you be my wife?"

"Yes!"

People nearby clapped, surprising the newly engaged couple.

CHAPTER 29

Stephanie let Daniel into her apartment and kissed him. "I'm almost done with dinner." She went back into the kitchen.

He took his coat off and hung it up in the coat closet before sitting down in a chair near to where Karen sat reading a book. "Hi Karen, so what are you doing for Christmas?"

She pulled a book mark from the back of the book and put it into the current page before closing it. "My parents sent me a plane ticket so I can go home to visit them. I guess you're going to be pretty busy."

"I am?"

Karen laughed. "You have to pick out items for your gift registry, select invitations, figure out what you're going to wear, pick a place for the wedding and the reception, choose what meal to have served, pick a cake. Oh, and you need to find a photographer. It's going to be a very busy two weeks."

"I had no idea there's so much involved."

"That's just the part you're involved in. Stephanie has more to do than that."

Daniel's eyes went wide. "She does?"

Karen shook her head as she stood. "Men. You have no idea what we go through for you. I'm going to see if Stephanie needs some help." She went into the kitchen.

"A surprise?" Mary walked with Lucas in the airport.

"That's what she said. Which direction…?" He looked around.

"I think it's this way. It was nice of Rose and Mark to bring us down for Christmas."

"They definitely have room to accommodate all of us in that house of theirs. How much you think they paid for it? Ah, here it is."

At first Mary stood by the window and watched as the jets took off and landed while Lucas sat down. After a while, she sat in the seat next to him and pulled a book out of her purse and read while Lucas made faces at a toddler waiting with his mother, making the boy laugh. He stopped when the door to the jetway opened and people started to come through. Lucas craned his neck to see into the jetway as people passed by, smiling and standing when he saw Stephanie.

Stephanie held Daniel's hand as she came through the jetway. When she saw her grandparents, she grinned and pulled him forward. As she got near them, she let go of his hand and hugged Lucas. "Papa!" She then hugged Mary. "Grandma!" She let go and stepped back toward Daniel, with a smile she could not control, and grabbed his right hand. "Papa, Grandma." She took in a breath. "This is Daniel, I've told you about him." Lucas opened his mouth to say something when Stephanie continued. "We're getting married."

"What?" Mary reached forward and pulled up on Stephanie's hand to reveal the engagement ring. Her eyes glistened as she looked up to Stephanie. "That's wonderful." She hugged her again and then hugged Daniel. "Welcome to the family."

"I can't believe you kept this from me." Lucas hugged Stephanie as Mary hugged Daniel. "I assume this is the surprise?" He shook Daniel's hand.

"Yes, but don't tell mom. I want to surprise her myself. Where is she, anyway?" She looked around as they headed toward the luggage claim area.

Mary put her hand onto Stephanie's back. "She had a doctor visit. Nothing serious, just one of those things a lady sometimes has to deal with. You can talk to her about it later."

Stephanie nodded.

"Stephanie?" Rose called out as she entered the house through the kitchen.

"Right here, mom." Stephanie got up from the couch and ran toward the kitchen, Daniel following more slowly behind her.

Rose hugged Stephanie. "It's so good to see you. How's the job? Are your roommates doing okay? Are they... well hello." Rose saw Daniel as he walked into the kitchen.

"Hi I'm Daniel." He extended his hand and Rose shook it.

"I've heard so much about you." She looked to Stephanie with a smile on her face, still holding his hand.

Smiling, Stephanie stepped next to him. "We're getting married."

"I knew it! I just had a feeling." Rose hugged Daniel. "Welcome to the family." She turned to Stephanie. "Let me see." She held onto Stephanie's hand as she looked at the engagement ring and sighed. "It's beautiful." She looked up. "When's the big day?"

"We want to do it in March."

"March? So soon? We have a lot to do." She gasped. "I know just the place to have the wedding and reception!"

"Awesome! Hey, can Julie come down a couple days after Christmas? She's going to be the matron of honor and wants to help us get started."

"I don't see why not? We definitely have the room. You already asked her?"

"Yup. She was so excited when I told her."

"So I'm the last to know?"

"I wanted to surprise you! Surprise!" Stephanie turned to Daniel. "Can you excuse us? I gotta talk to my mom."

"Sure. I'll just go watch some T.V."

She waited until Daniel left and then turned to her mom. "Grandma said you had to see the doctor?"

"Oh, they found a lump in my breast during my checkup, turned out to be a cyst."

"Okay. I was worried. Let me call Julie and tell her that she can stay here."

Rose grinned and walked away. "Okay. I'll go and get to know my future son-in-law better!"

"Stephanie Rachel Starr daughter of Mrs. Rose Phelps and the late Raymond Starr and Daniel Michael Clark request the honor of your presence..." Rose continued reading the printed invitation to herself. She looked up at Stephanie. "It's beautiful. Your dad would be so proud."

"I want Papa and grandma to get the first one so I'm going to give it to him myself since he's in New York now."

Rose handed the invitation back to Stephanie. "It's a shame they both had to go so quickly after Christmas. I'm always surprised at how busy they keep themselves."

Stephanie took out an envelope that had a name and address already written on it and put the invitation into it, licked it, and then handed it back to her mom. "That one is yours."

"Well, thank you. I thought Papa was to get the first one."

"After yours, of course."

"I'm heading up to New York next week. You mind if I join you in presenting the invitation?"

"That would be great. Okay, I think I have everything." Stephanie looked around the bedroom and then hugged her mom. "Thanks for everything."

Rose wiped her eyes. "I'm so happy for you. I'm glad we were able to get so much done." She let go of Stephanie and turned to Daniel who stood nearby and hugged him. "You take care of my baby."

"I will." Daniel hugged her back. "I promise." He turned to Stephanie. "You ready?"

"Yes."

Stephanie opened her apartment door as she ate a sandwich and heard the phone ringing. She ran across the carpeted floor to pick up the phone, licking her fingers before picking it up. "Hello?... Hi Mom, when did you get in?" She looked at her watch. "I can't tonight I have to work, but I can tomorrow morning... Uh huh... Okay, I'll see you then." She hung up the phone and took off her coat, and left it on the couch before going into the kitchen and finishing her sandwich. She returned to the living room. "Karen, we gotta go." She picked her coat up and put it on.

Karen came out of her room, putting her hair into a ponytail. "You know I heard Melody may be leaving the company." She got her coat out of the closet.

Stephanie stepped out into the hallway and zipped up her coat. "Who'd you hear that from?"

"Brittany said she heard her talking to Allison."

"Sounds like gossip to me. We should ask her about it."

The two women took the elevator down and walked out of the building to the bus stop just outside and waited for the bus.

Karen shivered. "I'm glad you didn't want to do one of those New Year's weddings. Can you imagine?"

"I know, right? I saw all those people doing it in Central Park. I would be freezing." Stephanie stepped back a little from the curb as the bus rolled to a stop beside them. She went up the steps and dropped in her token before walking to the middle of the bus and sitting where Karen could sit next to her.

"I'm so glad Christmas is over. I don't think I could perform The Nutcracker again to save my life."

Stephanie giggled. "I know what you mean. I'm looking forward to something …" She looked out the window and stopped. Her mouth hung open as she stared across the street, her head moving as the bus moved along. Eventually she couldn't see what she was looking at anymore and just looked forward, her eyes wide and her mouth open.

Karen looked back as best as she could. "What? What did you see?" Stephanie didn't answer. "Steph! What did you see?"

"Papa. And he was kissing another woman!"

CHAPTER 30

"What?" Karen looked back, but couldn't see anything for they had gone too far past the spot. "Are you sure it was him?"

"I know my own Papa. Yes, it was him." Stephanie raised her arms and her voice. "What is he thinking!?" She looked around and lowered her arms when she realized others on the bus were looking at her.

Karen put her hand onto Stephanie's shoulder. "He is an actor. Maybe you just caught him practicing a scene."

Stephanie frowned at Karen. "They practice that kind of stuff on the stage, not on the street." She tightened her lips. "You know, she did look familiar. I wonder how long he's been seeing her. I have to call him." She pulled her phone out of her purse.

"You're pretty upset. Maybe you should wait until you've had a chance to cool off first."

Stephanie glared at Karen for a second before dropping her phone back into her purse. She looked forward. "You're right. I'll yell at him tomorrow."

Stephanie went into her apartment with Karen behind her. She grabbed a hanger from the coat closet and went to hang it up, but the coat fell to the floor as she did so. She glared at it and slammed the closet door shut before walking to the couch yelling into the air. "Focus? I'll give him focus. He can focus on my foot as I kick him!" She gave a guttural grunt as she plopped down on the couch.

Karen picked up Stephanie's coat and hung it up properly. "Well you are distracted. It's no wonder you missed those steps. Just be glad it was a practice night." She watched as Stephanie picked up the phone. "Who you calling? Not your grandfather?"

"Daniel." She dialed the phone and listened. Her face relaxed and she leaned back onto the couch. "Hi. You would not believe what I saw on the way to work..." She grinned. "Don't you wish. No, I saw Papa kissing a woman!... Yes I'm sure it was him. Why do people keep asking me that?"

Karen smiled to herself as she watched Stephanie relax. She went to her bedroom and closed the door, leaving Stephanie alone in the living room.

Stephanie tossed and turned in her bed as she thought about what she saw. Eventually, she got up and went into the living room and sat on the couch. She interleaved her fingers and rested the palms of her hands on the arm rest and put her chin down onto the tops of her fingers and looked at the phone. She sighed and closed her eyes as tears stung them. Shaking her head, she got up and went into the kitchen and got a glass of water. After drinking, she stood by the phone for a minute before picking it up. She set it down and then picked it up again. She stood there holding the handset as the dial tone droned into the stillness of the night. After a minute, a loud honk-like tone replaced the dial tone demanding her attention. She set the phone back into its cradle.

Karen came out of her bedroom, yawning and squinting her eyes. She saw Stephanie standing by the phone. "Hi. I thought I heard the phone was off the hook."

"Sorry, I didn't mean to wake you up. I couldn't sleep." She plopped down on the couch and sighed.

"Pretty upset over this, huh?" Karen walked over and sat in the chair by the couch sideways so she could face Stephanie.

"It makes sense. He's always away from grandma, of course he's going to get lonely. How could he not?"

Karen leaned her head sideways and then shook it as she formulated her response. "Mmmm... I don't think so. He doesn't seem to be the type. I've met your grandfather. He's a gentleman. I can't see him doing something like that."

"He's human. He has needs. I wonder if my dad knew. He always hated how Papa traveled so much." She sat upright. "Maybe that's why he didn't want me to become a dancer. Great! Now I'll be the one that's looking for comfort on a cold night." Her eyes got wide. "I gotta call off the wedding!"

Karen's eyes went wide and she stood. "What!? Now, hold on." She crossed over to Stephanie and sat beside her. "Obviously you're upset and probably even nervous about your own wedding. There's no need to make rash decisions while you're feeling like this."

Stephanie looked at Karen. "Maybe I should quit dancing."

"Steph." Karen closed her eyes and sighed before opening them again. "You and Daniel both live here. The only warm body you'll be looking for on cold nights is Daniel. You've got to calm down. You can dance and go home to your husband on the same night."

"Oh yeah. Maybe I should get some sleep and talk to Papa in the morning."

Karen laughed. "Yes, I think so."

Stephanie put her hand out onto Karen's arm. "I'm sorry. Thanks." She got up and headed to her bedroom. "I'll call my mom first thing and then we can go talk to Papa." She lowered her voice and nearly growled the next part as she disappeared into her bedroom. "And then he can explain why he's cheating on grandma!" She slammed the door closed.

Karen flinched as the door slammed. "Glad I'm not in his shoes."

The light from outside shone on Stephanie's face, waking her. She looked at her clock and groaned. "Ten? How did I sleep so long?" She got up and picked out some jeans and a sweater to wear and took them into the bathroom to shower and get dressed. When she went into the living room, Karen sat reading another book.

Karen looked up. "Morning. How do you feel?"

"Coffee." Stephanie walked into the kitchen and found some coffee still sitting on the warmer. She poured it into a cup and went into the living room. "Thanks." She pulled both of her legs up onto the chair and criss-crossed them before sipping her coffee while Karen continued to read. After finishing the coffee, she set the cup down on the end table. "I'll have to ask Mom to stop by someplace. This is a two-cup morning." She paused as Karen bookmarked her place. "Sorry about last night."

"You're all emotional. I get it. I think I would be the same if I saw my dad kissing someone else. What are you going to say to him?"

"I don't know." Stephanie uncrossed her legs and took her cup into the kitchen to clean it.

"Are you sure it was him?" Rose sat next to Stephanie in the back of a cab.

"Yes, mom. It was him. It upset me so much I could barely dance. I was up all night with it."

"I'm sure there's a logical explanation."

Stephanie sighed as they pulled up next to the apartment building. After her mom paid the driver, Stephanie got out first and stepped into a pothole, soaking her foot with icy water. "Great!" She pulled her foot out and shook it. "I just got these."

"I'm sure it'll be fine. We just need to wipe it off and dry it." Rose avoided the pothole.

"Maybe. All the salt they put onto the streets, it could be destroyed too."

They walked together into the building and rang Lucas' apartment bell. He let them in and they took the elevator up to his floor. Lucas stood outside his door with a smile on his face as they exited the elevator.

"Hey Dad." Rose gave him a hug before entering the apartment.

Stephanie gave him a brief hug. "Papa."

Lucas scowled as he followed Stephanie into the apartment. "Everything okay?"

Stephanie looked around the living room and moved a couple of the magazines that were on the end table. "I gotta use the bathroom."

"You know where it is."

Stephanie went into the bathroom and closed the door. She opened the medicine cabinet and looked inside. Some medicine bottles were inside along with some deodorant, toothpaste, some bengay, and stuff for shaving. "Hmmm" Stephanie picked up the medicine bottles and looked at the labels. They were written out to Lucas or his roommate. She came out of the bathroom to find Rose and Lucas talking.

Lucas looked at Stephanie. "Everything okay, Sweetie?"

"Yeah." She sat down and listened as Lucas and Rose finished talking about her new effort to go back to school to get a business degree. Her mom was mid-sentence when Stephanie scowled and stood, her eyes tearing up. "How could you!?"

Lucas sat up straight. "How could I what?"

"How could you kiss that woman?"

"What woman?" He scowled and glanced at Rose before looking back to Stephanie. "What are you talking about?"

"I saw you! On my way to work yesterday. I saw you kissing that woman! How could you do that? You once told me that I should be true to myself, true to my family, and true to God. And you... you haven't done any of that!" She took in a breath.

"Sweetie..."

"I really..." Stephanie shook her hands in the air. "really don't want to hear it!" She sat and then stood. "I... I gotta get out of here." She frantically opened her purse, pulled out the invitation and threw it down on the table before grabbing her coat and walking out the door, letting it close behind her. She could hear her grandfather calling her name.

She strode down the hall and paused at the stairs before running down, tears streaming down her face. Outside, she ignored the people looking at her as she wiped her eyes and pounded out each step. She had barely gotten out the door when her mobile phone rang. She ignored it. When it stopped and rang again, she stopped and looked at her purse. Sighing, she pulled out her phone. "Yes?"

"Stephanie! Let me explain." Lucas watched as Stephanie stormed out and sighed. He looked down at the envelope.

"It's her wedding invitation. She wanted you to have the first one."

"Oh." He picked it up and opened the envelop.

"Dad... is it true? Were you kissing another woman?" She watched him nod as he read the invitation. Her mouth fell open. "What were you thinking?"

Lucas smiled and then snorted a short laugh.

"What's so funny?"

He looked at Rose. "She must be a bundle of emotions right now. Let's see if we can get her up here and I'll explain everything." He walked over to the phone and dialed Stephanie's cell phone. "She's not answering. Let me try again." He held down the button on the handset for a couple of seconds and then let it go to dial again. "Steph... Yes you're right, but it's not what you think... No, I wouldn't... I have some news. Come upstairs to hear it." He hung up.

Rose watched as he hung up the phone. "What news?"

"Let's wait for Stephanie and I'll tell you both."

"I don't know. She's pretty mad."

Lucas sat down in the middle of the couch and looked at the invitation again as he waited. "This is really lovely. I'm impressed you got it printed so quickly."

"Papa..." Stephanie came inside the door and approached him. "I know what I saw. You can't ..."

"I'm retiring."

Stephanie faltered. "Retiring?"

"I told Veronica about it and she wanted to take me out to dinner. What you saw, was her giving me a good-bye kiss." He shrugged. "It's her way. You remember Veronica don't you? I've been working with her for a long time."

Stephanie sat down next to him. "Retiring?"

Lucas nodded. "It's past time, really. I'm having a hard time keeping up to the demands of the job. I told your grandma about my decision last week and she agrees."

"What will you do Dad?" Rose came over and sat on the other side of him.

"I thought she looked familiar." Stephanie looked at Lucas. "So you haven't been cheating on grandma?"

He took Stephanie's hands. "I would never ever want to hurt your grandmother. I'll be honest, life on the road is hard and sometimes... " He saw Stephanie's eyes getting large. "Well I could never hurt her so no. I haven't cheated on your grandma."

Stephanie smiled and hugged him. "I'm glad."

"I feel bad about lying to her... I know. Still, I need to see you... today? Yes, I can be there... Great. See you then." Lucas hung up the kitchen phone and sat down at the table to finish his breakfast.

Mary walked in as he put his plate into the dishwasher. "Who was on the phone?"

"Sales call. I was thinking. Since I'm supposed to walk Stephanie down the aisle at her wedding, maybe I should get a new suit."

"What about the one you wore to Rose's wedding?"

"It's starting to fade. Remember how you commented on it afterward?"

Mary thought about it a second. "The dark blue one, yes. Now I remember. Why did we keep it?"

"Laziness I suppose. Anyway, I'll go out today and get a new one."

Mary smiled and kissed him. "That's good. You need to do something with your time anyway."

Lucas smiled. "When do you think you'll be home today?"

"Oh you know how mid-terms are. I'll be home late. Just eat without me." She headed to the garage door. "Love you."

"Love you too." Lucas watched as she walked out the door.

CHAPTER 31

After Mary left, Lucas moved quickly. He made his way to the guest bathroom and opened the drawer in the vanity. He pulled out a medicine bottle and took the last two tablets from it and set the empty bottle onto the vanity. From there he went to take a shower and put on some fresh clothing. After brushing his teeth and hair he spent an extra minute examining himself in the mirror, turning his entire body to one side and the other. He weighed himself and then left the bathroom.

Lucas grabbed his wallet and mobile phone from the top of the dresser along with his keys and headed to the car, stopping by the guest bathroom and grabbing the empty medicine bottle. He drove to an upscale department store and made his way to the men's department and looked around.

"May I help you sir?" A man greeted him from nearby.

He smiled. "Yes, I would like to get a black suit. My granddaughter is getting married and I need to look my best."

"Well congratulations. That is certainly a special occasion. When is the wedding?"

"Three days. My wife and I are flying down tomorrow night, is that enough time?"

"It should be, let's see what we can do for you." The man turned. "If you'll just walk this way." He led Lucas to an area that had three racks of suits in different styles and colors. "I can immediately think of two different suits that I think would suit you just fine." The man chuckled at his own joke.

Lucas smiled and let the man show him the two styles. "Let's try this one." He pointed to the one in the man's left hand.

After setting the other aside, the man helped Lucas try on the jacket and showed him to a mirror. "We'll obviously need to adjust it. Do you like it?"

Lucas stood looking in the mirror for a few seconds straight on and then turned a little to look at himself from the side and nodded. "This should do just fine. When can you have it ready?"

"It's still early. We could probably have it ready by tonight. Would you like to pick out a shirt and tie while you're here? Perhaps something that matches your granddaughter's wedding theme."

"I hadn't thought of that. That's a good idea" He followed the man to get a shirt and then he selected a tie.

"An excellent choice sir. Do you need a new belt? Socks? Shoes?"

"I hate getting new shoes. They always make my feet hurt. I think the ones I have should be fine. I'll just have to polish them."

"Very well sir. Let me introduce you to our tailor and he will make sure that everything fits perfectly. Now James is a deaf-mute so don't be offended." He led Lucas to a small desk where a man sat. He handed the clothing to James and went away.

James smiled and silently stood and shook Lucas' hand. After looking at the selected garments, he nodded and put his hand onto Lucas' back and pointed to the nearby dressing room. He held onto the jacket and handed the rest to Lucas. Lucas went inside and put on the pants and shirt and returned to find James waiting with a tape measure in hand. He mimed the position he would like Lucas to take and took measurements.

He adjusted the pant legs and pulled pins out of his mouth to hold the cloth in the right position. After the pants, he adjusted the length of the shirt sleeves and pulled onto the shoulder area, inserting more pins. He pulled the jacket off a hanger on a nearby rack and put it onto Lucas and made more adjustments. Smiling, he pointed back to the dressing room.

Lucas changed back to his regular clothes, making sure he didn't pull any of the pins and came back out to find the salesman had returned.

The salesman looked at James and tapped his thumb to his pinky. James nodded and took the suit from Lucas. The salesman turned to Lucas. "He said that he should have it ready by six o'clock tonight."

"He did? Should I pay now or then?"

"Tonight after you're satisfied with the look and fit of the suit. It's our way of making sure customers are 100 percent satisfied." He shook Lucas's hand. "See you tonight."

On his way out the door, Lucas dropped the empty medicine bottle into the trash.

Lucas looked out the car window at the building in front of him and sighed. He sat there for several minutes before getting out and entering the medical complex. He walked without hesitation to one of the offices and went inside.

The receptionist smiled. "Mr. Starr. How are you feeling today?"

"Not bad." He signed his name on the paper and was about to sit when the nurse called his name. He followed her to an examination room where she asked him about how he felt and took his vitals before leaving.

After a few minutes, the doctor came in and closed the door. "Mr. Starr, you're putting me in a difficult position." He sat down on the stool and wrote out a prescription.

"I know Dr. Shaw. I really appreciate this."

"You should at least tell your wife. She has every right to know."

"I feel bad about lying to her, but I don't want her spending every day wondering if it's my last."

"You could start treatment as we discussed."

"How much time would that buy me? Four more months? Maybe five? How long do I have without?"

Dr. Shaw turned away from the desk and handed Lucas the prescription. "Probably a month, more or less. I can only tell you the numbers. God's the one that makes the final determination. Your granddaughter's wedding is this weekend isn't it?"

"Yes. I just got done picking out a suit. It will be nice for the wedding." Lucas paused. "And the funeral."

"You look so handsome in it." Mary put her hand on the sleeve as Lucas modeled the suit to her. "Stephanie will love you walking her down the aisle with this on." She turned to James and smiled. He gave the okay sign with his hand and sat down at his area and packed things away for the evening.

"I'm glad you like it. Let me get changed and we can get to the airport." Lucas went to the dressing room and changed back into his street clothes.

On the way home, they discussed what they knew of the wedding and who would be there. As they gathered their stuff to take to the airport, Lucas took his toiletries bag and slipped in a freshly filled medicine bottle along with some other medications and put it into his suitcase. He called for the cab and put the suitcases by the front door as his wife made sure they had their airline tickets ready for use.

Lucas looked at his little bag of peanuts and glass of cola. "I miss the days when we got full meals on the flight." He opened his bag. "You know why we used to have the nice meal back then don't you?"

"For the same reason you used to dress up to fly. It was considered an up-scale environment." Mary sipped her drink.

"Actually it was because of federal regulations. There was an arm of the government called the Civil Aeronautics Board that spent a lot of their time artificially keeping the prices high. To be competitive the airlines would add amenities, such as full meals, because they weren't allowed to lower prices. When they had the deregulation, it was the late 70s or early 80s I don't remember which, one of the first things to happen was the lowering of airline prices."

Mary held up her peanuts and smiled. "And now they can't afford to give us more than peanuts."

Lucas stood to use the lavatory and walked down the aisle a few steps before he stumbled and fell.

"Lucas! Are you all right?" Mary reached her hand out toward him.

The flight attendant came over and gave assistance, helping him stand and steadying him. "Are you okay, sir? Do you need to sit down?"

Lucas grabbed the back of another seat to steady himself as he stood there. "I guess I stood too fast. Give me a second." He stood there with his head hanging low until the wave of dizziness had passed. He looked to the attendant and thanked her and then looked to Mary. "I'm okay."

"Thank God. You need to be careful at your age."

He smiled and then went to use the lavatory. While returning he saw Mary watching him until he sat down. "See, I made it there and back. I just stood too fast."

She put her head on his shoulder and clasped her hand into his. "You know I love you."

He patted her hand. "I know. I love you too."

Rose picked Lucas and Mary up from the airport and took them to her house. Mark met them as they arrived and took the larger suitcases into one of the spare bedrooms while Rose brought in the rest. He excused himself to wrap up some work so he could have the next two days free.

"Stephanie's hairdresser is sick so she, Julie and I will be finding another one first thing tomorrow." Rose talked as she walked toward the living room. "I just hope that's the worse of the problems. It was a miracle we were able to get everything put together so quickly. The rest of the wedding party is showing up tomorrow morning."

"I would think in an area like this, it would be easy to find a new hairdresser." Mary sat down on the couch.

"Thankfully March is a slow wedding month. That's been our saving grace in getting everything scheduled."

Lucas sat down next to Mary. "Where are the girls, anyway?"

"Julie and Karen took Stephanie out. Julie told me…" She widened her eyes and she held up her finger. "… and I quote, 'Don't bother staying up.'"

They all laughed at that as Lucas stood. "Well, maybe they can stay up all night, but I can't. You ready for bed?" He turned to Mary.

"You go. I'm going to stay up a bit and talk to Rose."

"Okay. Night." He kissed Mary and gave Rose a hug before going to bed.

The faint noise of clinking dishes brought Lucas to consciousness. He laid there for a moment before sitting up in the bed. As he stood, he winced and made his way to the bathroom where he took his medications and attended to his other needs. From there he walked into the kitchen where Mark was putting away some dishes.

Mark saw Lucas as he came into the kitchen. "I'm sorry. Did I wake you?"

"No, I'm normally an early riser. Perhaps not as much as I used to be, but I still like getting up early."

Mark smiled. "Coffee?"

"Yes, please."

Mark pulled out a cup from the cabinet and filled it with coffee. He set it on the counter and pulled out a spoon from a drawer and a tray from a lower cabinet that had creamer and sugar on it. He set these items next to the coffee. "Tomorrow's the big day. I guess you've been looking forward to this for a long time."

Lucas smiled as he helped himself to the sugar. "Yes. Almost her entire life we've had this promise that I get to have the last dance."

"That's what Rose was telling me. Even I've noticed how quickly she's grown up. I can only imagine how you must feel."

"Yeah. Seems like yesterday she was sitting in my lap to watch television. Tomorrow I have the privilege of walking her down the aisle. What time does the rehearsal start?"

"Seven o'clock at the church. From there we go to where the reception will be held to have dinner."

"When the time comes, you'll come from this side door and walk over to this spot." The minister led Daniel from the door at the front corner of the sanctuary to the center.

"How will I know the time?"

"Because I'll tell you."

"Oh. Okay."

The minister smiled. "You, Stephanie, will be in the back along with the rest of the wedding party. Do you have a flower girl and ring bearer?" Stephanie pointed to a girl and boy, each about the age of five. He smiled at them and continued to talk as he walked toward the back, everyone else following him. "You'll want to keep them close to you since they go just a few minutes before you do. The other members of the party will, of course, go before them." He paused and turned around to face them. "Now, when you're coming down the aisle you count to yourself like this." He counted out loud and took a step. "One, two, three, four."

As he said 'One' he put his right foot forward and then put his left foot next to it. He repeated the count, but started off with the left foot and brought the right next to it. He repeated this sequence several times alternating the foot he started with each time. After a few times of doing this he quit counting out loud and continued the pace until he reached the front. "Let's try it all together." He led them to the back and had them practice together, reminding the children that they're supposed to count in their heads.

After that, he led the group through the sequence of events from the time the wedding march played to when the bride and groom kiss. "Of course…" he put his hands between them. "… that will wait until tomorrow." Everyone laughed as he kept moving his hand to keep Stephanie and Daniel from going around his hand to kiss each other.

"I recognize this place." Lucas looked around the hotel as they entered to do the rehearsal dinner.

Stephanie held onto his arm. "Oh yeah?"

Lucas closed his eyes and groaned.

"Papa?" Stephanie looked at him and her eyes went wide as he slumped. "Papa!" She tried to hold him up as others ran over to assist.

CHAPTER 32

Stephanie felt some hands pulling her away from Lucas as Mark came forward and administered CPR. She watched as he did the chest compressions and some-one else did the breathing. Next to him she could see her mother on the phone while others kept their distance. Her grandmother stood next to Rose with her hand to her mouth. Watching. Tears streaming down her cheeks. She focused on her grandfather, seeing her world fall apart as they continued to do what they could to resuscitate him. How could this be? He was supposed to walk her down the aisle. He was supposed to have the last dance at her reception.

"Stephanie!" Stephanie jumped and turned as she saw some paramedics mov-ing forward with a gurney. Had that much time already passed? She got out of the way and watched as they moved Lucas. Was that his chest moving? Yes! He was breathing on his own, oh thank God.

Rose grabbed her by the hand and they walked out to the car with Mary and Daniel following. "It will be okay, Baby. He's stable." She helped Stephanie into the back seat of the car to sit with Daniel. Instinctively, she held onto Daniel's hand and leaned her head onto his shoulder.

Stephanie noticed that they had driven to the house instead of the hospital. "What are we doing here?" She looked at her mother. "We have to go to the hos-pital."

Mary stepped out of the car. "They'll want to know what medications he's tak-ing so we're stopping by here to get his bag." She went inside and a few minutes later came out with the small leather bag Lucas used to hold his toiletries and medicine. "I didn't think they would need to see his razor and stuff so I took out everything except his medications."

"That's good, Mom." She waited until Mary had buckled then drove to the hospital.

Rose walked up to the desk in the emergency room. "I'm looking for Lucas Starr. He was just brought in."

The woman behind the desk tapped on the computer keys and looked at the screen. "Yes, he's in room 12."

Rose led the way toward the room. "If I know Mark, he's already taken charge of Dad's care."

When they got to the room Mark sat next to Lucas' bed writing some information down on a sheet of paper. He stood and took the bag offered by Mary. He took the bottles out and set them onto the counter by the sink. "Cholesterol, thyroid, blood pressure, and pain killer." He looked at Mary.

Mary blinked. "Pain killer? No, he shouldn't be taking that. He has only the three."

Mark held the bottle up and looked at it again. "Hmmm has his name on it. I'll call the doctor that prescribed it." He held onto the bottle and left the room.

Mary turned to Rose. "I didn't even notice the extra bottle in there, I was just focused on taking out the other items."

"Don't worry, Mark will find out what's going on."

Stephanie let go of Daniel's hand and sat next to Lucas, and took his hand into hers. As if seeing his hand for the first time, she stared at it; noticing how the veins and tendons were clearly visible as a result of weight loss. She ran her finger along one of the tendons and continued to stare at it for several seconds before wrapping her hand around it. Daniel brought in extra chairs so they could all sit. While they waited for Mark's return, a nurse came in and hooked up an EKG to Lucas and took a reading. After she left, they sat in silence.

Mark came back into the room, a deep frown on his face. He opened his mouth and then shut it.

"They were his?" Mary's voice choked.

He nodded. "Apparently he's been taking them for a few months." He took a deep breath and removed his eyeglasses. "His cancer is back and has metastasized."

Upon hearing that, Stephanie gripped Lucas' hand.

"Sweetie… that hurts." Lucas pulled on his hand.

"You're awake? How could you keep something this important from me?" Mary drew her lips into a thin line.

Lucas looked at her. "I didn't want you to worry."

"I'm your wife. You let me worry about worrying."

Stephanie couldn't help but smile at that.

"I'm sorry, I should have told you. I really didn't want you to worry. With something like this, every day becomes a waiting game."

Mary put her hand on his arm. "How long?"

"Four, maybe five months." He held her gaze for several seconds. Lucas turned his head to Mark. "What happened?"

Mark held up the EKG output. "Looks like you had a heart attack." He looked at Mary. "I'm sorry."

After a long silence, Daniel walked over to Stephanie and put his hand on her shoulder. "We can always postpone the wedding."

Stephanie looked up to him and gave a brief smile. "You're the best, you know that?" She looked at her grandfather. "No, it wouldn't be right to everyone. We should still proceed."

Rose yawned. "I guess we should get going so we can get up in the morning. You're hair appointment is at 10."

Mary continued to sit. "I'll be staying here." She looked at Stephanie. "I know your wedding will be beautiful, Honey, but I need to be here with Lucas."

Stephanie's eyes met Mary's and held them for a few seconds before she nodded and then stood and went around the bed to give her grandmother a hug. "I love you." Then she turned and leaned over the bed to give Lucas a hug. "I love you, Papa."

Lucas wiped a tear from his eye. "I should have been there more often for you. Been a better grandfather."

Stephanie stood, wiping tears from her own eyes before grabbing his hand. "You were the best."

He squeezed her hand. "I love you too. You go, get married. Be the best wife you can be. Who knows? Maybe I can still be there. I've known some guys to have a heart attack and get on the stage the next day." He smiled.

The flower girl looked back. "Now?"

"Yes, go now. Remember to count."

The flower girl gave the ring bearer a little nudge with her basket, prompting him to move. As she approached the open door, she reached down into her basket and spread the rose petals, the initial handful landing in a pile at her feet.

To the right Lucas' voice could be heard. "She's so adorable." His figure came into view. "You are so beautiful, just like I knew you would be." He raised his hands up and lowered the veil.

"I'm glad you could make it Papa. You look so handsome in that tuxedo."

"It's the same one I wore when your grandmother and I got married." He held his left arm out. "Maybe after this, we should go get some pancakes with some extra crispy bacon. How does that sound?"

"We need to bring Daniel too."

"Of course."

Stephanie reached out to take his arm when she heard her mother's voice calling her name. She woke up.

"Good morning." Rose opened the blinds.

Stephanie continued to lie in her bed as she looked at her mom. "I had a dream that Papa was walking me down the aisle."

Rose remained by the window. "Mark and I were talking, would you have a problem with him walking you down the aisle?"

Stephanie took in a deep breath. "Can I wait to decide?"

"Still hoping Papa can make it?"

With a nod, Stephanie sat up and put her legs over the edge of the bed. "Is that wrong?"

Rose sat down next to her and put her arm around her. "Of course not. God does miracles every day. We can decide once we get to the church, okay?" After Stephanie agreed, Rose hugged her and stood. "Julie called to say that she and Karen will meet you at the salon."

Stephanie came into the kitchen to find a cup of coffee on the counter next to the tray with sugar and creamer. Her mom stood by the counter making toast. She sat down and spooned some sugar into her coffee when her mom asked if she would get some butter from the refrigerator. She stood and went to the refrigerator and got the butter from the door. On the shelf, a package of bacon caught her attention. "Was this for Papa?"

Rose came over to see. "Yeah. Knew he would appreciate it." She continued to stand there with Stephanie for a few seconds when the toast popped up. She put her hand on Stephanie's shoulder and took the butter. "You better hurry, you don't want to be late."

Stephanie closed the door and returned to her coffee. She sipped it. "This is really good. I've been meaning to ask, what kind is it?"

"We grind our own beans now. See?" She opened a cabinet to reveal a small coffee grinder. "Makes it so much better."

After Stephanie finished her coffee, she went to get ready. As she approached her room, she could hear her mobile phone ringing. She ran in and picked it up. "Hi Danny. Are you allowed to call me?" She listened and giggled. "Not until the wedding. I have a lot to do before three o'clock." She smiled. "I love you too. See you then." She closed the face of her phone and got ready.

"Stephanie!" Julie hugged Stephanie as she entered the Salon. She looked at Stephanie with concern clearly on her face. "How's your Papa?"

"Not good. He had a heart attack and he probably won't make it to the wedding. We also learned his cancer is back."

"I'm sorry."

"I'm sorry too." Karen put her hand onto Stephanie's arm. "Your step-dad going to walk you down the aisle?"

"My mom was asking me about it this morning. I told her I wanted to wait and see."

They stood there in silence for a few seconds before Julie took a deep breath and smiled. "Today's the big day!"

"Yes!" Stephanie looked at Julie's hair. "I love your hair!"

Julie smiled. "Thanks. I found someone willing to do a quick weave first thing this morning."

"I cannot believe how much this woman eats!" Karen grinned at Stephanie. "Her breakfast could have fed me for an entire day. Maybe two!"

Julie laughed. "I didn't eat that much." She patted her slightly swollen belly. "I have to eat for two now, you know."

Stephanie laughed with them. "I think you were eating for two before you got pregnant. Do you know the sex yet?"

"We find out next week."

Karen held a small gift bag out to Stephanie.

"What's this?" Stephanie took it and, after she pulled out the tissue paper, pulled out a hair clip with artificial flowers on it. "Oh. It's your hair clip." She looked up at Karen. "Thank you, but I have lots of hair clips. And this is your favorite."

"No, it isn't a gift. You're borrowing it." Stephanie scowled. "You know, 'Something old, something new, something borrowed, something blue.'"

Stephanie's eyes went wide and she looked at it again. "Oh! Of course. This is my something borrowed."

"For the something blue, you should be wearing that sexy combo I gave you the other night under your wedding dress." She gave a dramatic wink.

Stephanie blushed as she smiled. "Maybe I already am." This drew broad grins from the other ladies. "For the old, I'm wearing the necklace my dad gave me and the wedding dress is the something new. That counts, doesn't it?"

Julie shrugged. "Works for me. Now let's get all pretty. I can hardly wait to see how you and Karen get your hair done before we do our nails."

Stephanie held her nails out against the others. "Perfect. This will go great with your dresses."

"At least they're not hideous. When my sister got married, you should have seen the dress she made her bridesmaids wear." Karen opened her mouth, stuck her finger in half way and made a gagging sound.

Julie looked at the clock. "We better go get them. Think we have time for lunch?"

Karen gasped. "We just ate!"

Stephanie giggled.

The seamstress pulled on Julie's dress. "It should be okay, but I can let it out a little."

"Maybe it's me. I feel like I've gained another inch these past two days."

Karen laughed. "Probably because of all the food you've been eating." She stood next to Julie with her dress on, both of them facing a large set of mirrors.

"I think you guys look great." Stephanie stood behind them and off to the side while the seamstress worked on Julie's dress. "The peach color draws out Karen's natural blush and it goes nicely with Julie's dark skin."

The seamstress stood back. "You're all set. Take these off and we'll get them into boxes for you. Now you remember how to help Stephanie get her dress on?" They both nodded. "Good."

Stephanie looked at the time on her phone. "Almost 10 after one. That gives us enough time to get to the church and put on the make-up and get dressed." She looked out the window. "My mom should have been here by now. Let me call her." She opened her phone and dialed her mom's number. "Mom?" She listened for several seconds, her expectant face falling into a frown as she listened. "Okay, see you at the church then." She hung up and put her phone away and sighed. "She stopped by the hospital. Papa isn't much better. She's going to meet us at the church."

CHAPTER 33

Rose sat in the car with Mark at the church talking as Stephanie arrived. She got out of the car and greeted her daughter.

"Mom, you look beautiful." Stephanie paused to admire her. Her mom wore a new salmon pink dress that complemented the dresses of the bridal party and her hair had been professionally done.

Rose turned around for her. "Didn't it come out nice?"

"Mrs. Phelps is trying to show-up the bride." Julie laughed.

Rose laughed. "Hardly think that's possible. Look at you! You're all so beautiful." As she was talking, another car drove into the parking lot and a woman got out. She opened her back door and pulled out a square case and walked over next to Rose. "You're just in time." Rose held her hand out to Stephanie. "This is my daughter, Stephanie."

"Pleased to meet you."

"This is Sophia. She's the best makeup artist I know." She looked at Sophia. "She's even done work in the movie business."

Sophia smiled. "Your mom hired me to do your makeup today."

Stephanie's eyes got big. "Mom! That's so nice." She hugged her mom. "Thank you so much. I was going to do it myself."

As they were hugging, the click of a camera got their attention. "Perfect." A man, standing off to one side put his camera down.

Stephanie pulled back from her mom. "Thomas, when did you get here?"

Before he could answer, the church door opened and a woman came out and walked toward them. "You remember my wife, Natalie? We got here about 30 minutes ago to set some stuff up." He pointed to a van parked in the corner of the lot.

Sophia looked to where Thomas pointed. "TNT Studios?"

Natalie smiled. "Thomas and Natalie Turner Studios. Together, we're dynamite."

"I'm not sure if that's good or bad."

Thomas and Natalie looked at each other and laughed. Thomas looked back at Sophia. "I think it depends on the day. But it's mostly good and that's what counts."

Sophia smiled and turned to Stephanie. "Let's get you inside to start on that make-up."

As they all proceeded into the church, Thomas and Natalie followed behind with Thomas giving some instruction. "I'll be doing still shots and Natalie will do still shots and video. Just ignore us until we do the formal shots after the wedding. Is there anything specific you have in mind that we didn't cover on the interview?"

Stephanie shook her head. "No, I don't think so. Mom?"

Rose looked over her shoulder. "Your portfolio is amazing. I think you have it all covered."

Thomas took a few photos of Stephanie getting her make-up done and then disappeared to find Daniel while she got dressed. After another half hour had gone by he came back in after knocking and getting clearance. "Let me get a few shots of you putting on your veil and then I'll go to the main sanctuary to get some shots of people arriving. Nervous?"

Stephanie took in as deep of a breath as her dress would let her. "A little."

Julie adjusted Stephanie's veil. "I was nervous too. You'll be fine." She looked at her watch. "I think it's time to get into place."

The bridal party made their way to the foyer where Daniel's groomsmen were waiting with the flower girl and ring bearer.

Rose went over to the children's mother. "The twins look so adorable!"

The mom beamed. "I think if they see another camera, they'll run away." She bent down to the girl's ear and whispered.

The flower girl listened and nodded and then walked over to Stephanie and handed her a blue sapphire ring.

Stephanie took it. "What's this?"

"Something blue. My mom says you might need it. She told my dad she never liked it anyway."

Stephanie covered her mouth to hide the smile. "Awww, thank you so much." She hugged the girl. As the girl walked back toward her mom, Stephanie looked at the ring and then looked up at the girl's mom. "I can't take this. It's too expensive."

Still red in the face from what her daughter said, the mom walked over to Stephanie. She took the ring and put it into Stephanie's hand. "It's a man-made sapphire, so it's okay." She hugged Stephanie. "Congratulations. I gotta get to my seat."

Stephanie smiled and tried the ring on her right hand. It wouldn't fit over the glove on any finger except her pinky, so she left it there. She stared at the door to the church.

"Watching it won't make your Papa appear." Rose put her hand on her daughter's shoulder.

"I know. It's just… Papa is strong. I thought that maybe…" Stephanie took a deep breath and waved her hand at her face while she blinked several times.

Rose nodded and kept her hand on the shoulder. When she heard the organ music change, she took her hand off and looked at Stephanie's face. "I need to go sit down. I'll send Mark back." She hugged Stephanie. "I'm so happy for you. Daniel is a good man." She opened the door enough to let herself through and disappeared inside.

After a couple minutes, Mark came through and walked over to Stephanie. "You doing okay?" Stephanie nodded. Mark gave a nod to Karen and the groomsman that were waiting. They opened the doors and locked them open before proceeding down the aisle. When they were half-way down, Julie gave a smile to Stephanie and then proceeded with the first man.

The flower girl looked at Stephanie. "Now?" When Stephanie nodded, she took the ring bearer's hand and walked down the aisle, completely forgetting to drop the flower petals. When a guest whispered to the girl that she should be dropping the petals, she became animated. "Oh yeah." She let go of her twin brother's hand and ran back to the door and dropped the petals from there while her brother waited for her.

The door to the church opened. Stephanie gasped and looked to see a man dressed in jeans and t-shirt walk in. He looked at Stephanie. "I'm sorry. Is there a wedding today? Obviously yes. I'll come back later." He walked out, being careful to not let the door slam. The organ shifted to the wedding march.

Mark held is right arm out for Stephanie.

Stephanie took her eyes away from the door and looked at Mark. "Wrong side." Stephanie walked around to his left side.

"Of course, sorry." He held out his left arm and walked her to the open doorway. After everyone stood, they started down the aisle.

Stephanie looked at Daniel as he stood there in his tux and smiled.

"You look great." Thomas looked at the wedding party as they stood in a line in front of the pulpit. "Natalie, her train is wrong. Can you fix that?" He watched through the camera eye-piece as Natalie came behind Stephanie and quickly arranged her sweep and train. "Perfect." He stood straight up. "And smile. This is a wedding after all." When everyone grinned, he took the picture.

After taking several pictures of various combinations of the wedding party, the bride and groom with their parents, and just the twins who were getting tired,

Thomas and Natalie went outside followed by everyone else, leaving Stephanie and Daniel alone.

Daniel smiled at Stephanie. "You are stunning, Mrs. Starr." He kissed her and held out his hand. "Think we can do this?"

Her eyes glittered as she looked at him. "As long as we're together." She took his hand and they walked to the church door where the pastor stood waiting.

He shook each of their hands. "Good luck you two. May God bless you with a joyful and long life together." He paused. "The car is waiting with the door open. Ready?"

Stephanie and Daniel looked at each other and answered in unison. "Ready!"

The pastor opened the door and they ran through the cheering mob and rice-filled air into the waiting safety of the limo.

As the couple got driven through the streets, other drivers would occasionally honk in response to the 'Just Married' sign on the back of the car. On one such occasion, Stephanie and Daniel stood through the moon roof and waved at them.

When they came down, Daniel held onto and kissed Stephanie. "We should just skip the reception and go straight to the honeymoon."

She laughed. "Papa wouldn't like that! He..." Her laughter stopped and the smile slowly faded from her face.

"He wouldn't want you to miss your wedding cake."

She smiled. "Right. Or the eating and dancing and socializing."

After meandering through the streets for 30 minutes, they arrived at the hotel for the reception. As they got out of the limo and entered the hotel, people who saw them clapped and congratulated them. Thomas was also there to capture the moment.

When they got to the reception hall, Natalie stood outside. "Just a moment." She disappeared inside and then came back out. "Okay, they're ready for you. Just give us 30 seconds." She and Thomas went inside so they could record the entrance of the happy couple.

"You okay?" Daniel took Stephanie's hand into his own and pulled her against himself.

She looked from one eye to the other and kissed him. "I am."

"I love you."

"I love you too."

They turned toward the door and went inside.

The dance floor dominated the room with floral arrangements decorating the tables surrounding the open space. At the end of the dance floor sat a wide table for the wedding party. A buffet of food and a bartender mixing drinks for guests hugged the right wall while a table laden with gifts occupied the opposite side. In the corner, the DJ stood next to his equipment.

As they walked in, the DJ stopped the music. "Ladies and gentlemen, please join me in welcoming the newly wed couple, Daniel Clark and Stephanie Starr!"

Everyone stood and clapped. Some talked to each other, questioning the use of her maiden name. While they clapped, some tapped their spoons onto glasses and soon everyone was doing it. After Stephanie and Daniel grinned and kissed each other, everyone gave a cheer and clapped some more.

The wedding party had been interspersed among the guests talking to them as they waited for Daniel and Stephanie to arrive; they came forward and joined the couple at the main table. As they sat, Stephanie looked at the nearest table and saw the two empty chairs next to her mom and Mark.

Attendants came from by the buffet table and gave the wedding party some food and drink. Then parents and grandparents were served before everyone else was allowed to serve themselves.

The night became a blur of activity. From the first dance to the taking off the garter belt, to the tossing of the bouquet. Guests offered congratulations and danced with the bride or groom, for a fee of course. The money dance was fun as aunts and uncles would try to give more than the last had given. After they had danced and mingled with the guests for an additional hour, the DJ announced the cake cutting.

Stephanie and Daniel made their way to the cake table where the three tiered cake sat next to a smaller cake. They took the cutting knife and held it together for the photographer and then cut two small pieces from the small cake. Each taking a piece they brought it near the other's mouth. Daniel grinned as he got near to Stephanie's mouth.

Stephanie smiled. "You wouldn't dare."

On her words, Daniel smashed the cake up against her lips and cheek. As he did this, Stephanie mashed her piece up against his face too. Both of them were laughing along with their guests. Then Daniel kissed the pieces of cake off her face. She took some of the icing from his face and ate it. The guests clapped and cheered.

Stephanie kissed Daniel and put her head onto his shoulder as they danced. Someone stopped by and wished them well before he departed.

Daniel kissed Stephanie's cheek. "Aren't we supposed to go before they do?"

She nodded her head and sighed. She looked at him. "You ready, Mr. Clark?"

"I am if you are, Mrs. Starr."

"Let's go say goodbye to our parents." As they stopped dancing, the DJ also stopped playing the music and the room grew quiet. "What?" Stephanie looked around and saw everyone looking toward the main entrance of the hall. There, in a wheelchair, sat her grandfather with her grandmother standing next to him. Stephanie took in a shuddering breath as tears blurred her vision.

She blinked the tears away and looked at Daniel to see him smiling. He kissed her on the lips and let go of her hand. She ran to the edge of the dance floor and stopped as Mary rolled the wheelchair up to it. Mary helped Lucas up out of the wheelchair and onto the dance floor.

"Papa! You made it."

"You think I could ever go back on our promise?"

Stephanie smiled and took his hand and put her head against his chest as they started to sway.

"You know, this hotel has a very interesting history."

Stephanie laughed and kissed her grandfather's cheek.

A note from the author

Thanks for reading my story. Please go online and provide a review at the place of purchase. It's surprising how much of a difference two minutes can make.

As an author many people ask me, "Where are you in the story?" I think in this case it's obvious. I'm the grandfather.

This is a great read for young
adults/teenagers. We read it on a
long road-trip and everyone was
in suspense. We really enjoyed
reading the parts about the
Chesterton, Indiana area since I
grew up in Chesterton. The
author developed the characters
very well and was adept at
engaging us with their struggles as
teens. The story is not too scary
for young pre-teens. We have a 13
and 11 year old and they loved it.
The ending is very unexpected.

This was a very good book for
middle schooler's. It reminded me
of when I read the original Hardy
Boys when I was young. I liked
the way he mixed the mystery and
the coming of age of the main
character. Very entertaining! I will
not spoil the ending, but it was
total surprise, and I remember
saying out loud, "What ???"

Download today for **FREE**
http://AaronLBratcher.com